MEET
THE COSMIC CORRESPONDENTS
OF SATELLITE NEWS . . .

RIKKA COLLINS—ace reporter. She's got brains, beauty . . . and a built-in microphone.

HARRY SNYDER—anchorperson. As an intergalactic newsman, he's tops . . . when he's not tipsy.

JHONNY—cameraman. He's a robot, he's illegally employed . . . but no one's perfect.

MICHELANGELO—technician. He may look like a grizzly bear, but this alien troubleshooter knows his nuts and bolts and microchips.

"ACE" DEITRICH—the brains, literally. His body died almost three decades ago, but his scientific mind is still ticking.

"BOX" AMBOCKSKY—program director. He gets the team into the heat of the action, brings them back to the studio . . . and sometimes bails them out of jail.

They're the Satellite News Team—beaming your broadcast light years ahead of the competition.

Catch all the news! Don't miss
Satellite Night News . . . Only one thing stands in the way of the Satellite News Team and a nova-hot story—an interplanetary war.

Satellite Night Special . . . The Satellite News Team will blow the lid on a plot to kidnap a Martian prince—if the Martian war fleet doesn't blow them away first!

Ace Books by Jack Hopkins

SATELLITE NIGHT NEWS
SATELLITE NIGHT SPECIAL
SATELLITE NIGHT FEVER

SATELLITE NIGHT FEVER

JACK HOPKINS

ACE BOOKS, NEW YORK

This book is an Ace original edition,
and has never been previously published.

SATELLITE NIGHT FEVER

An Ace Book / published by arrangement with
the author

PRINTING HISTORY
Ace edition / June 1994

ISBN: 0-441-00065-7

ACE®
Ace Books are published by The Berkley Publishing Group,
200 Madison Avenue, New York, NY 10016.
ACE and the "A" design are trademarks
belonging to Charter Communications, Inc.

PRINTED IN THE UNITED STATES OF AMERICA

10 9 8 7 6 5 4 3 2 1

To Phil Foglio and Kaja Murphy,
my best friend and his very special lady.
Thanks, folks.

CHAPTER ONE

"YOU'RE TOO LATE!" cried Professor Ketter, his lab coat flapping like the wings of a crazed albino bat trapped in a sickly laurel bush—which showed signs of someday getting well again, unlike Ketter.

"Too late! Late! Late!" he added as an afterthought, and then did a little war dance.

Standing breathless in the underground laboratory before the mad scientist, the four members of the Satellite News Team could only wheeze for a moment in reply. Dressed in standard white spacesuits with the helmets tucked under whichever arm the owner preferred, their frantic dash up the 247 flights of stairs from the valley floor below had been reminiscent of kissing an electric fan: awkward, slightly painful, and very embarrassing when performed in front of friends. Obviously they were consuming just too damn many Danishes during coffee breaks. Why the prack didn't this loony have an armed elevator or a military space dock like everybody else on Venus? He was a good dancer, though.

"If . . . you . . . wanted people to arrive on schedule," panted Rikka Collins, her long brunette hair disarrayed and sweat-damp, "then why did you have the invitations printed in code?"

"Because I only wanted smart reporters to arrive!" cackled the professor. At the far end of the room, the defrocked physicist began adjusting some of the endless controls adorning the wall-spanning console. Meters started to flick wildly and lights flashed in preprogrammed madness. In the corner, a coffeemaker turned on, then off, then began making tea: a

1

sissy drink outlawed on the hard-boiled, two-fisted world of Venus. A person needed a permit to not carry a gun on this world, and Hallmark greeting cards required antidotes.

"Smart reporters?" queried Michelangelo. The huge alien lifted a thick eye ridge of dark hair high on a noble bestial brow of fuzz. "Are you crazy, sir?"

Standing three meters tall and apparently forged of nothing more than muscle, fur, and teeth, the giant technician sported a silver Lavalear mike clipped to a brown ear and a ridiculous pair of tiny pince-nez glasses perched on the end of his elongated black snout. Neither did anything to relieve the overall impression of bestial power.

SO IT'S AN OXYMORON, scrolled the IBM computer strapped to his arm in lieu of a dinky little human wrist secretary. SHADDUP! THIS GUY IS DANGEROUS!

After a moment, the alien agreed. Yes, it would take serious oxygen deprivation to make anybody goofy enough to search for smart reporters. If any of them were truly intelligent, they would have become journalists. Or garbage collectors.

"It took us days to decipher what you threatened to do!" scolded Harry Snyder, trying to establish himself as an authority figure. Dark-haired with wings of silver at each temple, Snyder was the visual epitome of dignity, which accounted for his vaunted position as the Face and Voice of the SNT. Painfully distinguished, the dapper fellow radiated confidence and the faint smell of twelve-year-old Scotch.

Scowling with disapproval, Rikka agreed. Coded letters, bunch of damn foolishness. If the facts in his invitation were correct, then this was either the biggest news story of the year, or the worst disaster. Which would, of course, make it the biggest news story of the decade!

Backing into a corner, a slim youth braced himself and quick-drew a pair of hand cameras from his double shoulder holsters. Detaching itself from the top of the spacesuit helmet lying on the floor, a small minicamera extended metal spider legs and climbed directly up the torso of the youngster to settle comfortably on his left shoulder. A glance at the sensor panel on his armored forearm said there was sufficient illumination, and with a revving whine the three cameras booted live as Jhonny started recording everything; one camera trained on his frowning teammates, the shoulder cam focused on the giggling Ketter, and the third aimed toward the nearby open window.

Visible outside the underground bunker was a staggered wall of mountains forming the northern rim of the Whatadump Crater. So named because that's what everybody said when they first viewed this unsightly planetary bog hole. A near perfect circle of ragged lumpy mountains devoid of mineral wealth, beauty, or even skiable snow, ringing a not very deep hole whose sides were childishly easy to climb, the crater lacked caves to explore, was sans thermal currents to make hang gliding a remote possibility, or even any night-flying rodents that a comic book might be based upon. In fact, the only known less hospitable terrain was the deadly tundra of Sunset Blvd. in downtown Los Angeles.

Only minutes ago, as the SNT rocketed through space to keep their impromptu appointment with the mad Dr. Ketter, they were not surprised to discover that he had purchased the whole damn crater for fifty-nine cents cash, two subway tokens, and a free sample subscription to *"OH YEAH?" The Belligerent Magazine for Venusians with Guns.* Oddly, Ponticlift & Ponticlift, the real estate agents who had conducted the sale, gleefully believed they had swindled the old scientist something awful.

Which was certainly bizarre. Sir Comrade Dr. Prof. Major Gregor Ketter of the Dreamhaven Institute for Advanced War Sciences and College Bookstore was the most famous general scientist in the entire solar system. A scrambled alphabet followed his name that few sentients could even pronounce in a single breath, much less match. A truck attempting to carry his accumulation of awards and medals had once broken down under the amassed tonnage. And above anything else, Ketter worshiped brains. It was rumored that he had a five-pound clone of Ben Franklin's on a secret altar in his asteroid condo where he privately danced about naked with logarithms painted on his body. But it was only a rumor. Locked in their world of hard unyielding facts, most scientists simply loved to gossip about each other. But just then Rikka spied what resembled a large grayish cauliflower sporting antique bifocals in a pickle jar over on a dusty lab shelf.

Nyah, couldn't be.

"Yes! Too late!" screamed Ketter, returning her to the present. Flecks of whitish foam stained his lips. "Too late to even discuss it!" He threw another switch and a mighty humming sounded in the floor below the bunker. "Call me mad, did they? Insane? A xenophobic sociopath with subliminal delusions of egalitarian divinity, eh?"

There was a pause.

"Eh?" asked Michelangelo puzzled, typing quickly on his IBM.

"Really really insane," breathed Harry, clenching and unclenching his gauntlets. Oh, Lord, here we go again. Another last-ditch effort to change an entire world into the deluded perfection of a techo-madman! Hmm, maybe Ketter should try his hand at politics.

"Bah! Phooey!" growled the scientist, his lips twisting about with a life of their own. "Well, let's see what the government of Venus calls me after this!"

And before the reporters could take a step, the little man yanked down another switch, this lever plainly marked VICTORY or DOOM. Lead shutters slid over the windows and the massive door to the bunker locked-locked-locked. Obviously, a complete lack of subtlety was the hallmark of both journalism and science.

"Ten!" sang out Ketter, pulling a brew from a shoulder holster and tossing it off in a single swallow. "Nine . . . eight . . . seven . . . six . . ."

Sealed in the subterranean bunker, the four members of the Satellite News Team frantically searched for an air vent or garbage chute, but every external passageway had been tightly sealed with great slabs of military steelloy adorned with garishly painted signs reading: "Ha-ha!" "I win!" or the immortal classic "Einstein was a sissy!" The news reporters were less than pleased.

"Aw, to hell with countdowns," decried Ketter and he threw yet another giant switch prominently marked THE.

Instantly, the floor shook as if a heavy truck had driven by.

The walls shook as if the truck had rammed the bunker. Then the ceiling shook as if the truck had detonated. Then everything wildly shook, rattled, and rolled as if God had extended a mighty leg from heaven and was brutally stomping His holy combat boot on the fiery ruins of the vehicle.

That was when the underground room exploded.

Or, at least, that was the overall impression. The walls danced, the ceiling jiggled, the floor did what no proper floor should and gave an excellent rendition of a Tilt-A-Whirl. The lights dimmed, then came on blindingly bright and promptly died away again. The physical maelstrom buffeted and shook the SNT reporters to their very bones and souls. And the madness increased until an egg timer sitting calmly on the main control board gave off a cute musical ding and the tumultuous gyrations ceased in ragged stages.

"Whee!" cried the scientist, his face pressed hard against the viewport of a hooded monitor. "I've done it! Success! Success!"

In a rumble of pocket thunder, the massive slabs of metal retreated into the walls leaving the sides of the bunker open space. Piled on the floor, the SNT could only gasp at what was now exposed, because the mountains were no longer as they had been. Indeed, the titanic range of eon-old granite was as no natural mountain range had ever been. Or, quite possibly, would be again.

As the news team looked out the windows, large stone faces peered back in at them. In triumph, Ketter giggled and hugged himself. Struggling to his feet, Jhonny swung a second camera, then the rest of them, toward the view outside. Wow!

"Deitrich, do you copy?" whispered Collins into her throat mike as she extracted herself from the jumble of friends. Clothing was adjusted and modesty prevailed once more.

There was a crackle of static.

HERE, scrolled the tiny monitor of her wrist secretary. BUT JUST BARELY.

"What happened?" breathed Snyder in astonishment, unable to tear his eyes away from the window.

THE WHOLE DAMN MOUNTAIN RANGE WAS BLANKETED WITH OVERLAPPING NUCLEAR BLASTS, said the MainBrain pilot of their shuttle. MY ANTIMETEOR SHIELDS JUST MANAGED TO WITH-

HOLD THE EXPLOSIONS. BUT, WOW! WHAT A SHOW! HAVEN'T SEEN
ANYTHING LIKE THIS SINCE THE AIRPLANE FULL OF FIREWORKS
CRASHED INTO THE GASOLINE TRUCK DURING THE ANNUAL VOL-
CANO SPECTACULAR ON NEW POMPEII.

"Nuclear?" Instinctively, Harry's gauntlet pulled a hip flask
into view, and the news anchor undid the cap. But then he re-
capped the container and stuffed it back into his belt pouch. If
the force shields and armor of the bunker hadn't stopped the radiation, it was far too late for a dose of DNA-stabilizing whiskey. At this very moment, the reporters could be mutating into
some slavering, oozing, subhuman life form; something even
lower on the evolutionary scale than a corporate lawyer.

"There's no fallout," stated Michelangelo, studying a small
box in his paw. "The atmosphere and surrounding grounds are
totally clear?"

CHECK. THE ONLY THING RAD AROUND HERE IS KETTER HIMSELF.

Heartfelt sighs abounded.

"Never mind that," said Jhonny, angling about for a better
look. In the belt pouch of his spacesuit, a smashed minicam jin-
gled loosely. Damn. "Deitrich, can you give me a horizon
sweep?"

TONES AND BARS, PAL, replied the aviator.

"Just don't forget to remove the lens cap this time."

PICKY, PICKY.

With a swirl of color, the main view screen above the water
cooler/gun rack came to foggy life. As the screen cleared, the
surrounding mountains showed to be transformed into a circular tableau of historical scenes: Adam and Eve being expelled
from Eden by a large off-stage landlord, Ug the caveman in-
venting fire and accidentally discovering the barbecue at the
same instant, Alexander the Great rudely finding out that he
couldn't swim worth a good goddamn, Emperor Claudius of
Rome creating the public TV miniseries, Hannibal riding his
famous escalators across the Alps, His Royal Majesty Clint
Eastwood signing the Magnum Carte, General George pat-
enting World War II, Neil Armstrong landing the Eagle on
Luna, and the ever popular destruction of the Jupiter moon Io,
along with its secret military base of the oh-so-hated space pirates, the Free Police—who were neither.

Next came a frozen sea of stony waves lapping at the granite shores of four large islands, decorated with perfect stone trees, bushes, and surfers. Adorning each island was a stout column of scaled leg reaching upward to form the body of a giant turtle. Standing brazen upon the animal's back was a human in ancient loincloth and girdle, his mighty muscular torso supporting a perfect replica of the Greek goddess Venus holding her namesake planet balanced on top of a dainty digit. Followed closely by a reproduction of the mythological monarch King Kong, in his early days before booze and drugs gave him mange; a perfect Statue of Liberty—launching a salvo of ICBMs from her torch; an exact duplicate of the Eiffel Tower—whose pinnacle frothed with champagne and can-can dancers; and a final section shrouded in misty clouds.

"Let's see the Venusian Board of Tourism laugh at me now!" smirked the scientist, thumbs hooked into his camouflage-colored belt. Even his smart-ass brother would be impressed!

"But . . . how . . ." gasped Rikka, utterly flabbergasted.

Ketter gestured dramatically. "Nuclear sculpturing."

"Eh?"

"What?"

"Quarl?"

"You!" accused Snyder, leveling a stern metal finger. "It was you who destroyed the Empire State Building last week! Blew it into a million pieces?"

Contorting his face, Prof. Ketter managed a grin trying to appear guileless, and failed miserably. "Well, yes," he admitted sheepishly. "My test explosion was only supposed to open the windows. A slight miscalculation there. But I did implode the building back together again the next day, and added a few extra stories as an apology. Subsequently, I have corrected that minor technical problem. My Blast Sculpture process is perfect! Absolutely perfect!"

"Shaped nuclear charges," whispered Collins, staring out the bunker window at the manly knees of Atlas. "I wouldn't have believed it could be possible. Where did you buy these things?"

"Buy?" Prof. Ketter spoke as if he had never heard the word before. "Buy? I made them!"

"Really?"

A shrug. "Some plutonium, a wad of superconductor foil, some twine, a banana . . . they're actually quite simple."

"Excuse me, sir, but what is that foggy section over there?" asked Jhonny, pointing with a camera. The spidery camcorder on his shoulder exactly duplicated the motion.

"Ah!" exclaimed Ketter, beaming a smile. "That was a toughie. Forming an endless steam geyser from the underground springs to permanently hide that area from casual view."

"But what is in there?" demanded Rikka, her curiosity piqued. "The world's biggest sauna? The ultimate laundry? A planetary dumpling factory?"

"Something naughty?" asked Snyder hopefully. Sex always made good TV copy, and sadly Venus was fully clothed in a toga.

"Hardly," drooled the scientist as they gathered around him.

Palming the control board, Ketter manipulated the main view screen into a tight zoom through the steam and suddenly the SNT reporters found themselves staring at a double-barreled shotgun.

Eh?

"A nose?" asked Mike, touching his own snout.

"No," corrected Rikka. "It's a bust!"

The alien frowned in concentration. The sculpture was of female sex glands? A failure? Ah, no. The head and shoulders of a human. Esperanto was such a difficult language.

"Pretty damn impressive," stated Harry honestly. On command, a tiny mechanical arm reached out from the miniature control panel encircling the neck ring of his spacesuit to thoughtfully scratch his chin. "But is it art?"

Just then a tremor shook the entire facade of the sculpture, a rain of pebbles cascaded down the face, and with a crack of thunder a seam split wide across the bust, bisecting the right cheek and making the nose fall off. Shocked murmurs sounded as the nasal meteor tumbled down into the misty distance.

"My God," cried Jhonny, almost losing focus. "It is Art!"

"A perfect likeness," agreed Collins with a smile. "Sgt. Artwald Bonniter, the founder of Venus. Wonderful! Fabulous!"

At last, Venus finally possessed a tourist attraction worthy of public notice. Now humanity had another reason to come to this blighted planet aside from cheap beer and no extradition. Why, this could save the floundering world economy! At least it was certainly a better idea than the Free Air Festival and the Moonlight Tanning Saloons. Especially since Venus didn't even have any satellites, aside from that silly plastic thing floating over the North Pole. An inflatable Aurora Borealis. Pitiful.

Walking from window to window scrutinizing the milieu of contorted granite, Michelangelo found it interesting that nobody had yet made a passing comment on the fact that shrapnel from the blast had filled the crater about them, raising the level to only a dozen or so meters below the bunker. And the larger chunks had settled atop each other forming benches, decorative walls, tiered fountains, and assorted concession stands. Very impressive. Briefly, the alien wondered what the human could do for Halloween with a grenade and a pumpkin?

"But why is Art masked?" asked Collins suspiciously, tapping a computer stylus against the sleeve of her spacesuit.

A sly scientific grin. "So that the visiting yokels will be forced to pay extra to see what's inside!"

The news team exchanged pleased looks. By gad, Ketter was a genius. A scientist who knew how to make money. Amazing. But then, his parents did come from the molten world of Mercury, a fiery planet where turning a profit was considered as vitally important as air-conditioning and #99 sun block.

"So, how does this work?" asked Harry, crossing his arms. "You attach a bunch of miniature atomic bombs to a block of marble and kaboom, you get an instant copy of Michelangelo's David?"

"The turtle?" asked the alien technician. "Oh, that artist fellow."

"No-no-no," ranted Ketter, waving his arms. "To do a Blast Sculpture—"

TRADEMARKED, PATENT PENDING, scrolled across their wrists.

"—requires thousands of massive charges, years of precise calculations and endless experiments to fine-tune the precise vector tangent vortices and secondary shock-wave schismatics.

"I got the idea from watching loose shopping carts wheel about in an inclined parking lot," admitted the scientist candidly.

Stepping to the sill, Harry gazed out the window allowing Jhonny's camera to catch his highlighted profile. "Your brilliance and expertise in these matters is without question."

A certified genius his whole life, Ketter merely shrugged. The task had not been particularly difficult. It wasn't as if he had solved one of the four remaining mysteries of the Time/Space continuum, finally come to understand the British tax laws or anything major like that.

"And this central column is a nice touch," added Jhonny.

A blink. "Eh? Whatever do you mean, lad?"

The android dollied in for a close-up on the professor. "I mean that the entire mountain range has been molded in exquisite detail, except for this central column of irregular stone. A somber reminder of the way the crater was originally. A perfect artistic counterpoint. My congratulations!"

"Irregular?" repeated Prof. Ketter, frowning. "What the prack are you babbling about?" In angry strides, the professor crossed the bunker and began regulating the controls on the console.

"Okay, folks, let's prep for broadcast," said Rikka, typing notes into her wrist secretary.

Harry looked down and copy was already scrolling on the teleprompter set strategically below his chin. In a glance, it was memorized. This minor mental talent had served the anchor well in his twenty-five years in the news biz, and earned him a small fortune playing poker.

"Ready when you are," said Snyder, and he started removing his spacesuit. Underneath the adamantine garment, the ever dapper news anchor was wearing a natty, five-piece, neon-green jumpsuit with a pink paisley ascot and transparent carnation.

Extending telescoping legs from the bottom of his big 3-D

cameras, Jhonny plugged in a directional mike and booted the EM transponder. "Deitrich, am I hot?"

AS A TWO-DOLLAR LASER, BUDDY, replied the MainBrain. LINK ESTABLISHED WITH THE LOCAL QSNT AFFILIATE, I'VE RESERVED US A Z-BAND TRANSMITTER AND MEDIA HAS ALREADY ALLOTTED US A SPONSOR.

"Wow. Good work. Who?"

THE INTERPLANETARY BOOK CLUB IS REISSUING THE CLASSIC ASIMOV TRILOGY: *CHOOSING THE GROUND, DIGGING THE HOLE, FOUNDATION.*

"Hey, neat! Order me a copy of the Deluxe Land Fill set."

NO PROB.

Using a small can of spray paint, Jhonny made an "H" on the floor before the control board. "Just stand there, Harry." As Snyder complied, the android checked the light levels with a hand meter. The camera-op frowned, and reaching into his shoulder bag produced a second spray can. A quick sprintz tinted the overhead light bluish and he nodded in approval.

Assuming a stance, Harry started his solo preamble and Rikka watched the professor working feverishly at the control board. Ah, like any perfectionist he was probably fiddling with the sensors and furious over the fact that this statue was an inch too wide, or facing a full millimeter in the wrong direction. Nothing important could have gone wrong, or else they would be surrounded by umpteen tons of driveway gravel.

Suddenly a strangled cry sounded from Ketter and as the reporters watched he clutched wildly at his hair and his eyes began rotating in different directions, as if each orb were valiantly trying to escape from its owner.

Adjusting the focus on the big camera, Jhonny was vastly pleased. Great reaction shot! But what caused it?

"Ah, very nice, sir," acknowledged Rikka politely. "But kindly save it for the interview."

"Prack!" cried the man, thumping an elderly fist onto the controls, electrical sparks spraying out from the impact. "Prack, hell, damn, crap, and whistle! Double whistle!"

Interrupted in the middle of a sentence, Snyder stopped his spiel and turned from the camera. "Sir, what the hell is wrong?"

"This butte was supposed to be converted into a sculpture of naked Mae West soaping the buxom form of a nude Marilyn Monroe!" cried the scientist. "I was going to hollow out the bar of soap for my retirement home. That way whenever I open the living-room curtains the horizon will be completely filled with . . ." He shook himself. "But it's completely ruined! The bombs dysfunctioned!"

"They didn't go off at all?" asked Michelangelo, unreeling rainbow-colored superconductor cable from his white arm. Darn, what a disappointment. Although his species was rather new to human civilization, he was fast becoming a diehard movie fan. James Cagney, Earl Flynn, Zusu Pitts . . . and that Mae West, hubba-hubba, what great hair.

"Apparently not a single bomb detonated," sighed the scientist. "And I spent sixteen years on designing their torsos alone!"

Privately, Harry and Rikka snorted in amusement.

GEEZ, THIS GUY REALLY NEEDS A DATE.

"However, the nouveau of this central column opposite the deco of the artificed mountains makes a splendid counterpoint," noted Jhonny soothingly. Artists were so temperamental.

"But I didn't want a bloody counterpoint!" screeched the scientist. "Oddbotkins, are you trying to dis me, homeboy?"

Collins placed a comforting hand on the oldster's shoulder. "So try again later. The rest is truly beautiful."

"No!" wailed Ketter, clawing at the console. "You don't understand! If I set off the blasting under these conditions, the remainder of the range may be destroyed! Decades of work blasted into rubble!"

Softly, a whispery wind full of heat and dust blew past the assemblage as the angry Venusian modulated readouts and twirled dials. "Damn, the circuits are still operational, but the charges have failed to detonate. How annoying."

He stated this so calmly it took a good two seconds to percolate through the collective minds of the news team.

"The bombs are live?!" they cried in loose chorus.

A nod. "Yes, malfunctioning, not dysfunctioning. The whole six hundred and three of them. Armed, but unexploded."

"But . . . there's no danger," ventured Snyder, nervously loosening his necktie. "We're safe inside here?"

Closely studying a readout panel, the professor furrowed his brow. "What? Oh, of course not. Don't be silly. If the charges should go off now, we would be annihilated in the first microsecond."

"Sir, could you repeat that, please?" requested Rikka in a strained voice.

Gnashing his teeth, the professor did so. "Of course, it's theoretically possible that if any of the nukes explodes, then maybe merely the top of this butte would be broken off and we'd simply drop the fourteen meters to the new gravel floor of the valley," added Ketter, throwing tripbars and pressing buttons.

"And survive?" squeaked Jhonny hopefully, sliding a fresh video disk into a handcam that already was holding two more than maximum. The camera made a gagging noise and spewed the disk back out like a shiny tongue. Hey, enough was enough already!

Lost in concentration, Prof. Ketter continued to fiddle with the complex controls, adjusting slides and typing commands onto a keyboard roughly the size, and oddly the exact shape, of Nebraska. "Survive? Nonsense. However, we'd get an extra thirty seconds of life. But even worse, without the cushioning shocks of the surrounding explosions, the shrapnel might damage my other mountains!"

The semisentient Toshiba on Jhonny's shoulder fainted.

"And whatever you do, don't make any vibrations," admonished the professor grumpily, both hands busy. "The slightest additional shock could trigger an immediate detonation sequence."

"Whoa there, amigo," barked Rikka quietly. "We're sitting on top of six hundred nukes and not supposed to move?"

"Yes."

"Are you insane?"

"Madam, do I look unstable?" snapped the scientist, his eyeballs bulging out slightly and his hair starting to stick straight up.

Diplomatically, the reporter said nothing in reply.

"Jhonny, you recording this?" asked Harry, nervously tugging on his mustache. If they lived, it would be a hell of a story!

The android looked up from manually rebooting his unconscious camera. "Of course. Why?"

A gulp. "This may be our last broadcast."

AT LEAST IN THIS DIMENSION.

"Ho-ho. I laugh." Damn big-mouthed Brain.

"Let me finish." The camera-op cleared his throat and returned to his taping. ". . . being of sound mind and body, do hereby leave my worldly possessions . . ."

On the main view screen above the control panel, Prof. Ketter was diligently flashing through a series of scenes displaying dimly lit crevices. Thick cables ran everywhere like the web of a deranged spider on cheap drugs. Shielded coaxial cables connected to massive cylinders of burnished steelloy marked with cryptic black numbers, red radiation symbols, and the silver silhouettes of buxom women.

Annoyed, Rikka snorted disdain. "Shaped" charges. Ha. But it also gave her an idea.

Finished composing his death poem, Michelangelo raised a questioning paw. "If we're going to die, should we take this opportunity to call the boss and tell him off?"

"Tempting," said Collins, gently loosening the sleeves of her spacesuit. "Or better yet, we could strip."

"Beg pardon?"

"When we walk, our clothes will cushion our footsteps and bare feet make softer impacts than boots."

Instantly, the news team began to disrobe as fast as safety allowed. They hadn't done anything like this since the last office Christmas party. But what the heck, real journalism was about the naked truth anyway.

"Cut, rewind!" stated Jhonny, ceasing in his striptease. "This is useless. 'Cause when Deitrich lands our 160-ton shuttle on the roof, or near the door . . . boom!" He pantomimed an explosion using both hands and a small pile of papers.

FLOAT LIKE A BUTTERFLY, LAND LIKE A BRICK, THAT'S ME, admitted the MainBrain pilot honestly.

Grudgingly accepting that as the truth, Snyder eased off his cummerbund anyway and allowed his stomach to expand that extra half inch. Ah, freedom. "Okay. Fine. No problem. Deitrich, rendezvous at the south window of the bunker. Just hover there on antigrav and we'll crawl on board."

GOTCHA.

"And keep the FTL engines running," added Rikka, Velcroing the front of her jumpsuit closed again.

HUH? YOU WANNA GO FASTER THAN LIGHT INSIDE AN ATMOSPHERE?

"Know a better way to outrace a nuclear blast?"

WELL, IT'LL CERTAINLY BRING NEW MEANING TO THE TERM "GOING FATAL," noted Deitrich tactlessly on everybody's wrist monitors. ON MY WAY.

"Damn, damn, damn!" shouted Ketter, shattering the somber tone in the bunker. Bubbling obscenities, the elderly professor then grabbed a nearby chair and started pounding on the control board with pyrotechnic results. "Take that! And that! And this too!"

At the noise, hearts stopped for so long that their pocketdocs almost declared a cardiac emergency, and the numb reporters had to wait until their blood started to move again before speech returned as a viable option.

"Is the danger over?" whispered Collins, staring at the floor as if she could see the coming nuclear blast. In her mind, atomic holocaust was a cross between bad chili, a volcano, and an executive board meeting. Shudder.

"Yes. Certainly. Who cares!" ranted the scientist, pulling a Bedlow laser derringer from his coat and firing blindly at the console. Sparks sprayed in the air and a section of the board burst into flames.

"Then what the prack is going on!" demanded the reporter at the top of her lungs.

Snorting with ill-controlled rage, Prof. Ketter spun about, his face contorted with frustration and a glowing laser in his fist. Whatever the man had to say, everybody was going to listen.

"Sabotage!" cried Ketter furiously. "These bombs have been deliberately short-circuited to prevent detonation!"

"How do you know for certain?" asked Harry, feeling the

knots in his shoulders loosen. His body desperately wanted a drink, but his mind demanded the facts. Story first, martini later.

Baring his teeth, the professor gestured with the laser, the scintillating energy beam annihilating another panel of controls.

"Just look at those readouts!" he stormed as the smoke wafted out the window. A pause. "Oh. Well, you should have seen those readouts! The testing circuit had been looped back into itself. So when I tested the main circuit, the testing circuit only tested itself. Which was, of course, working on the test!"

Silence reigned for a minute.

"I understood that," Mike admitted reluctantly.

YEAH, RIGHT.

Ketter snorted agreement. "And the firing circuit had been rewired to a common VCR. When I asked for detonation, instead the machine dutifully recorded a local Historical/ Science Fiction sitcom!"

FORBIDDEN PLANTAGENETS, supplied Deitrich. GOOD SHOW.

"So how did this happen?" asked Snyder curiously. After so much preparation, a mistake of this caliber was fantastic.

"Must be those damn idiot union electricians I hired!"

But in spite of the vehemence of the scientist's declaration, the SNT reporters did not consider that an option. Maybe if the bombs had simply been broken, sure, but sabotaged? Nyah, that would have required overtime. Then again, maybe it was only somebody disguised as a union electrician. Hmm.

"Do you have any enemies?" asked Collins, getting to the core of the matter. "The New Mafia? Free Police? The Sons of Uncle Bob? Spacial IRS?"

"Enemies?" raved Ketter, waving his laser pistol about to cool the glowing barrel. "A nice guy like me? Enemies? Of course not, you blithering dolt!"

"What union did you use?" inquired the unflappable Rikka, touch-typing on her wrist secretary. If any major criminal power got ahold of these superbombs the consequences could only be described as pure front page. That is, if there was anybody remaining to hear the broadcast.

"Ah . . . 'Ion New York.' "

"From Manhattan Island, Earth?"

"There's another?"

Tolerantly, the reporter smiled. "Just checking."

"Still, you're lucky the only sabotaged bombs are in this central column," noted Jhonny, studying a vector graphic on his flashing secretary. "If even a single bomb in any of the statues had failed to go off, the resulting unbalanced forces would have annihilated everything. It's a miracle this column survived undamaged." Curious. Very curious.

Holstering his derringer, the scientist petulantly kicked at an inoffensive bit of broken chair on the floor. "Well, I suppose."

"Not necessarily," growled Michelangelo in his stentorian bass. Crossing the bunker in two strides, the goliath alien ripped open his spacesuit and started removing tools from a bulging vest. "I'm going to run a diagnostic on the primary inducers."

"Eh! Why?" demanded Ketter, craning his neck to peer around the alien's waist. "Nonsense. There's no response pulse and the multiphase cybercubes are totally limp. I.e., it's broken. What else could possibly be the problem?"

Impatiently, the leviathan delicately picked Ketter up with one huge paw and placed the obstruction aside. Ye gods above and below, the majority of humanity was so damn stubborn in its beliefs that they certainly couldn't have evolved from monkeys. Must have been mules. Or used car dealers.

"Deitrich, give me a deep scan with the WatchDog sensors," Mike requested, ripping off a service panel and removing a pawful of wiring. Ah, there was the proximity accelerator!

WORKING. AND I KNOW WHAT TO NOT LOOK FOR.

"Not look for?" asked Rikka, but then bit her tongue. She was out of her depth on the technical angle of this business and always allowed the techies to run amuck whenever possible. Got a lot of good stories that way. Also the occasional prison sentence, but what the heck.

Joining his friend at the ruined board, Jhonny parted the sleeves of his spacesuit and was hardwiring his pet camcorder to the security camera set in the smoking wall. "Doing a pas-

sive loop," he said, jacking into the secretary on his wrist.
"On line . . . got an internal picture from the fiberoptic cables
. . . tracing the mains . . . to the photovoltaic transformers . . .
ah-ha!"

"What?" asked Harry, frozen in the act of lighting a cigar.
The android blanched. "Oh, no."

"What?" asked Rikka, standing near a cluttered desk and in
the act of stealing a sealed manila folder marked SECRET AND
PRIVATE.

"I have the same result here," muttered Mike, his huge
paws moving with fluid grace across the shattered console.
"Deitrich?"

ZERO, BIG GUY. NADA. THE MAGIC GOOSE EGG.

"I told you the charges were sabotaged," snorted Ketter in
disdain.

The technician turned about and raked a set of talons across
his hairy face. "No, sir. They are not broken."

"Oh, yeah?" sneered the Venusian, belligerently fondling
his gun. "Then why didn't they detonate?"

Michelangelo merely stared down at the minuscule human,
the expression on the alien's face unreadable to the professor,
but the familiar fuzzy countenance spoke volumes to the reporters.

"Gone," said Rikka, feeling that old surge of excitement
tingle in her spine. "The bloody bombs didn't go off because
six hundred and three of the canisters are empty!"

"Sir, apparently six hundred and three of your precious
shaped nuclear bombs," stated Snyder, in his best on-camera
voice, "have been stolen!"

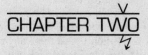

CHAPTER TWO

"YES!" CRIED RIKKA, raising a clenched fist into the air. At last, they had a real story to cover, not merely a picturesque series of controlled nuclear explosions forming a thousand-kilometer-long statue detailing the evolution of life and civilization. That was old hat. Sunday supplement stuff at best.

Eyebrows up and mouth down, Ketter stared at the woman, aghast.

Quickly she lowered her hand. "Ah ... I mean ... that is ..."

"While the importance of your contribution to the fields of demolitions and sculpturing is without peer," soothed Harry, stepping in front of her. "It must behoove us, if only in passing, to note that the theft of such incredibly advanced technology has broad and far-reaching eco-sociological implications of a dire and illicit nature."

"Okay, I buy that," said the professor.

"What he say?" asked Jhonny, undoing the wires from the console.

Shutting down the trace, Mike shrugged. Perhaps it was sort of a human religious thing. Whew. He had been afraid that the bombs might be used for criminal purposes.

ALERT! scrolled the wrist secretaries. INCOMING!

"Shrapnel? Missiles? Pirates?" demanded Rikka aloud.

WORSE. THE LOCAL AFFILIATES OF QINS, QCNN, AND QBBC EACH SPOTTED THE DETONATIONS AND THE NETWORKS ARE ON THEIR WAY!

"The networks? Crap!" cried Snyder around his pipe. Their exclusive just deteriorated into a race. "ETA?"

TOO DAMN SOON, replied the pilot. AND THEY'VE GOT COMPANY.

"Who?" demanded Rikka, pulling on her spacesuit as a prelude to action.

THE VENUSIAN ARMY, NAVY, SPACE FORCE, POLICE, INTERPLANETPOL, AND THE UNITED SOLAR DEFENSE ALLIANCE.

"I didn't send them any coded invitations," scowled Ketter, stuffing hands into lab coat pockets. "How could those cretins be aware of what happened?"

GEEZ, HOW COULD THEY NOT? THOSE DAMN BLASTS ILLUMINATED HALF THE HEMISPHERE AND KILLED TV RECEPTION FOR THE REST OF THE WORLD! Deitrich chuckled. UH-OH, THE NEILSENS JUST PUT OUT A CONTRACT ON THE PROF. AND THE WHATADUMP HISTORICAL SOCIETY HAS JUST PLACED A BREAKFAST ORDER FOR YOUR PRIVATE PARTS.

"Prack 'em," stormed the professor in a surge of Venusian pride. "It's my crater, and I'll do with it as I please!"

Collins spun about fast. "Professor Ketter, we need to finish the interview, pronto!"

The scientist seemed unsure of himself. "The interview? Ah, well, I'm not sure . . ."

"We're the only ones who answered the invitation," reminded Jhonny sagely.

"True."

"And it's free advertising for the park," puffed Snyder. "The Gregor Ketter Technological Park d'Triumph!"

"That is, unless you want us to spread the story that your security was so shitty that some milk-drinking wimp from Earth simply strolled in off the street and took your bombs?" asked Rikka with a sly smile.

"Earth!" spat Ketter in disgust. "Those buffoons couldn't take a bath! That story would make me look like a total idiot! Where did you get that puerile notion?"

Silence. Four evil grins.

"Pax," sighed the scientist in resignation. He had dealt with blackmail before and knew when to surrender. On the other hand, it was also how he had gotten his tenure at Annihilation U. God bless zero-G motels. "What do you want?"

"Stick to the artistic counterpoint story, answer Mr. Snyder's questions, and comb your hair," ordered Rikka, handing Snyder a computer clipboard. "Here are the basic questions. Mike, get us a hot link to the shuttle."

"Done!" rumbled the giant technician, nimble talons wiring the standing camera to a booster relay on the back of his spacesuit.

Her mind revving to overload, Rikka turned to snap more commands, but Jhonny was already busy with a light meter and checking the sound system. What an android! Best damn camera-op in the whole system. Too bad he was legally un-employable as an android or else the manchine would have a closet full of Pulitzers instead of only two. But then, every-body had secrets. Even her.

ENEMY NEWS SERVICE IN FIFTEEN.

Fixing his clothes, Harry spun about facing the camera and caught a hand mike tossed to him by Jhonny. "Good evening, ladies and gentlemen and all the ships in space," boomed the anchor, flashing his famous smile. "This is Harry Snyder broadcasting live from the violence-filled badlands of lower Venus with an exclusive QSNT report on the most amazing technological advancement in the Arts and Sciences since the creation of frozen MTV dinners."

Just then a new message flashed on the teleprompter. "This special report is brought to you by The Interplanetary Book Club: "Bound for glory under the covers," and by Hanover Trust brand condoms: combining fiduciary responsibility with safe sex you can bank on!"

A thousand kilometers away, a sleek white needle of steel and lithium plummeted out of the starry black of space. Re-sembling a flat-bottomed airplane with stubby wings and a great cluster of chemical jets in the rear, the space shuttle smashed through the ionosphere of Venus, shattering the sound barrier with a strident boom. On the side of the shuttle was emblazoned the logo "QINS: News NEWS, NEWS!" That purportedly brilliant slogan had been the brain child of the station owner's nephew, who charged the Interplanetary News

Service a cool million for his work and who had been promptly executed upon its embarrassing delivery.

Behind the sleek craft, contrails of dirty smog formed two hard lines that quickly cooled, condensed, and broke into pieces that rained down toward the distant ground. On most worlds, this would have been considered littering. On Venus it was deemed urban beautification.

"Found 'em! We're going in!" cried the pilot, tightening the seat harness across the chest of his embroidered spacesuit.

"And no sign of the SNT!" cried the copilot, adjusting the trim of the wings and booting their stolen WatchDog scanner jamming system.

Black hair, blue contact lenses, tan, and muscular to the point of immobility, the pilot was a painfully handsome man who reveled in the fact. Indeed, hidden in the inner recesses of his velveteen wallet was a photo ID proclaiming him as Jason Hardcopy, a former president of the Narcissus Fan Club. A Nikon 35mm military assault camera was slung over a powerful shoulder and the butt of a signature model Torkamada Truth Stick peeked out of the top of his right boot.

A blond riot of natural curls cascaded down across the stunningly lovely face of the copilot, the breathtaking beauty marred only for a moment as the woman spit a stream of black tobacco juice into a nearby cuspidor. And not even the thick protective material armor of her spacesuit could disguise the delightfully ample female curves of her amazing form. A combination video recorder/lie detector was strapped about her dainty armored waist, the explosive ID tag bearing the moniker "Susie Sunshine." The ace reporter had once been asked to join the Narcissus Club, but declined, not believing that they were good enough for her.

In the rear of the Interplanetary News Service craft, their bedraggled camera-op continued berating himself for not paying more attention when he signed the guest ledger at a party. Only this morning the man had rudely discovered that he had just renewed his service contract with QINS—at half his usual pay rate. Privately, the camera operator hoped for a quick, clean crash. With the pilot and copilot going first.

Happy retirement, indeed. Bah. Humbug.

* * *

Skimming among the rocky planetary surface at near lethal speeds, the heavily armed Venusian school bus "The Hall Merrimack" streaked over the desolate mud flats of the Achilles Foothills and headed straight toward Whatadump Valley. The Tombstone City Internal Defense League and Thursday Night Bowling Society had publicly hemorrhaged when the report came in of the multiple nuclear blasts and immediately requested a reconnaissance strafing run. The first rule in the Venusian military was "Shoot the Unexpected." Even among the civilians, sneezes were considered rude, jack-in-the-boxes were strictly outlawed, and practical jokes were merely a more sophisticated form of suicide.

Sitting bored in the back seats of the scholastic assault vehicle, a group of small children played with their live hand grenades and watched Road Runner cartoons.

"Target located, sir!" announced the helmsman, both hands working his glowing control panel. Meters ticked, scanners swirled, and gun safeties were clicked off. On the port screen, a robotic ore freighter arced the horizon and the automatic cannon swiveled about to lock on target. But fire was withheld as the computer records showed the freighter was registered to carry only minerals bearing rocks and rarefied gases. Ether, ore, the craft was nonoffensive.

"Coordinates?" barked the Captain Sister Mary Petard. The dour educator was dressed in spitball-proof ninja fatigues, with three and a quarter inches of a yardstick extended from the scabbard attached to her belt, which was about to fall off from the collection of notches in the thick leather strap.

"The valley is at, mark, 14.60 degrees," announced the driver, strong and loud. But then his voice started to fade away. "Directly past that giant granite gorilla and the drowning guy in a toga?"

"Say what?" barked the Captain, snapping on a pair of binoculars to stare at the video monitor.

"What!" chorused the children obediently.

Instantly, the yardstick was out searching for a target. For-

tunately for the children, that was when the scanners detected
the QINS shuttle.

Ah-ha, intruders!

"Thank you, Professor," smiled Harry, turning from an undamaged section of the control board to face the camera and
bright lights.

"No. Thank. You. Mister. Ah, Snyder," replied the scientist,
woodenly reading his response from the teleprompter.

Off camera, the SNT reporters made pained expressions.
Lord, what an amateur! Good thing Ketter wasn't in the theater or else he would really become the master of bombs.

Struggling not to laugh, Harry nodded benignly and struck
a pose as the camera zoomed in for a close-up. "And this is
Harry Snyder signing off for the Satellite News Service.
Please stay tuned for the following program lower-my-voice-
and-have-the-studio-computer-insert-the proper-slug here.
Thank you and may the good news be yours. Aloha!"

On cue, Mike activated a castanet-sized clapboard and
Rikka killed the auxiliary lights.

"Cut!" announced Jhonny, capping the camera lens and
folding the support legs closed. "That's a wrap. More than
enough. I can do an edit in the shuttle on the way home."

"Check," said Harry, wiping the cosmetics off his face with
a moist towelette. Oddly, the anchor actually looked younger
without the cosmetics, but Snyder knew he had an image to
uphold. The public didn't want the hard news from snot-
nosed youngsters, but from crotchety old farts. It didn't matter
that Harry was scrupulously honest, if he didn't appear scrupulously honest. Ah well, such was the news biz. You gotta
lie to tell the truth.

A billow of warm air filled the bunker and a familiar shape
filled the windows. "All aboard!" sang out Deitrich's voice
from an external speaker.

As her comrades grabbed their equipment and dashed for
the window, Rikka yanked a pen and paper from the scientist's hands. Climbing over the sill into the airlock she waved
the contract to help dry the ink. It had required little effort to
convince Ketter to sign a standard release form giving QSNT

an exclusive on the stolen bombs story, although the five thousand Venusian buckaroos in exchange had soothed his wounded ego.

The last to leave, Michelangelo pawed the scientist a stack of prepared press releases to give to the other news services when they eventually arrived. And on the way out the alien slapped a QSNT EXCLUSIVE sticker on the exterior of the bunker. In revenge and business, it always pays to advertise.

As his huge form wiggled into the tiny human airlock, the doors slammed shut and the craft angled away from the bunker on a soft blue field of antigrav.

"Brace yourselves!" cried the overhead speaker, and deep within the bowels of the spacecraft the disembodied MainBrain pilot leveled the trim of their wings and kicked in the after-turbo thrusters. In an explosion of power, the SNT space shuttle thundered away from the bunker and knifed through the cold muggy air above the newly formed park. The billowing gouts of green flame blasting from the jets rudely volatilized the contrails formed by their wings.

Gawd, he loved doing that.

Hurrying to the cockpit on the bridge, the news team quickly strapped themselves into their assigned seats. Filling the bow windows was a rapidly growing statue of Hercules as he permanently rearranged the columns of a Roman arena. As the shuttle rocketed between the great hairy legs of the historic accountant, Rikka couldn't help but glance upward under his loincloth and was astonished at the amazing detail on the statue. Wow, so much muscle, and Jewish too. Neat!

Seated at the navigation console, Jhonny was frantically typing commands onto a keyboard and adjusting slides. "Prack! QINS is almost dead ahead of us!"

"Evasive maneuvers?" asked Michelangelo, his paws busy on the engineering console as he prepared to remove the safety stops from the engine controls. A black-palmed paw was poised expectantly above the glowing red button that would ignite their solid-fuel boosters, kick in the emergency rockets, activate the auxiliary turbo-thrusters, and automatically serve them with a $1,000 speeding ticket.

"There's no room or time," spat the android.

"Deitrich, can we do a Deadman?" asked Rikka, seated in the copilot's chair. Her hands were tight fists held before the console. "Kill our power systems and slide by underneath them?"

"No way, chief," replied the ceiling speaker. The pilot's seat was empty, but the controls depressed and dials turned by themselves as the human brain deep in the bowels of the ship expertly did his job. "The relative distance is so short, they'd see us through the windows!"

Poised at Communications, Harry ground his teeth and started booting every radar jammer and WatchDog scrambler device they possessed, which was a lot. Most of them legal.

"Mike!" the anchor barked. "Did you get a chance to repair our hull after that crash on Jupiter last month?"

"Yes, but so what?" asked the alien, urging a few more ergs of thrust out of their straining engines. "No matter what our hull says, QINS will automatically assume it's us!"

"Oh, no, they won't," said the ceiling, and somehow the words carried the feeling of a smirk.

On the outside of the speeding craft, the black bow lettering of QSNT melted to spread out in a smooth blanket of gray that extended across the entire outer surface of the craft. Lightening in color and rippling with texture, the shuttle assumed an entire new appearance.

Seconds later the two news shuttles passed within a few kilometers of each other with a combined speed slightly greater than that of greased, unchained lightning on a light gravity world.

"Eh! What the heck was that?" demanded Jason, twisting his neck to glance out the port window.

Focusing an aft monitor, Susie scrutinized the WatchDog scanner. "A stone space shuttle?"

"Look!" cried Hardcopy, pointing with his dimpled chin. "Statues!"

Facing forward, the blonde blinked in surprise and then grunted. Okay, that shuttle was just another display. Odd though, it had appeared to be moving. Plainly just an optical illusion.

Relaxing a bit, the INS reporter wiped sweat from her brow with a sleeve. Thank goodness, for one dreadful moment she was horrified that the SNT had beat them to another story.

Aft rockets thundering in unrestrained fury, the QSNT news craft rose in a screaming climb above the clouds.

"No response from the INS shuttle," announced Deitrich in gleeful victory.

Rikka cried, "Yes! Made it!"

"Home free!" added Mike, wiggling his ears in celebration.

"With an exclusive interview under contract and a secret lead to the most dangerous robbery this year," capped off Jhonny proudly.

"Ladies and gentle beings," announced Harry, rising from his seat and taking a stance. "It's Quiller time!"

The colored hull condensed on the prow again forming the words "Quiller Geo-Medical Plumbing." It was the SNT's favorite fake ID and there was still several Venusian sentry satellites to sneak past. Reporters were often considered muckraking troublemakers, but everybody ignored a plumber.

"First thing we have to do is find who stole those bombs," admonished Collins, checking her notes. "And have the police recover 'em before lives are lost."

"You got that right, kid."

"Check, chief."

"Agreed."

"Xar'nl su-if," growled Mike as he bared his teeth. "In spades!"

At maximum atmospheric speed, the spacecraft lanced through the ethereal boundary of the Van Allen belts that girdled every planet in the manner of a magnetic truss, and erupted into the starry black of space. Freed from the confining restraints of air, the ionic flame blasting out of the main rocket array trailed behind them like a long, radioactive putting green.

Dutifully, the four-pound pilot altered the design on the hull to again read QSNT. It was boring but functional. Deitrich hated boring. Privately, he decided that someday the team must assign this noble craft a fitting designation, and if

they couldn't come to a decision, then he'd just name it any-
way himself! How about The Knightly News? The Spacial
Report? Or perhaps Star Reporters? Nyah, too plebeian.
Maybe he should just stay with the original Deitrich's Flying
Loony Bin. It was undignified but painfully honest, which
were two big points in its favor.

"Forward flight path is clear," stated Jhonny, double-
checking the navigation scanners.

"Course plotted and laid in," added Rikka, punching buttons with oft-practiced ease.

"Check," responded Harry, keying in a standard response
signal. "Life support is operational and we have VD . . . ah,
we have clearance to go off-world from Venus Defense."

"Sterlings are at ninety percent," finished Mike, twiddling
dials and thumping meters. "Mains are on-line. Power levels
are 10/10. And I'm chilling a six-pack." Fuel for the crew.

"Going Fatal . . . now!" announced Deitrich.

To the reporters, Venus vanished as the stars before them
took on a definite reddish hue while those behind turned blue.

"Next stop, Media!" gaily called their MainBrain pilot.

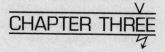
"MEDIA ON SCREEN!" announced Deitrich as the stars cleared into sharp points of white and went infinitely still. The visual always reminded him of having sex with a girl from Connecticut.

"Took long enough," growled Rikka impatiently. Earth had inconveniently been on the other side of the solar system and the reporters had been forced to circumnavigate the sun to reach their goal. Even traveling faster than light, the journey had taken so long Jhonny had already edited up a broadcast version of the interview with Ketter and beamed it, scrambled, encoded, and in three separate pieces—nouns-verbs-adjectives—back to Media. It was an old, but reliable trick. The only news department that flatly refused to use it was Classified Ads, as their weird alphabet ciphers were quite confusing enough as it was: SWF, DBM, REHI˜99/BRB:). What did this stuff mean anyway?

Filling the main view screen of the shuttle was the dark rocky ball of Luna. Illuminating most of the moon's hemisphere was the sprawling electric wonder of Starlite City. The biggest city on the dark side of Luna. There were a dozen other enclaves: CrashTown, Green Cheeseville, Hole-In-The-Ground, No Meteors Here! including four United Planets military bases, thirty-two independent mining outposts, and six interplanetary observatories—who actually were studying the military bases for rival planets. The largest of the observatories was permanently pointed at Media in a vain attempt to keep track of those damn troublemaking reporters. It had

never worked, but the spies kept trying. Besides, they were
paid by the hour.

Reclining in his seat, Harry puffed a victory cigar at the
monitor. In the mere three hundred years humanity had been
in space, Starlite City had evolved from a bare rock plain of
vacuum and dust into a domed metropolis with a population
of fifty thousand mostly law-abiding residents. Which annoyed the reporters no end. A major population center only
kilometers beneath their home base and not a single good
story had ever come out of the place. It was positively mad-
dening.

With perfect lunar symmetry, the bustling city was neatly
bordered by the Royal Black Mountains. The soaring cliffs
were formed entirely of dark volcanic glass, a crude symbol
of primordial nature unleashed and apparently very pissed off.
Thankfully not at anybody the SNT knew personally.

Partially eclipsed by the gray horizon was the blue-white
glory of Earth. Originally the reservoir of humanity, the
planet presently boasted a population of less than one billion.
But the old homeworld still housed the United Planets General Assembly, the military headquarters of the United Solar
Defense Alliance, and more Automatic Teller Machines than
could be easily counted in a single life span. Backed by
money, guns, and lawyers, Earth was still the top dog in the
solar food chain. And they liked it that way.

Soon a dark blob was discernible, silhouetted by the poin-
tillism splendor of Starlite City. Tiny, at first, the irregular
shape grew into a large lumpy structure resembling a white
beach ball stuffed into a stainless-steel doughnut.

Media Station. Home.

Permanently locked in a geosynchronous orbit above the
moon, Media's outer hull was dotted with huge dish antennas
set in triplicate, proof against any possible accident so that
nothing could interfere with the Z-band transmitters that connected the news station to the rest of the solar system. A single lost minute of airtime could equate to millions of lost
revenue dollars with an estimated viewing audience of 4.5
trillion. The very thought of such a horrible catastrophe had
forced the station owner, Gardner Wilkes, to install a saloon

in the space station. An act that he subsequently regretted on an almost hourly basis.

A wonder of the ages, Media consisted of fifty-seven million tons of state-of-the-art communications machinery, jammed into thirty-seven climate-controlled levels operated by five thousand highly trained professionals, whose sole concern was the proper dissemination of the news, the whole news, and nothing but the news. Occasionally some truth slipped into a broadcast, but aside from the SNT reports, it was mostly by accident.

Surrounding the busy space station, shuttles, tugs, freighters, military gunships, paddy wagons, and executive singleships came and went with amazing regularity. Starry space was sprinkled with the assorted green flames of their distant chemical engines. Colorful buoys blinked lanes for traffic, with hologram arrows indicating the direction of the flow and precisely to whom the ever-vigilant Lunar Police were currently addressing their remarks.

"Traffic Control, this is SNT shuttle #1," spoke Harry into his spacesuit collar. "We have a priority story. Repeat, a top priority story. Request landing clearance and docking instructions."

"And keep it clean," added Deitrich.

"Acknowledge #1," replied a smooth voice. "Traffic is sparse and you have immediate clearance. Use approach lane 4, vector of 19, and dock at landing bay 23."

"Acknowledged," answered Deitrich, the pilot controls moving to new positions.

Soon the steelloy curve of Media centered on the main view screen. Under Rikka's adroit fingers, the midsection of the cockpit monitor zoomed in on a glowing rectangle of light bars that marked the opening of the landing bay. The hull doors cycled apart exposing a runway deck edged with blinking lights and brilliantly marked with the number 23. Her view was distorted by the presence of a sonic screen that kept the station's air inside, but the reporter was still able to see that the distant interior wall was packed solid with a towering mound of bulky sandbags and plastic crash barrels.

Aw, how nice. Something special just for them.

The console speaker crackled. "Media to SNT #1?"

"Yes?" puffed Snyder curiously.

"Please try not to crash, okay? We just painted the place again."

"I'll do my best," sang out Deitrich. "But we are in a hurry!"

Nimbly, the MainBrain pilot adjusted the flight plan of the shuttle. Belly jets vomiting flame, the spacecraft tumbled stern over bow and rigidly realigned itself aft toward the station.

"No!" cried the speaker horrified. "Don't come in backward!"

Obediently, the attitude jets flared and the shuttle spiraled about and came straight at the station broadside.

"Jesus, no! Not sideways either!" Clearly in the background could be heard sirens, Klaxons, warning bells, and assorted cries of "Oh, no!" "Run for cover!" and "I quit!"

As the reporters chuckled at the obvious panic, the MainBrain pilot spun the craft around, leveling out neat and trim toward the station with nose front.

"This is great!" laughed the ceiling. "Those stuffy flight controllers will never again complain about us landing too damn fast. We were never a danger to Media. Those bureaucrats just needed a better reference as to what a really bad landing might look like! Thanks for the idea, Harry."

"You're quite welcome, old man," acknowledged the anchor, tapping cigar ashes into a waste receptacle where they were sucked off to a recycling bin to be packed into a fresh new low-cal cigar. Waste not, want not. "What are friends for?"

"Loans?" asked Rikka, smiling, fluffing her hair.

Photographing a passing tug, Jhonny cracked a grin. "Alibis?"

"Trouble," answered Michelangelo, adjusting his pince-nez glasses as he closely studied a meter. "Deitrich, aren't we far exceeding the maximum allowable approach velocity by even more than our usual factor?"

"Oh, don't you start on me," retorted the Brain, and he ordered the nose retros to fire full power, in a series of split-second bursts. But only weak flame sputtered out from the nozzles and then nothing at all.

Faster than ever, Media swelled to engulf the stars.

"Ah, alert. There appears to have been a slight miscalculation on my part," stated Deitrich as every control on the pilot console endlessly moved to new positions. "We used too much chemical fuel blasting off of Venus. The brakes are exhausted."

"Ooops," the pilot added sheepishly as an apology.

"Emergency jets!" barked Snyder, tightening his chest strap.

"Exhausted."

"Reverse the mains!" growled Mike, trying to urge a last spurt from the nose rockets, and failing.

"Engaged and overheating."

Locking her seat immobile, Collins ordered, "Abort the landing!"

"No room to maneuver."

The open metal mouth of the landing dock zoomed toward them at frightening speed.

"Crash procedures!"shouted Jhonny, finishing the litany. Grabbing his camcorder, the android tucked his beloved pet into his helmet and slammed the headgear onto his shoulders.

Safety harnesses automatically tightened about every chest, crash balloons billowed out from the control consoles pinning everybody into place, and a fire sprinkler by the arms locker squirted a stream of foam directly at Harry's cigar, neatly extinguishing the potentially dangerous heat source.

At twice the regulation velocity, the SNT shuttle streaked into the space station, punching through the sonic curtain as if it was no more than air. Angled too low, the craft lightly tapped the deck, lithium tiles exploding out from the glancing impact, forcing the shuttle upward where it hit the ceiling with a resounding clang! Once, twice, thrice, the spacecraft musically bounced between the ceiling and deck to finally slam into the thick sandbag wall. Sand, water, foam, and burlap geysered from the meteoric strike, spraying debris everywhere. Rebounding from the resilient cushioning, the shuttle hung in the air for a full heartbeat before dropping impotently to the deck, indenting the hard surface.

A minute of reverberating silence passed as everybody worked their jaws to stop the ringing in their ears.

"Ah, another perfect landing," said the ceiling speaker, wafts of black smoke arising from the woofers and tweeters.

"Perfect?!" roared Snyder, turning red in the faceplate.

"Hey, at least I landed inside."

As the crash balloons deflated, Rikka unsnapped the safety harness and mumbled in agreement. True enough. As the Legal Department always said: No corpse, no crime.

"Come on," said Jhonny, rising and stretching. "We've got to go talk to Box. Agreed?"

A chorus replied yes.

Extracting themselves from the cockpit, the reporters gathered their gear and cycled out the airlock. Incredibly, it still worked, although the dilating metal leaves made a noise very similar to Michelangelo's real last name.

Climbing out of the shallow pit and picking their way through the broken tiles and exploded sandbags, the SNT gang headed directly for the bank of turbo-lifts. Safe behind a meter-thick barrier of scarred Armorlite glass, the flight control officers in the operations tower shook stern fingers at the departing team, while on the deck a small army of janitors started forward carrying an arsenal of brooms, mops, and an industrial-size tube of Mr. Fix-It superglue.

Ambling up a short flight of steps, the team walked quickly through a humming decontamination arch and a second sonic curtain. Passing the Damage Control kiosk, an exasperated technician took a computer stylus from his jumpsuit pocket and changed the markings on a digital tote board on the wall to read: 901-3.

Fuming in embarrassment, the team stormed down the hall and onto a turbo-lift, accidentally hitting the button for the main floor. As the express rocketed off to the requested level, the horrified reporters struggled valiantly to alter the instructions, abort the express, or shift the final destination, but to no avail.

As expected, the hatch to the roof of the lift was sealed,

and not even Michelangelo with his endless supply of tools could undo the expensive Scottish locks. They were trapped!

Minutes later the doors parted with a musical ding, and the rear wall of the lift extended forward with a hydraulic hiss to rudely shove the reporters into the foyer of the station.

Plush couches and comfy chairs dotted the reception area, along with potted Martian spider ferns and Venusian flytraps. The pretty blue-skinned android woman behind the front desk waved a hello and gave Jhonny a sly wink. Lustfully, the camera-op returned the favor. His status as a camera operator for the SNT was hinged solely on the fact that he looked human. In accordance to the Organic law of 2018 AD, no artificial being could own property or hold a job above secretarial. A stupid law that had almost started a war. It had taken him years of saving to get enough money for a full body tattoo to turn him pink. Few of his fellow androids knew his actual origin and even less were desirable females. And for Jhonny, sex with a human was like juggling raw plutonium: awkward, dangerous, and special shielding was required.

In a display niche behind the female was a six-hundred-year-old hand-held bell, and a black slate with a piece of white chalk tied to it with string. A humble reminder of the true origin of the team's vaunted profession. Professional bigmouths.

Then the air began to shimmer ominously. Quickly rummaging about in their equipment bags, Rikka and the team barely found what they wanted before the image focused into a hologram picture of a politically correct choir.

"WELCOME TO QSNT!" cheerfully sang the happy group. "ALL NEWS ALL THE TIME!"

Triumphant, the reporters strolled past the hated hologram, endlessly readjusting the sonic plugs in their ears. After twenty years of working here, they still weren't immune to that dreadfully cheery chorus. It was enough to make a reporter stop drinking. Almost.

A heavily armed security guard reading a book on advanced poker frowned at them as the news crew ambled victoriously through a set of swinging doors.

Pushing their way past the next double doors, the reporters stepped briskly onto the carpet of a cavernous, large, and generally really tremendous room.

Here in the exact middle of Media, the station was a huge undivided area; an ocean of desks, topped with white computer monitors extending off into the horizon until details became lost from the sheer distance. Aisles separated the different departments from each other and low-grade sonic curtains held the noise to a minimum. It also helped reduce the volume of paper airplanes and spitball volleys between rival sections.

Off to the left, the wall was composed solely of TV monitors, the fourteen screens showing the news broadcast of every other major service in the system. Rude mustaches and beards had been painted on the top three monitors designated QINS, QBBC, QCNN. To the right, was a single wall-spanning TV monitor, the same size as the rest combined. This showed what QSNT was currently broadcasting and although several attempts had been made, this glass had sadly proven to be totally mustache-proof.

Continuing onward in a stride, the team noted that yet another fistfight was occurring in Sports, with chairs bouncing off the sonic screens, so the SNT reporters did a detour. Must be the Worlds Series again. Going around Classified Ads, they stepped through the invisible pudding of a sonic curtain and entered the Advertising Department with the usual accompanying sound effect of scaw!

There a pentagram of desks faced each other, with half a dozen people typing madly on keyboards while a standing woman wearing a director's cap was savagely crossing lines off a sheet of paper with an editorial dagger, the red ink dripping off the blade in a highly suggestive manner.

The SNT reporters chuckled to themselves. Ha! Nothing symbolic there!

"Okay, let's go again," called the director, handing the paper to an assistant. "On the one, two, three!" And she leveled a finger.

In the center desk, a harried man took a deep breath and lifted the corrected paper before his face. "It's new! It's fan-

tastic! It's amazing! It's Socket Fisherman!" boomed the
skinny man in an astonishingly deep voice. "Just take one end
of Socket Fisherman, drop it into a nearby lake or stream,
plug the other end into a convenient outlet, and shazam! Hundreds of fish come bobbing to the surface. It's fantastic! And
if you order Socket Fisherman immediately, you'll also receive the cookbook *Cooking in the Wild*. Just sprinkle
breadcrumbs on top of the lake, add Socket Fisherman, and
shazam! FISHSTICKS! It's fantastic! It's amazing! It's Socket
Fisherman. To order your Socket Fisherman just send $39.95
to: U.S. Incorporated, P.O. Box 44, New York, New York,
New York, USA, Earth. Or dial 1-500-645-1196. Off-planet
call collect. Yes, SOCKET FISHERMAN! Just another fine
product from—"

A robotic chorus sang, "The Gunderson Corporation!"

"Cut! Cut!" cried the director, covering her face.

"Oh, what's wrong?" sighed the man, collapsing on the desk.

Crossing her arms, the director grimaced. "You said New
York three times, Rodger."

"Oh, crap," sighed the announcer. "There's four, isn't
there?"

"Yes."

On cue, a technician slapped a clapboard. "Okay, voice-
over for Socket Fisherman, take 156."

The announcer started to sob, and the SNT reporters quietly
hurried away. The poor bastard. Apparently there actually
were some things worse than working in the Weather Department of a space station. Incredible, but true.

Gardner Wilkes, the owner of Media, had once foolishly
tried to get Rikka and Harry to do commercials. The effort
had been as short-lived as Mr. Snyder's sobriety, while
Rikka's garish makeup had actually managed to explode a TV
camera. Albeit with a bit of help from Jhonny and Mike.

Scaw! The Crime News Department.

"Hey, chief!" called out a burly woman, lifting her head
from a hooded security monitor. "One of our scouts claims
they just found Jimmy Hoffa's body!"

The man addressed looked up from oiling the ammo clip of

his Smith & Wesson 1mm needler. "What, after so many centuries?" he snorted in disbelief. "Where?"

"Frozen in a glacier on Pluto!"

"How the prack could the Mafia of twentieth-century Earth have . . ." The man shook himself. "Never mind. It's too good a story to pass. Hannigan, go get some pictures! McMurphy, find any of his living relatives. Be sure to check Brazil. Schwartz, access the old UPI archive files and do a composite background sketch for the six o'clock."

"Check, chief!"

"Roger!"

"Gotcha!"

Scaw! Public Service.

As soon as the reporters crossed the curtain, a horrible siren cut loose to blast them to their knees with a strident steam whistle keen. "Oooooooooooooooooooooooooo . . . ! "

The hellish wail loosened the fillings in their teeth, cracked the lens on Jhonny's camcorder, and started Michelangelo's shedding season early when finally the deafening noise abruptly stopped and blessed silenced prevailed.

"This was a test," stated a mechanical voice. "This was only a test. Please put down your pens and hand in your papers. This will not count on your final grade. This was only a test."

As best they could, the gasping SNT limped hurriedly onward. Damn college radio, maybe they should have just fought their way through Sports. After all, what was the occasional football tackle to the groin among friends?

Scaw! Financial Reports.

"Hey, good news!" cried a corpulent man joyfully as he scanned a monitor covered with marching columns of incomprehensible math. "The Dow Jones/Ponticlift averages say that tin just went up!"

Half buried under a mound of computer printout a tall, golden-haired woman glared hostilely at the interruption. Denatured tin was what made FTL travel possible and the precious metal was deemed more valuable than even the Martian Youth Drug. "Don't be a putz. Tin is down!"

"Up!

"Down!"

Placing aside his stack of Chinese junk bonds, a beefy youngster reached over to cautiously tap the scrolling monitor and the indicators leveled out to new positions. "Actually, tin is both up and down," said the youth haltingly. How weird.

"Well, that explains everything!" cried the woman, delighted.

The plump man spun away from his monitor. "No, it doesn't!"

"Yes, it does," snapped the statuesque blonde.

"Doesn't!"

"Does!"

Taking their leave, the reporters exchanged amused glances. Apparently, the purported financial experts weren't exactly sure of what was happening in the Interplanetary Stock Market any more than anybody else. That did explain a lot.

Thank goodness their pension fund was invested in something stable and reliable like Jupiter's famous indelible cheese.

Scaw!

For a moment, this section resembled a junkyard, with old 8-track computer tapes, and vintage CD players piled higgledy-piggledy next to ceiling-high stacks of plastic books, damp scuba gear, an unfolded parachute, an overflowing glass file cabinet, a disassembled robot, a stuffed ocelot, an incomplete collection of "Heroes of the Sexual Revolution" drinking glasses, a suit of German medieval armor with a Zulu spear through its head, and general assorted unrecognizable stuff.

And seated like a king bum on a floating recliner was a short beefy man with close-cropped sandy hair. He wore a French denim jumpsuit, beaded Apache headband, Martian moon boots, and a pornographic Jupiter scarf. The solid brass nameplate on the file cabinet, the desk, most of the CDs, bore the name P. J. O'Ellsion. The same was embroidered on the parachute and imprinted on his pipe. He was a recent addition to the ranks of Media and was their sole freelance writer. Everybody loved his stuff, but hated him. Which was about par for a freelance journalist.

"Okay, thrill seekers, don a foam crash helmet and strap yourself into that easy chair," the short man spoke into the microphone floating near his head as a well-callused thumb opened another can of P. J. O'Ellision Brand Beer. "Because once more Uncle P. J. will tell you stuff you need to know, but don't necessarily want to hear. Too bad, shut up, pay attention."

A deep recorded slurp. "Ah! And today we're taking a much needed dip into the swirling pool of live theater again. That's pronounced 'theatre' by us slobs, and 'thea-at-tar' by the snobs, who are better than us 'cause they have lots of cash."

Another sip. "There have been many fabulous and worthwhile collaborations between different and occasionally conflicting authors. These range from such minor works as H. G. Wells and Zavier Hollander doing *The Whore of the Worlds*, to the classic by Ray Bradbury and the IBM Corporation: *I Sing the Body Selectric*, and of course that immortal work by Larry Niven and Frank Sinatra *Ring-A-Ding-Ding-World*.

A lowering of the voice. "But this latest work by Andrew Lloyd Webber XIV is a dismal failure. How he ever got backing for such a butterball as *My Fair Lady and the Tramp* is beyond my ability to comprehend. It was nowhere near as entertaining as *Seven Brides for Seven Brothers Karamazov* and lacked any of the subtle sophisticated slapstick of *The Incredible Shrinking Man of La Mancha . . .*"

Irritated, the Satellite News Team hurried on. Damn fool had no idea what he was talking about. Webber's new play was terrific. Even better than *Bob and Carol and Ted and Alice's Restaurant* and almost as good as *The Empire Strikes Back to the Future*. The original, not the remake.

Scaw! This area was empty, except for a plush velvet rope supported by brass stands surrounding a large, humming white box about the size of a space shuttle. A tiny speaker was mounted on top, and as they approached it crackled with static and then spoke.

"Yes, it's the Streamlined Download News! Bringing you

the top stories from the fourteen worlds every minute on the
minute. All the news which fits, we beep!" A pause. "Yes!
It's the Streamlined Download News! . . ."

Unimpressed, the Satellite News Team moved on and angled past the Society Editor, who was industriously polishing
her fragile ego, and headed straight for the center of the gigantic room.

Scaw! Suddenly the carpet changed from functional to decorative and grew a couple inches in thickness. Dotting the
downy acreage were a dozen islands of plush couches forming artistically pleasing conversation pits. Each was augmented with sound-dampeners, a private bar, Jacuzzi, and a
small executive trapdoor in case things got out of control.

Next came a squat fortress of polished mahogany cleverly
disguised as a simple desk, behind which sat a smiling old
woman frosting doughnuts. Beyond the formidable secretary
was the enclosed glass office of the Executive Producer for
the Satellite News Team, who was as close to a boss as they
would admit existed. The sign on the door read "Paul
Ambocksky" and etched into the glass underneath some long-
gone wag had added "The Box Stops Here."

The door did not possess a lock and the news team didn't
bother to knock as they piled inside. Busting in on folk unex-
pectedly was their patented specialty and too hard a habit to
break this late in their careers.

Across the transparent room was a sturdy steel desk backed
by a row of wooden file cabinets. And slumped in a swivel
chair at the desk was a pale, thin man in a rumpled gray
jumpsuit. He was watching the TV set in the far corner and
chewing on a sandwich that apparently had put up quite a
fight before finally surrendering and allowing itself to be
peacefully consumed.

"Greetings, sentients across the solar system," said the tiny
man on the screen. Behind him was a control panel and an old
man in a lab coat whose flapping hem seemed about ready to
launch him into space. "This is Harry Snyder, anchor for the
Satellite News Team reporting to you live from Whatadump
Canyon in the badlands of South Venus," said the edited version.

"Mercury has its awe-inspiring multicolored pools of molten metals and volcanic bingo system that makes Las Vegas pale into insignificance. Earth sports its Ten Wonders and oceans, ah, those oceans, something no other world has. Mars is adorned with the Grandest Canyon, those fabulous dust lakes, and more amusement parks than insurance brokers. Which is a damn fine thing, indeed. Luna is bristling with historic sights, numerous four-star restaurants and a truly impressive brothel. The Independent Asteroids have hundreds of specialty club and gambling casinos. The fifty-four colonized moons of Jupiter and Saturn are blessed with the natural wonders of their mother planets and cheap souvenir stands. The frozen methane slopes of Uranus are the ultimate skiers paradise, although the snow does have a nasty tendency to randomly burst into flames. Neptune, with its military prisons and secret government research labs, is closed to the general public, making it a trespasser's delight, and Pluto is a delicate fairy land of frozen ammonia spires colorfully illuminated by only mildly lethal meteorite showers that fall on an hourly basis.

"Only Venus, sadly named after the goddess of love, has nothing to offer the visiting tourist but a minimum of gun laws, free gravity, and very expensive air. Until today. This morning, the noted scientist Sir Comrade Dr. Prof. Gregor 'Did it Explode Yet?' Ketter corrected that terrible problem. And in the usual way the population of Venus handles their social and political dilemmas. With high explosives."

"Sound off," said Ambocksky, and the TV went instantly silent. Pushing at the floor with his shoe, the Producer swiveled about to face the grinning reporters. "Well done, people. You scooped the competition and delivered a hot story for the six o'clock. My compliments!"

"Ah, but there's more," smiled Rikka, pulling up a chair. "You see, the real story behind the headline is that well over six hundred of these superbombs have been—"

"Stolen," nodded Ambocksky, placing aside his bedraggled sandwich. "Yes, I know."

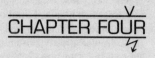

FOUR JAWS UNHINGED at those words and dangled loosely below stunned faces.

"You're surprised that I know?" asked Ambocksky, taking a bite of his sandwich.

Four silent nods.

A swallow. "Well, I don't presume this is a fact. But it certainly seemed to be indicated by what you didn't cover in the story. Gregor Ketter doing something creative as the counterpoint of that central column? Yeah, right. That man has less artistic instincts than a dead mackerel."

"Mackerel?" Rikka managed to say recovering some aplomb.

"At least the fish will eventually make a stink," smirked Box.

Harry stepped closer and gestured. "But he's an inventor! Winner of the Nobel Prize for Physics and the Pearl 20/20 Award for the most original thing too small to see!"

WOW, I DIDN'T KNOW THAT. BUT THEN, I'M FARSIGHTED.

"Ha. Very funny. You're fired," said Snyder.

AIYEE! RECEIVE MY BOSOM THIS FATAL BLADE!

"Yeah, he is an inventor, sure. But creation is entirely different from being artistic," chewed their boss, ignoring the tomfoolery. These were his best reporters, but not the biggest nuts of his staff. "Okay, how many were stolen again? Four? Five?"

"Six hundred three," said Jhonny, taking a chair.

Paul dropped his sandwich. "No shit!"

At first Michelangelo thought the cry was a note of culinary outrage about a missing ingredient in the luncheon fare, but then he quickly realized it was only an ejaculation of shock. Human slang was more outrageous than humans themselves. And that took some doing.

"Zounds," breathed Ambocksky, meaning every word of it. Absentmindedly, he pushed the sandwich and wrapper into a desk drawer already brimming with interrupted meals and one fat mouse. "Did you get photos? Any physical evidence? Clue to their whereabouts?"

With a wrist snap, Collins flipped up the top of her wrist secretary and accessed the pertinent file. "The butte under the bunker was sealed shut to aid in the explosion process, and there wasn't time to breach it before the other networks showed up."

"Signed and sealed?" interrupted Box with a worried expression.

Collins tsk-tsked. "Box," she scolded him. "Of course we got the professor under contract. Five K for us remaining quiet on his lack of security and Ketter claiming that the column was part of the planned design."

"Fine. Sorry. Go on."

The reporter reviewed the tiny screen. "What I saw on the bunker monitor seemed to indicate that the subterranean caverns were absolutely spotless; no trash, girlie magazines, beer bottles, flavor stick stubs, nothing. And with a union crew supposedly doing the installation, this can only mean one thing."

"They weren't," mumbled Ambocksky thoughtfully. "Somewhere on route, the thieves replaced the original crew, if the union ever even got the personnel request in the first place."

"Agreed," nodded Rikka, crossing her legs. "We'll check with the New York contractor as to their status. If a crew went out and never came back, then prack the story and we'll alert the authorities to start searching for bodies. However, it's eminently possible that Earth never even received the request for personnel. As for photos . . ." She turned to Jhonny.

"Mike and I got everything on disk," said the android grimly. "Haven't had any time to do an analysis yet."

"Need anything?"

"Time, quiet, and some lunch."

The discarded sandwich was offered and politely refused.

Ambling to the file cabinet, Snyder opened the file cabinet drawer "B" and withdrew a bottle of bourbon. Then paused and placed the bottle back. Reaching lower the anchor opened "S" and took out a siphon of Scotch. This was no time for halfway measures. Serious thought deserved serious booze.

"Where's the ice?" he asked, rummaging about in "C" for cold.

Box glanced over a shoulder. "I."

"For ice. Natch."

Adding a handful to his tumbler, Harry then slyly palmed the miniature freezer unit and slid it into "L"— for lost.

"Jesus, this is big. Really big. Bigger than big," said the Producer redundantly. "What can't be done with a couple of hundred shaped nuclear charges? Delicate enough to blow the bra off a nun and powerful enough to shift a politician out of office."

As the news team made noises of agreement, Ambocksky pursed his lips but refrained from whistling. He used to whistle a lot, but out here in space, he had quickly learned that a whistle had come to mean that there was a hole in your spacesuit and death was coming with an engraved invitation. There was no bigger taboo in outer space than public whistling. Except, of course, not killing a member of the Free Police. Or at least trying.

"So, what's the first move?" asked the pale man, running a nervous hand through his thinning hair.

"Congratulations," growled a voice from the doorway.

At the words, everybody turned and slumped. Oh, prack.

Filling the opening was two meters of solid blond cleavage, Maria Valdez, the Station Manager for QSNT.

BATTLE STATIONS, scrolled Deitrich.

A former Ms. Worlds, the tall blonde sauntered into the office with the sure certainty that every male wanted her and every woman hated her. Which was mostly true. Everybody hated her. Skintight, her lavender lace jumpsuit was molded so perfectly to every contour of her centerfold figure that a pulse was visible in several locations, and the only way Rikka could postulate that the woman got into the damn thing was a hydraulic press. Either that, or else it was merely a fantastically good paint job.

Ruby cluster earrings shone from within her coiffured hair, Maria's fingernails glistened with every color in the rainbow, and a costly tin Rolex wrist secretary gleamed on her wrist. It had been a present from the station's owner, Gardner Wilkes, and thirty-five separate attempts had been made by the staff to smuggle a stink bomb inside the device. But to no avail, because she never turned the blasted thing on.

Standing slightly behind her was a muscular youth with blue skin and silver hair. Sporting a black tuxedo jumpsuit with claw hammer coat and spats, Danny was her official butler and personal bootlicker.

Graciously, Valdez accepted a chair from Danny and, with ill-concealed hostility, glared at the SNT, who smiled innocently and immediately began rallying their massive arsenal of lies, evasions, and excuses.

"You're not here to rag our case about the shuttle crash?" asked Jhonny, dumbfounded. Busting their chops had always been Valdez's favorite hobby. That is, after doing a midnight mime of the Kama Sutra with the anatomically correct Danny. The two thought their affair was a secret, but in truth the only person who wasn't aware of their liaison was a deaf hermit on Pluto. And that was only because the fellow hadn't gotten his issue of the bulk mailing yet.

"The crash? A mere trifle," said Maria, forcing herself to smile benignly. The action made her face hurt. "After pulling in a wonderful exclusive like the Venus story, who cares about the breaking of a dozen traffic regulations and the destruction of a few thousand dollars' worth of the station?"

SHE'S BEING NICE, scrolled Deitrich. BEWARE.

Surreptitiously, Mike checked the environmental sensor in his toolvest and was not shocked to find that the sarcasm percentage in the atmosphere had just hit one hundred percent. But then again, truth was often like an onion: the closer you got to the core, the more it smelled. Maybe she really was proud of them. Another hot story meant more viewers, which translated directly into increased revenues from the advertisers.

"Gee, thanks, Maria," drawled Snyder and lifting the seltzer bottle he aimed the nozzle straight toward the Station Manager and pressed the trigger.

The stream of bubbling soda water only got halfway across the office before Danny stepped in front of the woman, taking the deluge himself. As the seltzer dripped to the floor off the android's sodden form, Harry almost dropped the bottle.

"What? You folks are here in person!" he demanded, croggled. "B-but, Maria, you always hologram in!"

OOPS, scrolled Deitrich privately.

"Not this time, Mr. Snyder," glared Valdez over the shoulder of her love butler. "And thank you, Danny."

"My pleasure, madam," loftily replied the manchine, licking his lips. "And the seltzer was a bit flat, Mr. Snyder. Might I suggest recharging the carbon dioxide cartridge?"

Knowing when he had crossed the line, Harry turned the bottle around and put a stream into his own face with gushing results.

"Yep," he agreed amiably. "Flat. Thanks for the tip."

Chuckling along with everybody else, Ambocksky released his death grip on the arms of his chair. Whew. Good move, that. The anchor had quickly defused a potentially awkward situation.

"You are forgiven, Harry," beamed Maria, batting her long eyelashes like tiny whips. "Besides, that was probably the first time you've ingested water without booze in years."

Ice tinkled in the tumbler as Snyder tightened his grip to dangerous levels. "Sorry, but you've hosed us down often enough," said the anchor good-naturedly, tilting his tumbler in response. "Just think of it as tits for tat."

YIKES! EGO WAR, TAKE 67. EVASIVE MANEUVERS!

Instantly, Rikka prepared to fake a heart attack as a distraction, Jhonny removed the safety from his camera flash, Michelangelo loaded a medical hypo with 20ccs of artificial lockjaw, and hands under the desk, Box activated the firing sequence of the explosive bolts holding the walls of his glass

office together. It was a last resort, but a doozy that always
worked. At least, it did on paper.

Her smile frozen harder than liquid nitrogen, Maria slowly
looked down at her tremendous display of cleavage and then
returned her gaze to the calm anchor.

"Are you addressing my body again instead of talking to
me directly?" she asked in a deceptively mild tone.

"Eh? Nonsense! You misunderstood."

"Perhaps you are trying to be amusing?" offered
Ambocksky as an aside.

"Well, it was the breast joke I could think of."

But the mispronunciation was heard clearly and Maria bris-
tled. "Listen here, you hasbeen—"

"Certainly," interrupted Snyder, taking a sip, "if there's
something important to get off your chest."

Furious, Valdez's face turned bright red, but just then the
air in the office shimmered and the translucent figure of a fat
bald man in a gold jumpsuit focused into view. About one
foot above the floor.

"Hi, boss," chorused everybody in a lackluster tone.

"Oh, hello, Gardner," purred Maria demurely.

Secretly amused, only Jhonny could tell that Danny's com-
plexion darkened with an aquamarine tint of pure raging jeal-
ousy. Wow, that droid had it bad, and he should know better.
Human females were poison. Literally.

"Hi!" said the corpulent image waving hello. Sporting a
herringbone jumpsuit with Oxford boots and a lime-green ascot, Gardner Wilkes wore a purely decorative watch chain
draped across his ample belly and a platinum-edge presidential pocket-doc was clipped to his hip. Polished platinum cuff
links on each wrist boasted the initials R on the left and L on
the right.

Glancing about, the owner tried not to show his disappointment. Oh, drat, this wasn't the barbershop. Lost again in his
own inherited station! Did they shift the position of things
around here when he wasn't looking?

"Welcome, sir," said Box, rising and spreading his arms.
"Always nice to have the boss come down and congratulate

our top team after they got the station another nova-hot exclusive."

"And a splendid job it was," said Wilkes, with what he hoped was a straight face. An exclusive? Swell. But he still needed to make an appointment for a haircut. Actually, it was time to dry clean his toupee, but the millionaire preferred to think of it as a haircut. Pure nostalgia.

"And what about that incident on Dock 27?" asked Valdez.

Wilkes gestured magnanimously. "Already taken care of."

"It is?"

"Of course. Nothing simpler." Whatever the problem was, Wilkes was certain that somebody somewhere was taking care of the annoyance. And there was nothing easier than avoiding the whole matter. It was good to be the boss.

Abruptly losing control of the hologram console in his apartment, Wilkes noticed that he was starting to sink into the floor and his employees seemed to be struggling not to laugh. Think quick, space ranger!

"Well, I must be going," he said to their assorted torsos. "Important business meeting on the next level." Carpet blocked his view. "Bye!" And he was gone.

"We will also be taking our leave," said Maria, rising to her feet as Danny offered her a helping hand of steel.

"Same meeting?" asked Rikka, at last grinning openly.

Icy blue eyes met those of warm earth brown. "No," said Valdez coldly. "I have some contracts to go over. The hard news department is up for a budget review and there's always some deadwood to prune." And spinning on a high heel, the woman and her droid marched from the office, leaving the veiled threat dangling in the air like an invisible hangman's noose.

"Well, now that the usual antisocial amenities have been observed, perhaps we can return to business," said Collins, massaging her temples. Oh, to be out in space again. She hated office politics. Hell, she hated politics. It was how she became a reporter and why she divorced her idiot husband. "So, in answer to your earlier question, Box, our first step is to check with Legal."

"Hmm, to confirm our obligatory status under the Ninety-

ninth United Planets Amendment. Good idea," stated
Ambocksky, folding his hands as an alternative to strangling
Harry. Damn the man and his private wars! "Although Legal
isn't always clear in their explanations. Lawyers are paid by
the word. Let's try Captain Hertzoff, instead."

"Oh, this ought to be good," chuckled Jhonny, taking the
vacated chair. The head of Security for Media had a bizarre
habit of answering questions with single word answers. Nobody knew why.

As there was no chair large enough to even chance sitting
in, Michelangelo stood and rested a large arm on top of the
wooden file cabinet. The stout antique creaked ominously, but
managed to hold its structural integrity. Yes, it was quite true,
having a conversation with Captain Hertzoff was a slow and
awkward affair, although she was a master of vocal inflection
and the money she saved on telegrams was incredible.

Shrugging agreement, Box touch-typed on a blank section
of his steel desktop.

"Security," replied a stern voice from the vicinity of the
stapler and a carafe filled with antacid.

Box leaned closer. "Hillary? Ambocksky here."

"Yes?"

"A question. Once I am in possession of information directly dealing with a capital crime, how long can the station
withhold that information from the proper authorities before
being held responsible as an accessory in any future crimes,
liable for interfering with due process, and/or endangering the
public safety?"

A pause. "Capital?"

"Yes, a capital crime. Stolen nuclear weapons."

"Hour."

The producer gaped. "What? Only sixty minutes?"

"Counting."

"Hey, no sweat," said Snyder, finishing his drink and placing the tumbler aside. "Only we have the facts. And if we're
a bit late in reporting, who's going to tell?"

"Me!" loudly said the ringing intercom.

"Hillary, you wouldn't!" gasped Ambocksky.

"Oh, yes, I would," corrected the intercom. "And that is an

hour from when the SNT received the information, not the station." And the desk went silent.

So did the office.

"Captain Hertzoff said a whole sentence," breathed Collins. "Wow. Guess she takes law enforcement very seriously."

"Swell," sighed Paul, glancing at his pinkie watch. "You have only twenty-five minutes of lead time before I have to tell the Venusian police." Then in ragged stages, a rueful smile grew. "After which I'll anonymously phone in a tip to the VD cops about the missing bombs and then send the UP the details of our legally required statement via the post."

A bumper crop of smiles.

"Mailed third class?" asked Rikka, smiling.

"Sublight."

"With a blurred address?" inquired Harry.

"I'll write it with my foot."

"And no zip code?" added Jhonny mischievously.

"Well, a letter without a zip code would be very suspicious. So it'll have, what I certainly hope, is the correct planetary number."

Rikka scrunched her face. "That will give us, say . . ."

"Twenty-four hours," said Box as the voice of experience.

Impressed, Michelangelo bit his tongue. Gods above, humans were a sneaky bunch. He liked that in a friend. However there was a minor ethical problem yet to be resolved.

"This isn't immoral, is it?" asked the huge alien with a woebegone expression.

"Hell no," stated Collins firmly. "If we were to merely broadcast that the bombs were missing, millions of people would panic, causing billions in damage and accidentally killing hundreds, maybe thousands!"

"While if we announce that the bombs were stolen," continued Snyder, using a handkerchief to dry his face, "but had already been recovered, then no panic, no deaths. *Comprende?*"

"*Sí.* Pax." Grudgingly, Michelangelo accepted the decision. Science was pure truth, and the technician hated this part of the job that required them to lie to save lives. It was such a moral quandary. Their job would be so much simpler if they only had to constantly tell the whole truth and let the bodies fall where they may. Death was inevitable, why hate it? However, his teammates thought otherwise on that subject. Humans were just so . . . defiant.

"Come on, big fella," said Harry, punching the alien on the biceps, which was as high as he could reach without a ladder. "Maybe we'll go up against the Free Police themselves this time! What a story that would be!"

"If we survive," added Jhonny, standing. "Hey, don't go soft on us, *bon ami*."

Soft? Ah, slang for a coward. Outrageous! "I don't know the meaning of the word 'fear,'" stated the technician proudly.

FEAR: A NOUN, USED TO DESCRIBE A STATE OF SEVERE EMO-TIONAL AGITATION AND DISHARMONY CHARACTERIZED BY A FEEL-ING OF SEVERE DREAD ACCOMPANIED BY LOTS OF RUNNING AROUND AND SCREAMING. SEE: CHICKEN.

Ignoring the rhetoric, Rikka set her wrist secretary to beep every ten minutes. Twenty-three hours and fifty minutes and counting. "Time to boogie," she barked impatiently. "Come on, guys, a crisis is afoot!"

Standing to his full height, Mike frowned. "I thought a crisis was an impending disaster?"

"Git!" laughed Jhonny, putting his shoulder to a spacesuit rump and pushing the huge being toward the door.

"Good luck!" called Ambocksky to the closing portal.

"Where to?" asked Harry as they piled outside. "The Toad?"

"Our office," stated Collins. "We need a full bio on Ketter, our secret files on the Earth unions, a list of weapons dealers, smugglers, disguise experts, and techno-thieves. Agreed?"

"Agreed."

Bold and sure, the news team trod off toward the turbolifts, halting only a moment at Mrs. Seigling's desk to grab a few handfuls of the fresh doughnuts. After that embarrassing disrobing on Venus, they had decided to start a diet. And a doughnut possessed less calories than a Danish. Didn't it? Certainly hoped so.

Munching their way across the news floor, the SNT were

supremely confident on only one subject; they alone knew the bombs were missing and still had almost a full earth day's advance start on the other networks.

Thank God.

In Whatadump Crater on Venus, a dry wind blew across the kilometer-high statues, bringing a storm of micro-fine dust down upon the crowd of attendees.

"Artistic counterpoint? Nonsense!" cursed the CNN reporter, crumpling the Press Release sheet into a ball and throwing it at the ground.

"Agreed," said the BBC reporter, neatly folding the sheet into a triangle. With a snap, he sent it winging across the field of gravel where it dropped directly into a granite waste can.

"Nice shot."

"Thanks."

Sporting a prim black bowler, a paisley muumuu, and high-top Oxford sneakers, Sir Alexander Hyde-White was the epitome of the old school gentleman. The designated representative of QBBC, from England, Earth, the aristocratic reporter found the shocking prevalence of handguns on this blighted world a horror and a shame. But even worse was the complete and total lack of any good restaurants. In the name of God, what were they supposed to do, order pizza?

Standing nearby in a white jumpsuit with a green bodice and a shoulder-mounted minicam was Hannabal O'Toole, ace reporter for the QCNN Venus and Mercury syndicate. Short and slim with red hair that told no lies about her temper when thwarted, O'Toole's original homeworld was Venus and it felt good again to be on a planet where everybody had a gun and was polite—or else.

Breaking a major unwritten rule in the news biz, the two reporters often worked together on big stories, sharing their tips and leads in a friendly atmosphere of camaraderie. It made the other networks positively ill just to contemplate the perverted partnership. And what was worse, the two weren't even lovers or sex partners, just friends. It was downright unnatural.

Both of the aces were annoyed that QSNT had purchased

a temporary exclusive, but were delighted to learn that
Hardcopy and Sunshine from QINS had been arrested for annoying the police. A very unwise move on Venus where the
Civil Liberties Union taught classes in advanced police bru-
tality. Apparently, the INS reporters would be doing yet another in-depth exposé on the jails of KaBoom City for the
next few days. It was part of an ongoing series for the solar
troublemakers.

Walking along the irregular floor of the crater, O'Toole
nudged a piece of stone shaped oddly like the tip of a nose.
Ketter was a weird guy.

"Is it my imagination," she asked aloud, "or are these
benches out of plumb?"

"You are correct," said Hyde-White, examining a pocket
WatchDog scanner his mater had given him for Boxing Day.
"And the raised lettering along the base of this mountain has
no punctuation."

O'Toole laid a hand on the older man's arm, stopping their
crunchy walk. "What with the incredible care and detailing
that Prof. Ketter did on this park, I can't believe he'd miss
such a basic engineering principle as things being level and
he got straight A's in grammar."

"Agreed," stated the BBC reporter, his arm tingling from
the contact of her hand. No. Friends. They were just friends.
"Which raises an interesting series of possibilities."

"Do tell."

"One," the Lord said, raising a manicured finger, "is that
these sculptures are not perfect, and thus, in fact, may be unstable and highly dangerous."

Glancing upward toward Samson in his barber chair, Hanna
shuddered. The last thing she wanted was some giant guy
thundering down on top of her. Then she coyly glanced at her
dapper business cohort. Well, maybe not the last thing.

"Agreed. Number two," added O'Toole. "Something occurred to disrupt the process."

"Doubtful. Or else this crater would only be a hole in the
ground."

"Okay. But then what did happen?"

In unison, the two reporters turned to stare at the irregular

column of stone soaring fourteen meters above them to crest
with the professor's armored bunker. On the side was etched
the name of a famous soap company.

"Malfunction?" postulated Hyde-White.

"Dysfunction, more likely," corrected O'Toole, her long
hair whipping about in the tangy Venusian breeze.

"Unless the bombs are gone."

"Stolen?" Born and raised on Earth, the BBC reporter gave
a whistle, causing the space-raised CNN reporter to nearly
jump out of her skin. Quickly, her hands raced across her
body searching for punctures.

"What are you . . . oh, sorry." He blushed. Dammit, Hyde-
White spent too much time on planets where a breathable atmosphere was a given, not a manufactured product that was
advertised on billboards.

Catching her breath, the Venusian waved the trifle aside.
"No problem. It was better than my morning aerobics. How
many do you think there were? Two? Three? A dozen?"

"Maybe dozens!" frowned the British Lord. "An unknown
number of ultra-special nuclear-shaped charges stolen by, high
probability, professional thieves. Maybe even the Free Police
themselves!" A slow grin expanded across his face, threatening to break his head in half. "Which would certainly explain
why the SNT purchased a twenty-four-hour exclusive."

"And why they departed so quickly they didn't even wait
to gloat or brag at us. Yes, it makes sense the bombs are stolen! Why, this could be a major disaster!"

"God, what couldn't some boom-happy Venusian do with
armaments of such caliber!"

"Where first? Try to wheedle an interview out of Ketter?"

"Better, let's hit the VD HQ and wait for Media to send in
its mandatory report."

"Which we will accidentally read?" asked Hanna, grinning.

Reaching into his billowing muumuu, Lord Hyde-White
fanned himself with a thick sheaf of BBC currency. "Well,
these things do happen, milady."

Yeah. Thank God. "Let's go!"

* * *

As the school bus cycled through the massive airlock of the domed city, Susie Sunshine turned away from the barred window of their cramped cell.

"Was this particularly clever?" asked Sunshine, scratching a damp armpit. Damn, her twelve-day deodorant must have expired.

Both scarred hands on the window bars testing the metal, Jason Hardcopy grimaced. "Damn straight it was. We had to get out of there fast and this was the easiest way."

"Why?" demanded the angry blonde, crossing her arms underneath her ample bosom.

In a side corner, their camera-op was asleep standing up with his 3-D camcorder dutifully photographing the view of downtown KaBoom City. The crowded city street was filled with hovertanks, armored taxicabs, horribly beweaponed sports cars, spiked motorcycles, and an ice cream truck that could have won World War II by itself. However, nobody was speeding or changing lanes without signaling first, and when a street sign said STOP everybody just sat there until it changed. End of discussion.

Reluctantly admitting defeat on the window bars, Jason gave a nasal laugh. "Prof. Gregor Ketter doing something as fancy as artistic counterpoint, balancing those big statues with that rough stone column underneath his lab? Nonsense! Those bombs must have malfunctioned. And when they do eventually go off . . ." The reporter left the sentence dangling.

Sunshine shuddered at the concept. There was no need to elaborate. Millions would be killed, and even worse, she could be among them. To die with their viewers. Yuck.

"Unless the charges were stolen," she added as an afterthought.

For a moment, the two INS reporters stared at each other, their trained professional minds whirling with possibilities and options.

"Nyah!" they chorused and sat back to enjoy the ride to jail.

Meanwhile, back in Whatadump Valley, a sprinkle of gravel rained down from the belly of Atlas, and from inside his manly navel a pinpoint of bobbing light enlarged until it reached the external ledge of the colossal godling and clicked off.

Standing brazen in the neatly rounded mouth of the natural cave, the amateur spelunker could only stare dumbfounded at the wondrous sights filling the transformed crater. Then with a decisive hand, the college student reached into a pocket of his twilled jumpsuit, withdrew a bulky package of Wacky Weed, and unceremoniously sprinkled the illicit narcotic into the gusting winds. Enough was enough, already.

When finished, he ate the bag, sat cross-legged on the hard stone floor, and started humming a mantra as he began contemplating his navel.

And how to get out of it.

CHAPTER FIVE

WHILE RIDING THE turbo-lift on Media, Michelangelo shifted uncomfortably in his spacesuit and loosened his collar a bit. But it didn't help.

"Rikka, would you mind if I stop off at my apartment for a quick shower?" the alien rumbled. "I've been in this suit for over a day and I am starting to feel like a shag rug."

"Honestly, I could use a quick rinse and spin myself," said Harry around his cigar. His gauntlet rubbed across his stubbly chin to the sound of crinkling cellophane paper.

"Me too," mouthed Jhonny, running a tongue over his teeth. The camcorder on his shoulder nodded vigorously.

"Agreed," laughed Rikka, tucking a loose strand of hair behind an ear. She had been ready to ask for a break herself. "Ten minutes for everybody to change their socks, and we rendezvous at the office. Check?"

"Check."

"Gotcha."

"Affirmative."

Easing the lift to a complete halt, the reporters punched in their respective levels and the turbo-lift moved off again to momentarily halt on the eighth, twelfth, ninth, and twenty-fifth floors.

On Level 25, section 9, corridor 16, Mike strode from the turbo-lift and happily hurried toward his apartment. Glancing about to make sure nobody was watching, he retrieved the key from under the welcome mat and pawed open the door. Stepping inside, Mike entered another world. Not literally, perhaps, but pretty damn close.

The door to the apartment swung shut, disappearing into a huge tree whose dimensions dwarfed a California redwood. The floor appeared to be an apple-red moss and shimmering rings arced across a deep violet sky. Low rounded mountains crested the horizon and giant ferns softened the hard landscape. As Mike walked into the alien glen, a flock of butterflies the size of condors exploded from a depression in the moss, filling the sky with wild colors, and then they were gone. In the lake, a school of fish softly hummed their group mating call. Amid the background noise, a bull ajak bellowed a brave war cry to its ancient enemy, the horned oilof, which had been extinct for a thousand years, but try to explain that to the ajak.

Normally few stars could be seen past the reflected light of the planetary rings, but a little fiddling with the hologram projector had fixed that and Michelangelo had a view of his home system beyond the wildest aspirations of any astronomers. Looking at the constellations, he felt like a cub again, camping with his father and learning the ancient solar signs: the Mage of Doom, the Avenging Fist of God, the Stampede from Hell, the Rabid Wildebeast, and the Insane Knives! Ah, such happy memories.

The rest of his team often came by for a night of poker, or just to relax by shooting the atmospheric currents. He enjoyed sharing the image of his homeworld with friends, old memories and new mixing into a pleasant blend. And the team loved the view. As Jhonny had once correctly stated, it was the closest they would ever get to a real alien world. Except for Mike who only had to take the noon ferry to Earth. That was about as alien as a world could get!

Moving past a huge natural gem shaped like a dancing fish, the technician meandered through a copse of swaying ferns and hopped over a decorative pink corral fence. Stepping through the laser illusion, the true wall of his apartment was discernible, plain steelloy. And before him was a proper sized door leading to his Closet-King, the lintel marked with a "G" for Gremlin. Other Closet-Kings would be marked "H" for human or an "A" for android. Although Jhonny's had been carefully remarked "H" to help foster his human disguise.

And Rikka owned a plush, executive Closet-Queen. But that was just a perk.

Gremlin was the humorous nickname given to his race when their sublight sleeper ship *The Reaching Hand* arrived in human space twenty years ago. By an incredible happenstance, it was a young cub reporter named Harry Snyder who coined the term. Mike still marveled at the coincidence. If he had read the event in a novel, the alien would have laughed uproariously and tossed the book aside. But then life was stranger than art.

Michelangelo's race called themselves the aaraa, and their world U'rth, which roughly translated into "Earth." It had long ago been agreed upon that there was nothing original under the sun, no matter whose it was.

Part robotic physician and part mechanical lackey, the Closet-King was a complex device capable of sharpening a talon, giving a full body shampoo, or performing minor brain surgery; almost anything requested of it, depending solely upon the operator's state of intoxication. That wise limitation had been installed by the TickDoc Manufacturing Company after an embarrassing incident involving a drunk hermaphrodite, an inflatable raft, and one small gerbil.

Next to the King was a rack with a stiff-brimmed North American ranger's hat dangling off the side. It was Mike's favorite party costume. He simply took off his toolvest, put on the hat, and spent the rest of the party telling folk how only they could prevent forest fires. It always got a big laugh.

Booting the Closet-King, Mike chose a Rush Job #3 from the computer menu. He punched in the correct sequence onto the keypad, the machine asked for a double check, ran a diagnostic on itself, and, when satisfied, turned the access light green and unlocked the door. Stepping inside, Mike was engulfed by wiggling warmth as the entry portal closed with a sigh.

Minutes later, the door opened and out wafted clouds of minty fresh steam. As the medicinal fog dissipated, Mike exited and palmed the wall to cycle up a mirror for a quick inspection. Shaved, trimmed, shampooed, sharpened, and brushed, he felt like a new aaraa. His black boots were polished to a mirror finish, his short pants were stiffly clean with only a touch of starch in the buttocks. His tan toolvest was unbuttoned and deliciously heavy with replacement items for those broken or abandoned during work. A quick check showed his Lavalier microphone was properly tuned to his IBM portable and both were fully charged. Mike knew his spacesuit was off somewhere being cleaned and recharged to be later delivered to the QSNT shuttle by robotic conveyor belt.

Cycling away the mirror, Mike bowed to the picture of a female Gremlin on the wall behind. Not a photograph, but an oil painting rendition of his lady love back on U'rth, who had driven him so crazy that the technician willingly went off into space to escape her bizarre romantic machinations.

Thankfully, she would be married and with cubs by now, as the long journey had taken the astronauts some forty years to complete. Of course, Mike had no recollection of the time lapse. While in high orbit above his homeworld, Captain Ezekiel (the sound of a toaster popping up bread and then bursting into flames) had lowered the lid of his cryogenic suspension tank—only to have it reopened one second later by a tiny, pink, bald being who cried out in fear and promptly fainted. A later translation of this historic first contact showed the initial words of greeting were not "Welcome, weary space traveler!" but were in reality, "Holy prack! It's a fucking grizzly bear!" Not a very auspicious beginning, but the history books had cleaned the phraseology for the children.

Pausing in the kitchen for a bagful of apples, Mike checked his wrist secretary, cursed, and dashed for the door.

Time for work.

The hirsute behemoth thundered down the branching hallways until he reached the main corridor. There, the rest of his team was clustered around a perfectly ordinary door, no different from a score of others—except for the stolen Holiday Inn DO NOT DISTURB sign hanging from the latch.

Smoking a fresh cigar, Harry sported a loose, four-piece, brown worsted jumpsuit with matching fedora and boots. Combing his black hair smooth, Jhonny was in his standard work uniform of a utilitarian blue jumpsuit covered with metal rings designed to hold a wide variety of equipment. Impatiently tapping her foot, Rikka wore a pastel jumpsuit with a white bodice and Lady Marine combat boots, eminently suitable for tapping the toe on the floor as a sign of impatience.

"Sorry, the elevator got stuck," lied the alien, joining them.

Reaching up, Collins removed a bit of apple from his jowl. "And it broke in front of a fruit stand, how convenient."

Wiggling his ears, Mike tried to appear totally innocent and failed totally. But the alien did somehow manage to faintly resemble a scolded puppy. It was a trick he had spent weeks rehearsing.

Her scowl melting into a grin, Collins chuckled and swatted her friend on the arm. Aw, what the hell, they still had plenty of time. Almost ten whole minutes until Box sent his notification in! Thankfully, this was one story where they possessed a clear lead from the rest of the news pack. There was no rush. What a pleasant change.

"Ready?" asked Harry, hand on the latch and his feet arranged for a quick exit should it be necessary.

"Ready," replied the rest of the team, each poised in the act of flight.

Twisting the latch, Snyder threw open the door.

Inside, the office was brightly illuminated, quiet, and empty. Whew. They had once found a most rude guest waiting for them and the reporters swore to never again enter this room without a clear and easy escape route available.

Four large desks formed a rude square in the middle of the room, the furniture set so that the occupants would be facing each other. Three of the walls were lined with file cabinets, a compact kitchenette, Closet-Doc, secret escape route, a Murphy folding bed sporting a giant poster of the solar system on the underside, and an empty liquor cabinet. The fourth was a solid expanse of video equipment, with a single chair positioned in the middle. In reality, the seat was a modified bosun's chair, mounted on a slide and could easily glide from one end to the other with a single push. It allowed one man

. . . er, alien, to do the work of three and made for a dandy cocktail shaker.

But the room was also draped with dropcloths, filled with ladders, cans of paint, brushes, welding equipment, empty lunch bags, videocassettes, reels of superconductor wiring, laser torches, spools of molecular monofilament, and the inevitable roll of duct tape. How had mankind ever survived without that invaluable substance?

"Oh, hell, the repair crew hasn't finished yet," said Snyder grumpily. "Well, we can't work here."

"Not in this mess," agreed Michelangelo. "It isn't our mess."

"The Toad," stated Jhonny.

Rikka shrugged. "Yep, The Toad."

"No, wait!" cried Deitrich's voice and there was a flash of light.

Standing in the middle of the office was a tall, muscular man in knee-high brown leather boots, whipcord breeches, and a leather World War One flight jacket with a white silk ascot tied jauntingly about his neck. Oddly, the material was constantly waving behind him as if the aviator were facing a strong wind, or forever flying.

"Uther!" cried Rikka and she started forward, arms spread for a hug, but then stopped.

"Oh, sorry," she apologized.

White teeth flashed in a manly grin. "No problem, chief. Mike fixed my visual broadcast unit weeks ago," admitted the pilot. "But I was waiting for an appropriate moment to surprise you."

Ruefully, Harry rubbed his chin. "This what you really looked like, buddy?" he asked at last. "We've worked together a long time and I have never seen a picture of what you once were."

The hologram crossed his arms. "This is me! Or what I used to look like."

Quizzical expressions melted into total disbelief.

"Okay, okay," relented the pilot. "So I have a tan. Sue me. I'm German. We don't tan. If my people get too much sun,

we go crazy and invade a neighboring country or invent the
car."

"Can you maintain an image anywhere?" asked Jhonny, his
mind already buzzing with the endless list of technical problems. And how to solve them.

Removing his soft leather hat, the hologram shook his
head. "Sorry, no. Only here in the station and on board our
shuttle."

"Then we'll see you at The Toad," said Snyder, giving a
salute and spinning on a heel.

AND ABOUT TIME TOO, scrolled their wrists.

With a musical ding, the elevator doors parted and the SNT
crew stumbled into a lobby reminiscent of pre-space times.
The walls were lined with real wood and decorated with ancient flat photographs of men and women. Brass railings
edged the floor that was covered with a fine woven plastic
carpet of tremendous durability. Great leafy bushes in wicker
tubs stood sentry in every corner and a velvet-covered chain
blocked the set of wood and brass doors. On the lintel was a
discreet sign of puce neon that audibly hummed with electrical power: THE HORNY TOAD. And underneath blinked ALL
BOOZE, ALL THE TIME!

Ah, home at last.

Inside, there was a noticeable change in the atmosphere.
The saloon was darker than the rest of the station and several
degrees cooler. The air was crisp and fresh, thick with extra
oxygen. The walls were massive horizontal beams for the first
meter, then red brick to the ceiling, whose acoustic tiles were
painted a nonreflective black. Optical charts of the solar system and Scotland adorned the walls in no discernible order.
Cushioned leather booths lined the room and huge hexagonal
tables dotted the floor. As this was dinner time, the tavern
was jammed with a score of people munching on sandwiches
or quaffing frothy drinks in tumblers the size of moons.

A vintage CD player stood solitary and proud near the
bispecies lavatories. Above the music machine floated a
hologram of a stick-thin crooner who was efficiently able to
hide behind the microphone stand he held on to with both

hands. His Adam's apple constantly bobbing, the thin, blue-eyed youth smoothly sang about some people in the night who didn't know each other, but where swapping visionary presents and calculating the mathematical probabilities of falling in love before dawn. The music was sweet, the words sad, and not even the crooner seemed sure if this was a ballad about unrequited affection or a cautionary message on safe sex.

At the far end of the spacious room was the bar, its counter a single slab of dark granite. The top was polished mirror smooth, but the sides were irregular and pitted deeply in several spots.

Situated behind the vast expanse of aged mahogany was Alonzo MacKenzie, the owner and sole bartender. A shaved bear was the usual first impression that came to people's minds when they met him. Barrel-chested, the man was dressed in an incongruous Highland tartan jumpsuit. His long strawberry-blond hair was tied off in a ponytail that hung to his waist and his hands appeared to be more scar tissue than healthy flesh.

Spanning the wall aft of the bar was an aquarium tank filled with water and plants and plastic mermaids who displayed their mammalian attributes with brazen glee. And in his aquatic wonderland swam a battle-scarred fish of Herculean proportions. Even its jagged teeth and bloodshot beady eyes seemed muscular, and vicious. A sign on the outside of the tank bore the badly spelled legend: THIS NOT BRUNO. HIM BADD MONSTER. THIS AM FLUFFY. NICE FISH. HE NO EAT YOU. PETTING ALLOWED. Underneath, the ancient warning of BEWARE had been crossed out with what seemed to be blood.

Alongside the big tank was a smaller glass cube filled with deadly South American piranhas. The sign on their tank read: WE WANT PLAY WITH FLUFFY. PLEASE USE HAND TO DROP IN WATER US.

In twisted amusement, the reporters could only gawk at the ridiculous attempt at subterfuge.

"Ach now, and top of the day to ye," canted the big Scotsman, his blue eyes watching the fish in the tank very suspiciously. In his big hands was a baseball bat, with a chunk bitten out of the tip. "And stay behind the ropes please."

"Mac, what is going on here? Some sort of demented joke?" demanded Rikka. "If some fool put their hand into that tank, nothing but bones would come out."

Harry displayed his glowing wrist secretary. "Bruno is actually listed in the dictionary under dangerous."

"And insane," added Jhonny, displaying his wrist.

MacKenzie nodded somberly. "Ach, naw, I agree. I dinna be sure by whom this was done, but I nea like the verrry idea."

Michelangelo scowled and pointed. "You don't seriously think that . . . Bruno . . . himself . . ."

A Highland head shake. "I conna say, lad. But I'm staying behind the ropes."

"I'm not," said Deitrich. Materializing and walking forward, he extended a hologram hand into the large fish tank. Instantly, the water boiled in a mad frenzy.

Unable to eat the tasty flesh in his water, Bruno grew so furious that the killer smashed himself against the Armorlite walls. Momentarily stunned, the deadly Oscar drifted about with a stupid smile. In the side tank, the piranha paled as they realized the trick to wreck revenge upon their human captors had failed miserably, and their doom was sealed. They promptly began eating each other.

"Aye, it's still Bruno," stated MacKenzie, laying aside his bat. "Vicious little devil, he is. Hey, look at 'em go!"

"Ah, yeah, it's a great show," said Collins, feeling slightly queasy. Watching the fish population dwindle rapidly, she could sympathize with their plight, having been married to a cold fish from Mars for over two years. "But we need a table, Mac. Lots of work to do."

"Table for five it 'tis," said the barkeep, laying aside his bat. "Take sixteen over in the corner by the picture of Horace Greeley."

"Would that be on the west side of the room?" asked Harry with a twinkle in his eyes.

A toothy grin. "Aye, young man, it is. Ye know your history."

Laughing, the reporters maneuvered through the crowded bar, greeting friends and receiving congratulations on the Ketter piece, until they reached the assigned spot. As they took seats, Mike pulled up a second chair and carefully eased his bulk onto the flimsy human structures. Ah. On command, the sound dampener in the ceiling kicked in and the area around their table became totally silent. Although the crooner across the room seemed to neither notice nor care.

Harry palmed the menu plate and a tiny hologram of MacKenzie appeared in the center of the table. This version of the bartender was incongruously dressed in full weskit, kilt, tam-o'-shanter, and knickers.

"By the by, I never remember seeing ye here before, Captain Deitrich," drawled the tiny Scotsman, his brogue infinitely worse than the original. "If that's wha ye be."

"Correct, sir." A translucent hand made to slap Michelangelo on the shoulder. "It was my good friend here who solved the problem of syncing transmission, and shazam, I have a body again."

Hologram scrutinized hologram. "Kin ye drink?"

A frosty glass of bubbling champagne appeared in the hand of the MainBrain. "Brought my own," smiled the pilot.

"Ach, naw, so ye did," agreed the bartender in somber disapproval. Reaching into a pocket of his kilt, the redhead extracted a squat black box. Pressing a button on top, the glass in Deitrich's hand disappeared just as the hologram was about to take a sip.

"But not in my bar, ye don't, laddie, my boyyo," calmly stated the tiny waiter.

The disembodied pilot flexed his empty hand. Fourteen levels above them, the Sterling generators of the QSNT shuttle revved to maximum and then went into emergency overload, but still the drink failed to re-form.

A sheepish grin. "Sorry, Mac."

"Ye order, sirr?" asked the flickering Mackenzie, stylus poised above his computer pad.

"Tappetan of usquebaugh, straight," requested the MainBrain hologram, exhausting his command of the Scottish language.

"Ach, na. A quart of whiskey? Good choice." The waiter pressed the button on the box again and a huge mug appeared.

"Thanks."

"First one is free. Welcome t' The Toad. Dinna bother the stuffed moose."

"In lavatory stall #3, yes, I have been told."

"Double Scotch," said Harry, interrupting the introduction.

"Martini X," added Jhonny. "And add some chocolate syrup to the grenadine, please." Then the camcorder nuzzled his cheek. "And a shot of glass cleaner."

Immune to the taste buds of androids, and the antics of the SNT in general, MacKenzie simply made the appropriate notations.

"Gin and tonic, lime and ice," ordered Rikka, resting an elbow on the table. "And will you cut the wind?"

Cocking an eyebrow, Deitrich tilted his head and the scarf went motionless in the air. "Better?"

Snyder nodded. "Better."

"Brb," said the miniature waiter in computer slang as he faded away. Less than a minute later, the center of the table irised apart and a collection of glasses rose into view on a support column.

"To business," said Collins, raking a healthy swig. "Jhonny, you get the report on the Earth union?"

Wiping his lips, the camera-op reached into his shoulder pouch and withdrew a thick sheaf of papers. He handed her the one on top. She flipped the page over and read the brief report.

"Hmm, Ion New York Limited never heard of Prof. Ketter." Damn, the removal of the union contractors simplified their job, and thus made it infinitely more difficult. So much for bribing the chief clerk, outwitting the officials, or raiding the files.

"Is that information hard?" asked Harry.

"Straight from our own SNT mole from the Crime Department."

A nod. "Good enough for me."

"And me."

"Ditto," said Mike, using his favorite human word.

"So the thieves intercepted his request somewhere between Earth and Venus, substituted their own men for the union electricians, and Ketter willingly gave them the keys to the armored tunnel where the bombs were stored." Snyder frowned. "That part is almost too simple. But then how did they find out about the plans for the park in the first place? They couldn't be listening to every transmission in space just hoping for something juicy to fall into their laps."

"Unknown," admitted Collins. "Any ideas? Notions? Theories?"

There were a lot of facial gymnastics, but nobody had anything worthwhile to offer. The matter was bypassed for the present.

"Okay, then why would they only steal the six hundred three? Why not everything?"

"Because the professor probably never left his bunker, and the only section of the valley that wasn't under his direct observation was the column beneath his lab," postulated Michelangelo, sipping his ice tea. It was fresh-brewed Lipton and already the alien could feel the caffeine start to tighten his body motionless. Whew, better add some gasoline to weaken the mix.

"Accepted as a working hypothesis," said Collins, biting a lip.

Placing a straw in the window cleaner, Jhonny offered the concoction to his camera. "Maybe it's an inside job," he said over the tiny slurps. "Venusians are constantly in a state of war with each other; they don't need any external enemies." Then frowning, the android shook his head. "No, that doesn't compute. What Ketter was planning to do was for the good of the whole planet's economy."

Removing his hat, Harry spun it across the room, where it hit the wall and stuck. Some of the people at other tables silently applauded. Curiously, he glanced about to see why. Oh, it was for him! How nice.

"Could some radical isolationist faction of Venus be against an increase in tourism?" asked the anchor, taking a bow. "Or an off-world group that didn't want Venus stealing their business."

"Perhaps it was Mars," suggested Jhonny, withdrawing the straw. "They're certainly crazy enough to steal shaped nuclear charges."

"They're crazy enough to play catch with shaped nukes," said Rikka bitterly.

Laying aside his spoon, Mike adjusted his glasses. "Venus did not publicly assist Earth in its war against the colony of Titan. Could the Terrans be doing some sort of subtle revenge?"

"Subtle?" gasped Deitrich, gagging on his ethereal drink. "Earth?"

"I'll consider that a no," sipped the alien politely. Ah.

"Besides, if somebody wanted Venus out of the game, then they would have sabotaged the bombs and blown Whatadump off the map," observed Rikka. She squeezed a lime into her drink. "No, there's no plot to destroy Venus. And you couldn't discredit Gregor Ketter even if you had proof he was trying to invent time travel. Hell, he'd get backing for the project! Unfortunately, the most reasonable theory seems to be that the thieves merely encountered a priceless opportunity, moved fast, and stole what they could."

The center of the table irised again and a bowl of popcorn rose into view. Everybody took some, except for Deitrich and the camera.

"For what purpose?" munched Harry. "Duplication of the bombs?"

"They'd make swell weapons," noted Jhonny pragmatically, sprinkling curry on the kernels in his hand. "So it is a tenable theory."

"No, it is not," stated Michelangelo and he started rummaging through a stack of papers. Where was that note?

"Why?" demanded Rikka eagerly.

The alien pawed over a document from the stack. "According to this report . . . ah, liberated by Ms. Collins from the bunker, these were hand-built prototypes by Ketter himself. And if the scientist ran true to form, his inventions have so many safeguards and internal destruct mechanisms designed as lethal protection against industrial spies, nobody, not even the professor himself, could open one of them after the final seal was in place."

"But surely you only need the access code," said Rikka as a question, glancing at the sheet before passing it on.

"Not only the word," corrected Jhonny, accepting the paper and then inverting it proper side up. "But also how it is typed."

Deitrich watched as the technical document went by. The mass of squiggling lines meant nothing to the pilot. "Eh? Don't you mean how it's spelled?"

"No, typed."

As this sort of electronic skulduggery was the android's hobby, Rikka asked him to explain. And keep it simple.

Dampening a finger in his drink, the droid started writing on the table. "Oh, say the code phrase is 'Happy Birthday.' Well, maybe the 'H' in happy is lowercase, but the 'B' in birthday stays uppercase. Or the first letters should be lowercase and the rest in upper. Or only the middle letters uppercase. Or maybe the two words run together with no space between them."

At the bar, MacKenzie paused in filling a row of baby shotglasses with Roe & Wade Chablis, the wine of choice, when he saw the dour faces of the news team. Must be another tough assignment. He promptly sent another round of drinks their way, and some aspirin.

"Difficult," admitted Michelangelo grudgingly, his pupilless eyes narrowed to black slits in concentration.

"Difficult?" squeaked Jhonny. "Pal, that ain't the half of it! There is also the style in which the code word is typed!"

"Style?" repeated Harry, puzzled. "You mean the communications protocol from the keyboard? The font used? The kermit?"

The android shook his head. "*Nyet,* I mean the typing style. Does the writer start hard and go soft?"

"A common problem among men," said Rikka, innocently batting her eyes. "Or so I'm told."

Everybody ignored her remark. It was a cheap joke.

"Anyway, does the genderless typist always pause in the

middle of words," Jhonny went on. "Perhaps he/she/it types slowly, using one finger. Or does he use ten fingers?"

"We're rapidly escalating into impossible here," snorted Deitrich, crossing translucent arms.

"Plus there's the chronometric brackets, and the command prefix and authorization suffixes and—"

"Enough!" cried Rikka, raising a hand. "We get the picture."

"And it's a Jackson Pollack," quipped Snyder, dropping a couple of aspirin into his glass and watching them dissolve. God bless Mac.

Collins grunted in agreement. Yes, things were a mess.

"Okay, duplication is a no go. Can they change the configurations of the blast zones, or should we be diligently searching for any giant nude woman floating about in space?"

"Nyah, configuration is a perimeter decision," said the android, pointing at a mess of squiggle lines on the computer printout. "See? You can get any shape blast requested."

"So much for giant nude women," sighed Harry, extending his glass so that he and Deitrich could pretend to clink glasses in commiseration.

Exasperated, Rikka rolled her eyes. Men! "So our nameless perps have stumbled onto a pile of one-of-a-kind superweapons. Do they save them, use them, or sell 'em?"

"Perp?" asked Mike, typing on his IBM.

Harry covered the portable computer with a hand. "You'll never find the word. It's slang. Perp is short for perpetrator."

"Ah, criminal, crook, bad guy, villain, desperado, deviant, mug, knave, rascal, blackguard," announced the alien, tapping away with a talon. "See: Abduhl Benny Hassan. Check. Logged and filed. Thank you."

Starting to get the spirit of the conversation, Deitrich chimed in with an observation. "Okay, so if our perps decide to save the bombs, we might never find them until too late. And if they use them, it is already too late and we'll discover their plan from the destruction when everybody else does. But if they're going to try and sell them on the black market . . ."

"There's an excellent notion," mused Rikka, working her

jaw. "If anybody could pull off a job like this it would be Abduhl."

"I thought he dealt with pornography?" asked Deitrich.

"Naw, gave that up years ago. After the war." Reaching into her belt pouch, Rikka whipped out a cellular phone and placed it on the table. As she punched in the access code, the video monitor unfolded like a flower until it was ten times larger.

A few people at other tables gasped in delight and awe at the casual display of advanced technology and immediately called their local Radioactive Shack to place an order for one of those phones themselves.

Rikka typed a long number into the phone. There came a click, static, and then the screen cleared into a picture of a painfully austere man in a butler's uniform. Behind him were rows of marble pillars, a splashing fountain, the "Mona Lisa," a reproduction of Da Vinci's Horse, and a live African elephant wearing a French maid's outfit and holding a feather broom in its trunk. The beast was busily dusting a crystal chandelier hanging from the mosaic tile ceiling.

"Yes?" asked a voice so thick with culture it could have been used to make yogurt.

Leaning forward, the reporter put on a big smile. "Afternoon, this is Rikka Collins of QSNT. I'm an old friend of Sheik Hassan and would like to speak to him, please."

"I am sorry, madam, but the *hassur* is out at the moment."

"The matter is important."

"If you would be so kind as to leave your telephone number, I would be happy to relay the message to the master when he arrives home."

Whew, wordy bastard. "I'm in his Rolodex. Just tell Abbykins his little desert oasis said hello."

There was a clatter of plastic hitting marble and the view changed to a close picture of a shoe.

"A-a-a-abbykins?" stuttered an off-phone voice in horror.

"Bye!" she gushed and disconnected.

As the table burst into laughter, Harry gave a thumbs-up. "You are a bastard, toots."

"Thank you, Obiwon," winked Rikka. "At least we can be

sure Hassan will get the message." She started punching numbers again.

"Who next?" asked Jhonny, wiping tears from his cheeks. Lord, he loved this job.

"Nobody."

"Ah. He's the best."

Utilizing the privacy mode, the screen swirled with colors and focused into the classic colored bars of a test pattern. Then the circuit disconnected.

"Impossible," breathed Collins and she hit redial to the identical result. Carefully, she again punched in the number from scratch. Same thing. Then once more. Ditto.

"What's wrong?" asked Harry, concerned. "Is the Phobos relay down? Too much interference from sunspots?"

"Worse. My top underworld snitch won't answer his phone." She said the words as if she could not believe them herself.

"So? Maybe he's taking a bath. Or out at the movies."

Frantic, Rikka ran a diagnostic on the phone. Nope, it was fine. Oh, hell.

"You don't understand," she told them, returning the useless phone to her belt. "Mr. Nobody has call waiting on the call waiting of the answering machine of his car phone's beeper! Whoever he/she is, they make a living selling information and a lot of it is time sensitive. An hour too late and the stuff is worthless. A missed conversation could cost Nobody millions."

"Coincidence?" asked Jhonny in a tone to suggest that it was anything but.

"Hardly," snorted Collins. "Nobody makes his money buying and selling information, and we know that illegal items worth billions have possibly just gone for sale on the black market."

Harry slammed a fist onto the table. "He's handling the sale for Hassan!"

"Perhaps Hassan is buying the nukes."

"Or running the auction," added Deitrich, using his sleeve to polish the silver wings on his lapel.

Everybody turned to stare at him.

"Well, it only makes sense," hesitantly offered the pilot. "If these bombs are so special, then nobody, not even Nobody, is going to simply sell them like tomatoes. An auction would treble, quadruple, the asking price."

Smiling, Rikka blew him a kiss. "Brilliant!"

"Then this should be simple," boasted Jhonny. "If it's an auction, they've got to advertise for buyers. We merely wrangle an invite, outbid the criminals, buy back the bombs, scoop the other networks, and save the solar system!"

"Yeah!" That was what reporting was supposed to be about!

"Geez, use your heads, guys," she retorted hotly. "If Nobody and Hassan both aren't answering the phone, then the auction is probably already in progress!"

"Quarl," cursed Michelangelo. "You are most likely correct."

Jhonny stood and Harry tossed off his drink. "Okay, chief. What can we do?"

Collins inserted her credit card into the table. A tiny warning bell chimed and she withdrew it. Darn, overdrawn. What a day! "Deitrich, warm up the mains. I have a second best informant, but he doesn't accept phone calls. We've got to visit him on home turf."

"Can we spare the time? What about your number three or four?"

"I'll phone them en route."

"Where are we going?" asked Harry, getting a bad feeling in his stomach that wasn't from the aspirins and Scotch.

She handed the anchor his hat. "We're going to the ultimate dive in the solar system. Where every slimy bastard and double-dealing scumbag in space congregate to plot evil and madness. Where death and murder are items on the menu and the only rule is that there are no rules."

"The Apocalypse Wow! Society in the Asteroid Belt?"

"Wimps."

"The Hellfire Club in England?"

"Sissies."

"The secret headquarters of the Free Police?"

"As if we knew where it was."

"Our own cafeteria?" asked Mike, going for broke.

"A hellhole, indeed," she admitted honestly. "And a nice try, but also wrong. We're going to The Tattoo Zoo!"

Faces blanched in terror. Even the camera dilated a lens.

"No! No!"

"Oh, my lumbago! Can't walk!"

"Anything but there!"

"Power . . . down . . ." slowly spoke Jhonny, slumping over onto the table. ". . . need . . . recharge . . ." Then he made a loud click and went still.

Not amused, Rikka grabbed her phone and raised it threateningly. "Get moving, you weasels, or I tell Maria and our beloved Station Manager who broadcast her and Danny playing 'Good Gynecologist, Bad Gynecologist' on the Adults Only channel last March."

Sprightly as woodland nymphs, the four males leaped to their feet and hurried toward the exit. But as the group exited The Toad, Collins's wrist secretary began to beep. Their lead time was finally over. Now the Ketter exclusive was a race.

And they still weren't even sure exactly what the story was.

CHAPTER SIX

BLASTING UPSIDE DOWN out of Media Station, just to show that it could be done, the SNT shuttle spiraled past the orbiting warning buoys, leveled out amid the floating traffic arrows, and then immediately banked 45.78 degrees galactic north by northwest, plus Z mark 4 degrees by Y axis 0.923 micro-degrees universal. And if that failed, then the reporters would stop at a gas station and ask for directions. As usual, they had left the damn map at home.

"We have permission to launch," said Harry as they streaked off toward deep space. "It's belated, but official."

"Mains are on-line," added Mike, operating the push buttons and boot controls of his Hammond design engineering console at if it were a giant church organ. Only the tunes this device played were songs of strictly temporal power. "Sterlings at ninety percent, energy levels are at 10/10. Sixteen hours of tin remaining. Life support is good, and I'm reeling in what remains of our umbilical cable. Next time, give me a minute, okay?"

"Sorry. We're running late as it is," stated Rikka, flipping switches on the overhead console. Then she touched the comlink in her ear. "Lloyd Peterson at the Media Control Tower has just authorized our flight plans to Seattle, Washington, Earth. I've reserved us a suite at the SeaTac Hyatt and ordered room service for four in the morning."

"Check. The real course for Jupiter and the Tattoo Zoo is laid in and locked," said Jhonny, typing with both hands. "Deitrich, watch out for that garbage scow full of Shriners."

Geez, those guys were everywhere! How long did one of their conventions last?

"Going Fatal in five ... four ... aw, I hate countdowns," announced Deitrich and the hologram pretended to press buttons. Instantly, the stars in the windows blurred to the standard Christmas color patterns of red and blue. Once they had draped green tinsel over the explosive bolts set above the bow screen and used a photograph of it as a holiday card.

"How long till we hit the Zoo?" asked Rikka, unfastening her seat belt.

Activating the autopilot, which was also him, Deitrich turned and smiled. "The orbit of Jupiter is ten minutes away, the planet is forty-five minutes."

"Just enough for a catnap," yawned Harry, and reaching up he killed the overhead light over his console. It had been a busy day and there was lots more coming. And at his age, beauty rest was nearly as important as medical insurance. "Wake me if we crash into a star or anything."

"I'll stand watch," said Mike, removing his glasses and polishing them on a furry arm. "Don't think I could sleep knowing those bombs are roaming about loose. I've had fun, and war ain't it."

"Well, it was only sort of a war we covered before," said Rikka, leaning over the back of her seat. "More of a punitive action than a retaliatory strike."

"No, I meant back home," rebutted the alien.

A bridge full of confused looks.

"What are you talking about?" asked Jhonny, puzzled. "You're a pacifist from a race of pacifists. Gremlins at war?"

Politely, the alien displayed his elbows to show they were covered with the pelt of an adult. "Just because we're nonviolent doesn't mean we never have wars," retorted Michelangelo. "Conflict is essential to evolution!"

"Nonsense!" scoffed Deitrich, swiveling around in his motionless chair.

Stunned, Mike recoiled. "Really? You disagree with the theory of dynamic evolution?"

"No, that Gremlin war thing."

A bestial grin. "For your information, I happen to be a veteran, twice decorated."

"What?"

Rikka glanced at the control board clock. "Well, we got forty odd minutes till the Zoo. Shoot us the straight poop on this, big guy." A Gremlin-style war. Fascinating.

"Yeah, this I have got to hear," said Jhonny, placing his camcorder into a recess in the control panel for a quick recharge and lube job. "To hell with a nap."

Harry muttered something inarticulate and began to snore.

Pawing open a refrigerated sideboard panel, Mike withdrew a huge bowl of apples and placed it in his lap. Popping one of the fruits whole into his mouth, Mike began alternating munching and talking.

Forty years away from Earth, on the other side of the galaxy, is the beautiful ringed planet U'rth. Located in a lonely little cosmic cul de sac, it is the home of the most peaceful, nonviolent race in the entire universe; gentle beings who had never built a weapon of any kind, participated in violent sports, or even had words for murder, arson, or jaywalking. However, this did not mean that the Gremlins never engaged in fighting, battles . . . or war.

The First World War, their most horrible escalation of savage conflict, began innocently enough when the Premier of the Northern Continent, while trying to entertain her guest, the Czar of the Western Continent, publicly made a joke about the outrageously huge mustache worn by the King of the Southern Continent.

Unfortunately, the joke came at a time in the King's life when his wife was divorcing him again, and had sighted his infamous facial growth as the third party. Feeling despondent, the King was delighted to have somebody to strike back at. And under the advice of his staunch ally, the Western Continent, he gleefully activated his most ruthless sleeper agent in the capital city of the Northern Continent, with orders to "do his worst."

As a glorious golden dawn broke over the enemy city, the startled population awoke to find every wall poster of their

beloved Premier defaced by a hastily scribbled set of devil
horns and a snaggle-toothed grin.

The Premier was incensed by the heinous crime, and under
the advice of her good friend, the Western Continent, she unleashed her best secret agent to even the score. During the
night, the master spy penetrated the defenses of the Southern
Continent, broke into the palace of the King, snuck into the
man's private office, dialed long-distance information for the
correct time in the Arctic Circle, and departed. Deliberately,
and with malice aforethought, leaving the royal phone off the
royal hook.

When the staggering telephone bill for twenty dollars was
received at the end of the month, the King had no problem
getting his furious Parliament to officially declare the two
countries in a state of war.

Less than a year later, their avenging armies clashed in
moral combat at the primordial jungles of the Equator, the
brave soldiers boldly taunting each other by making rude
noises and nasty monster faces. Soon though, the battle degen-
erated into hand-to-hand combat, and thumb wrestling became
rampant.

The cruel fighting waged for weeks. Beginning to fear defeat, the Premier, under the advice of her valued associate, the
Western Continent, got tough and unleashed a crack squad of
stand-up comics, who traveled the South performing devastat-
ingly funny impersonations of the King and his mustache.

Demoralized by the unrelenting act of terrorism, the King,
under the advice of his bosom companion, the Western Continent, retaliated by broadcasting to the North a daily television sitcom about a Premier who scratched her head with a
dinner fork and needed detailed instructions to operate a light
switch.

Luckily, before it was too late, the North and South somehow learned the truth of the matter, joined forces, and
launched a joint armada of their navies against their common
foe—the evil Western Continent.

But when both ships finally landed on the correct beach,
the invading fleet was viciously embarrassed by shameless
snipers who leaped out of the bushes, dropped their pants, and

mooned the entire assault force, sending more than one
shaken young soldier to the psychiatrist for much needed
counseling.

As news of this brutal slaughter was made public, every
country in the world put their military bakeries on emergency
status and began stockpiling ICBM lemon cream pies.

The rest of the sad story is history.

"We are not very proud of that episode in our past," admitted the alien, replacing an uneaten apple back in the bowl.
"And yet I myself saw rude action in the Clogged Drain Re-
volt of '06."

"Oh, give it a break," chuckled Rikka, rolling her eyes.

Mike seemed astonished. "But it's true! And I was socially
wounded in the Split Ends Rebellion of '12. A very sad affair.
Disappearing ink, whoopie cushions, and blow dryers littered
the streets! Tragic, just tragic."

"Gawd Almighty, can you tell pracking whoppers," smiled
Deitrich. "Hair wars?"

"I beg your pardon, sir," said the alien stiffly. "But didn't
humans once fight over skin colors? Religions? Well, we often fought over hairstyles."

As the team chewed over this unsettling tidbit, their reluc-
tance to accept his war stories made the technician glad he
hadn't told them about his old Imperial covert team, the Curl-
Up-and-Dye Commandoes. His squadron leader could split
ends in the dark, and Mike was a trained specialist able to tint-
and-fluff any enemy soldier in under thirty seconds. It was not
a skill the gentle being was overtly proud of. Particularly not
his involvement in the legendary Bay of Wigs fiasco.

"Fighting any war is damn stupid," mumbled Jhonny, taking an apple. And to that sentiment, everybody agreed. Even
Harry, albeit nasally.

"Come on," said Collins, rising from her chair. "Let's go
get our equipment together. We got a lot of work to do before
we're ready for the Zoo."

"Yeah," agreed Jhonny, fighting a smile. "It's a real zoo."

Deitrich groaned, Rikka covered her face, Mike threw an
apple at him and missed.

Deep inside the bowels of a nameless moon was a great cavern carved from the living stone by slaves using hammers and chisels. Originally, the slaves had been given the much more efficient laser torches. But when the tired prisoners discovered how swell these energy beams went through their leg irons, and the pirate masters holding the keys, these deadly tools were quickly replaced with the much safer, although slower, chisels.

In a spacious auditorium, a thousand chairs were aligned in neat rows. The majority of the seats were decorated with wreaths for the dear departed. Some of the evergreen boughs were freshly green, others were desiccated and crumbling with age.

At the head of the room, on a raised platform of natural stone, stood a long table forged from the keel of a police gunship. Sturdy chairs surrounded the rude trophy and a hundred men and women in armored spacesuits sat sullenly at attention.

"What the pracking hell do you mean we weren't invited to the auction?" stormed the Vice Admiral at the head of the table. The ranking was more than just a military title, it was also his job description.

"Hey, Hassan didn't ask us," offered a lieutenant as explanation. "And without his instructions, it's impossible to find the secret location!"

"Well, what about those snot-nosed, upstart geeks who stole those bombs!" roared the captain. "Who they are? What government they work for?"

"Nobody has any bloody idea."

"Gawd, I wish it were us," lamented another captain, fingering a nasty laser scar on his cheek. A somber reminder that lasers and roller skates do not mix. "Even in our ancestor's golden heydays we never stole anything as valuable as those shaped bombs."

A metal gauntlet slapped the metal table cracking the adamantine keel column almost in twain. "Well, I want those weapons!" roared the Vice Admiral. "Every day, every hour those whistling amateurs are still roaming about, the heat is increased on us. Security is getting so tight that we haven't been able to steal anything in hours! Already our cash flow is down to a trickle. If things don't revert damn quick, we'll have to find honest jobs and work for a living!"

The whole crowd shuddered in fear.

"Space is our hunting grounds and no bunch of Sunday afternoon pirates is going to come and rob what rightfully we should be stealing!"

Angry murmurs agreed with this convoluted theory.

"I want the thieves dead!" pounded the Admiral, finishing the job on the podium his fellow officer had begun.

A hand was raised. "Is the SNT on the story?"

"Yes," drawled an Intelligence operative. "Of course."

"Then let's follow them!" bellowed the Admiral. "They can find the thieves and we'll steal the bombs and kill everybody involved!"

The stars reverted to white status and the SNT shuttle slowed to a sedate ten thousand kilometers per hour. Rotating slowly below the news craft was the banded supergiant world of Jupiter, its multicolored surface strongly resembling a meltdown at the corner ice cream store. Its monstrous red spot, formed of a single hurricane ten thousand times stronger and larger than the mightiest storm ever to hit the puny Earth, stared out into space like the great swollen eye of a barroom drunk who lost last night's fight and was looking for a rematch.

And dotting that eye was a silvery cylinder, a billion-ton soup can, the private home and world of retired millionaire Hugh Hustler, inventor of the edible centerfold.

"Hey, Harry, wake up. We're here," said Rikka, removing her bra and dropping it on top of the rest of her clothes piled on the deck.

With a snort, Snyder joined the living, gasped, and averted his vision. "Geez, give a guy some warning will you?" he said.

A laugh. "Sorry, I am aware you prefer ladies with a fuller figure, but I did not think I'd shock you that badly."

"Hey, that's not the reason! I only ... ah ... oh, never mind."

Struggling out of his chair, Snyder started undressing, folding each garment carefully and placing them neatly in his chair. The Tattoo Zoo was a skin club specializing in artistic skin designs. You needed at least twelve separate tattoos just to get into the establishment, and over fifty percent of your body had to be covered to join as a member. Although some members went as high as ninety-six percent. But every club had zealots. As proof of the tattoos, and as a measure to hold out thrill-seeking fakers, nudity was the prevailing rule. Which was why reporters hated the place. There was no respectable place to pin a press badge.

As the rest of his team was disrobing, Snyder removed the last stages of clothing, glanced at his naked form, and gave a start. Hey, during his nap somebody had been busy with paint and brush, decorating his hide with a UP Space Marine emblem, a duplicate of his press badge, a heart with an arrow through it and the initial HS loves SP inside, and in bold Gothic script sprawling across his chest was the Latin phrase: *"Credo quia absurdum est!"* His personal motto. "I believe it, because it is absurd!"

"Damn fine work here, people," he acknowledged. "Who did the work?"

Timidly, Michelangelo raised a paw.

"Nice job."

"Thank you. But it wasn't difficult. Welding a tight seam underwater with an implosion neutron beam takes a much more delicate touch than a simple outline diagram."

"No kidding?"

A shaggy grin. "Besides, I traced most of them from the *Big Little Book of Funtime Coloring.*"

Harry nodded. It was always smart to copy from the classics.

"What's on my back anyway?" asked the naked anchor, trying to reach over a shoulder to scratch.

Collins slapped his hand away. "The stain is still damp, don't muck about."

"Okay, but what's there?"

Rikka, Mike, and Jhonny exchanged glances at the picture of Harry and Sasha Parsons at the altar getting married.

"Skyscraper," said Michelangelo casually.

"Swell. Any in particular?"

"The Martian Beanstalk."

Ah, the place where the Youth Drug was made and stored. At least the alien possessed the good taste to use a structure with some historic dignity!

Sliding her credit card under the strap of her wrist secretary, Rikka was demurely attired in a full body painting of a formal turquoise jumpsuit, with white boots and diamond necklace. Aside from some unrestricted jiggling, the resemblance was quite remarkable. And the diamond design perfectly hid the silver button on her collarbone of her surgically implanted microphone.

As Michelangelo had no bare skin showing except for the black palms of his paws, the alien had used watercolors to dye his fur into psychedelic patterns. Oddly, the alien didn't mind removing his boots and pants, naked was how you were born and went swimming, but taking off his toolvest made him feel positively frightened. What if something broke? What was he supposed to use, his teeth? Slyly, the technician removed an multipurpose sonic Swiss Army knife from the vest and slid it into his mouth. There, dressed again! He just hoped that nobody asked him to speak.

The stripped down Toshiba riding his bare shoulder, Jhonny was adorned with thorny vines that sprouted from his feet, twined about his body, and were resplendent with flowers of flame on his torso. Honeybees swarmed on his face and neck diving for the burning blossoms. Inside the reservoirs of his forearms, the android had hidden a tape recorder, additional disks for his camera, an assortment of burglar tools, and a small can of insect repellant. Just in case.

Out of politeness, Deitrich had made his own clothes vanish and highlighted his muscular torso with just the punchline of every MainBrain joke ever written: ... 'cause he wanted to get to the head of the line ... then he really had no body ... you know how many politicians I have to kill to get a full pound? ... Sorry, lady, but I can't do that fifty-seven more times ... etc., etc.

Maneuvering on chemical jets, the chuckling pilot pulled

the shuttle into a slotted parking dock at the end of the silvery space station and, with a hiss, sealed airlock to airlock with the Hedonism Station. What an apt name.

"All ashore that's going ashore," sang the four-pound MainBrain. "Boy, sure wish I could go with you."

"Good God, why?" asked Snyder, trying to figure out where to carry his cigars. There was a place, but his lighter and wallet were already there and it could only hold so much. "Do you like to walk about in the buff with pictures painted on your hide as if some exhibitionist zebra?"

"No. But I enjoy seeing other people do that."

"For shame," scolded Rikka jokingly. "And you're an engaged Brain!"

The hologram grinned lewdly. "Hey, they can close my eyes when I'm finally dead."

"And in a casket," finished Jhonny for him.

"A showbox, actually."

The reporters made faces. Ugh!

Assembling on the middeck area, the reporters waited patiently while Rikka palmed an access panel in the hull. A section of the steelloy irised, showing the veined metal door of a stout safe. After Rikka twirled the dial left, right, right, left, and then depressed it twice on zero, the stout portal swung aside. Reaching in past the manila package of blackmail photos, old speeding tickets, and stacked vials of illegal truth serum, she withdrew a bulky black nylon bag locked with a simple titanium twist clamp.

Opening the bag, she glanced inside and nodded.

"How much?" asked Jhonny, starting to close the safe.

"Everything, probably," said Harry, placing the cigar in his mouth. "And hope there's enough."

Rikka closed the satchel with a snap. "Check. Let's book, dudes."

As there was atmosphere on both sides of the airlock, the double doors opened with no resistance and the reporters trundled out into the station. A floor conveyor belt took them past photographs of welcome signs inked into various portions of bodies and posters advertising Statler Mars skin cream.

Hopping off the belt, the reporters strolled into a tastefully decorated lobby with lots of green leafy plants, soft carpeting, and thankfully no air-conditioning, mirrors, or marble chairs.

At the main desk was a metallic stick figure, an impossibly thin mannequin, the silver oval of its head reflecting a fun house mirrored version of the lobby and naked reporters. This was the latest model of a civilian-class robot. Very expensive and chic. Originally designed for warfare, the machines proved to be expert shots. But to the horror of the military, the robots flatly refused to attack even human-shaped targets. Humanity had built them, how could they hurt their creators? Despite millions of dollars and hours, the USDA scientists could do nothing to shake this twisted philosophical conviction.

As the SNT approached closer, the robot at the front desk interfaced with the asteroid's computer and lightning fast compared the visual characteristics of the oncoming beings with the blacklist file.

FULL AUTHORIZATION GIVEN, sent the computer directly into the palladium brain of the robot. IDENTIFICATION FACTOR SIX: SNT NEWS REPORTERS FOR QSNT: RIKKA COLLINS, HARRY SNYDER, JOHN SMITH, AND MICHELANGELO (the pictograph of an old door creaking open and then falling to the ground). TO BE TREATED WITH COURTESY, BUT DON'T LET THEM ANYWHERE NEAR THE GUEST REGISTER AND, BOY, DOES THAT RIKKA HAVE A GREAT ASS.

A what? electronically demanded the horrified robot.

ASS.

Cease data flow! Inquire origins of that last comment!

VERBAL REMARKS UNINTENTIONALLY INCLUDED IN THE FILES BY THE FORMER CONCIERGE.

Delete at once!

WORKING . . . REMARKS DELETED.

"Greetings, Satellite News Team," said the machine, trying desperately to conceal the terrible social blunder that the reporters could have no possible knowledge of. "And welcome to the Tattoo Zoo! I have already logged you in, the management waives the cover fee and wishes you a pleasant stay at the Zoo."

Stymied by the barrage of goodwill, the reporters mumbled

their thanks. This was a prime reason why they hated this place. There was no way to wear a disguise that the front desk couldn't see through, and once identified as reporters it was nigh impossible to do anything covert, which was half of their information-gathering process. The other half consisted of minor crimes and eavesdropping.

Allowing themselves to be stamped with the scented fluorescent ink logo of the establishment, the news team stomped off toward the frosted glass doors at the far end of the lobby.

"And I hope you and your ass have a pleasant stay!" called out the robot, waving.

Last in line, Rikka stopped in the doorway, paused, and then continued on. Nyah, couldn't be.

A naked man with gold tassels on his broad shoulders closed the door for Collins and she joined the rest of her team at the warm brass railing of the foyer.

The Tattoo Zoo was built in concentric circles, each ring set beneath the other. On one level people were dancing, on another eating dinner, on a third getting new tattoos, swimming in a circular pool, playing volleyball, skating, listening to a poetry reading, having a game of look-but-don't-touch football, and watching a big screen 3-D TV with Harry doing his report from Venus. Oh, brother, so much for anonymity.

And all around them were people dressed only in tattoos. But what tattoos!

Blazing comets and swirling galaxies filled countless acres of undraped flesh. Some fleshscapes were polka-dotted with hundreds of individual designs, while others committed entire bodily areas to a particularly large work. Mostly waterscapes or panels from a beloved comic strip, although one swaggering fop wore his own self-portrait. Obviously he was a prime candidate for the Narcissism Club. One slim woman was an entire library of classic books, while a plump man was marked as fireworks above the nighttime Titan skyline. There were floral prints and rampart dragons galore, patently popular themes this year. Jungle themes were also abundant, tiger and zebra stripes battling it out with leopard spots and the rainbow feathers of a cockatoo. Also prevalent were pictures of gritty motorcycle bikers wearing tattoos of the person wearing the tattoo. Very chic.

One group even came as full body flags from each member of the fourteen UP worlds. In passing, the reporters saluted Luna, which was as close to a homeworld as the reporters would accept. Though Rikka was much more impressed by the virile Neptune and Harry tried not to openly drool at Lady Mars. Wow, what great moons!

Graduated steps angled down through the different rings allowing easy access, and the news team walked along smiling and nodding their heads to the naked strangers. Some of them infinitely stranger than others.

"Should we take a table?" asked Jhonny, trying to photograph just the smiling heads of the guests. Otherwise, the only place he could use this footage would be on the Adult Channel X, and even then they'd only show it after midnight.

"No, keep circulating, we've got to find my contact."

Harry shifted the cigar from one side of his mouth to the other. "Who we looking for?"

"Henderson."

And the anchor chocked on his cigar. Find Bill Henderson? How the prack could they, could anybody, do that minor miracle? Early in his career as a news reporter, Snyder had encountered the legend of Henderson. But never the man himself.

William R. Henderson, Jr., was a bland man of average height, weight, and color. If there could be such a thing, he was a textbook nobody. It took considerable effort to notice him. William wore what the majority of the population did, smoked if they did, or not, either way made no difference to him. At bars, he ordered "the usual." He neither overtipped nor stiffed waiters, his clothes weren't new or old. Henderson was the ultimate invisible man. Like a chameleon, he blended into his surroundings to the point that you didn't even realize he was there. He did what everybody around him did, ate what they ate, talked in their style using the correct terms, slang, accent, cant, or vulgarisms. No official records of him existed anywhere: school, motor vehicle, police, or otherwise. But if they had, the reports would have shown that aside from

Broadway shows his one great passion was crime. Any crime, as long as he could rat on the crooks and make a buck. Interplantary cops detested the cowardly bounty hunter, crooks wanted him dead ten times over, but news reporters all but loved the man biblically.

On Level 3, the SNT gang passed a sonic curtain and could then hear the band onstage. Sans instruments, buck-naked musicians covered in musical notes and scales were hitting different parts of their bodies with pressure sensitive microphones, producing the most amazing tuneful sounds.

"Hey, that lead bass is great!" noted a beefy man sitting at a table and snapping his snake fingers to the beat.

"Not bad," agreed a busty friend. "But that soprano. Wow, what a body!"

Just then five slim laser beams took ahold of Snyder's arm.

"Excuse me, Mr. Snyder?" asked a young lady, removing her hand. The buxom lass was adorned with a winged unicorn breathing fire at a flight of evil alien starships.

"Um?" replied Harry, his mind elsewhere. Henderson, where are you? Oh, what now, an autograph seeker? And what did she want signed? Or could this be Henderson. Will ... Wilma?

"That tattoo on your ... ah ... your ... ah ..."

"Yes?" answered Snyder with a tolerant smile.

"Sam?" she asked inquisitively. "Why did you name it Sam? Is that your real name?"

Harry barked a laugh. "Oh, no, it's just an old joke."

Bouncing slightly to the musical beat, the girl waited for enlightenment.

"The gag goes that it doesn't say just Sam," he explained patiently. "But under the proper circumstances is says Samuel's Delicatessen."

The woman chuckled in appreciation.

"... open nine to four, Monday to Friday," continued the anchor without a break. "Saturday nine to nine. Closed Sunday. Ask about our luncheon specials. We deliver."

"Oh, my heavens," fluttered the woman, passion inflaming her starships. "Let's go somewhere private and see. Hetero?"

"Yep. But not available. Sorry."

"Monogamous?"

A nod. "Happily so."

With a shrug, the girl undulated away and Harry wiped the film of sweat from his brow. Whew, close call. Fans.

Moving quickly to rejoin his friends, the anchor concentrated diligently on baseball, then old nuns, IRS audits, and then on Maria Valdez.

Ah, that did it!

Descending to the volleyball level, Mike suddenly froze as an ancient scent came to his quivering nostrils. Where? There! Spinning about, the alien spied a magnificent female Gremlin on the other side of the net, dyed as the net. Their pupilless eyes locked in mutual appreciation and the technician took off at a hot run, bowling over sports players, netting, the referee, and the grandstands.

Shocked, then furious at the unprofessional behavior, the reporters finally relented with a sigh. Oh, well, if there was anything more important than the news, it was love.

At the TV level, the reporters started strolling toward the next set of stairs when somebody soundly smacked Rikka on the tush. Spinning about she grabbed the upstart by the throat and squeezed.

"What was that for?" she asked through gritted teeth.

". . ." replied the choking man, his chest emblazoned with the tarot deck laid out in the dreaded Allister Crowley throw. The reporter loosened her grip a bit.

"Wet birds do not fly at night," wheezed the nondescript fellow with the pentacles and swords on his chest.

Even standing in front of him, Collins would have been hard-pressed to give a description of the man's face. Henderson, without a doubt.

"Ice cream has no bones," she replied coolly.

He stepped closer. "SNT?"

"Henderson?" the reporter whispered.

"Yep, give me the new password."

"Ah . . . what was it again?" she asked sotto voce into the silver dot of her throat microphone.

THE PASSWORD, scrolled her wrist secretary, IS VEGETABLE.

Boldly, the woman stepped toward the other figure.

"Tomato."

"Fruit?" answered the man promptly.

"Fruit? A tomato's a fruit?"

"Internal seeds. It's a fruit."

Scratching her head for inspiration, Collins received it. "Lobotomy?"

"Vegetable!" cried the man, and they shook hands.

"What do you want?" asked Henderson.

Rikka spoke softly. "Hassan is holding a . . . meeting. We need a location." No sense calling it an auction and tipping her hand. A prime rule in the news biz was never tell nobody nothing. Except the camera.

"You have cash?"

"If you have the info."

The black satchel was snapped open displaying thick wads of rainbow-colored money.

"B-but that's way too much!" stammered Henderson.

"Oh, so sorry," apologized the woman. "But we didn't know what type of cash you wanted. Earth bucks? Lunar eagles?"

"So we brought an assortment," smirked Jhonny, a hand strategically over the lens of his camera.

The man seemed to have trouble speaking, as his eyes filled with the glory of the hard cash. Which was the desired effect.

Inside was Earth green bucks, golden martian sanddollars, black-'n'-white Venusian targets, bright red Jupiter pounds. Every type of currency available.

"You've seen the cash. Let's see the data," said Harry, trying to keep his body between the bag and any casual onlookers.

"Here," said Henderson and he peeled off one of his tattoos and gave it to them.

The woman took the sticky plastic sheet and tucked it under an arm. Snyder palmed off a thick wad of Earth bucks, the best currency in existence, and the fellow nodded in acceptance of the amount. QSNT was not reputed to be pikers.

"L. Ron Hubbard has no lips," Henderson muttered as a good-bye.

"Except on Thursday," answered Rikka, wishing him luck.

"When it rains," they said in unison. The man took one step away and was gone into the sparse crowd.

"Okay, where's the auction?" demanded Snyder, annoyed. How did he do that? Mirrors? Holograms?

Rikka retrieved the sheet from where it had obediently attached itself to her rib cage and scanned the few lines on the back. Her brow furrowed in puzzlement and she started to speak, but then one eyebrow raised as the other lowered. "Quadrant 99, subsection 12, zone 3."

Hmm, that was way too shallow for the Asteroid Belt. "The ice belts of Saturn?" the anchor guessed.

ONE OF THE ROCK RINGS OF URANUS.

"And when does it start?" asked Jhonny eagerly, his camcorder almost losing its grip on his smooth shoulder as he leaned forward.

"Two hours ago," she said without emotion.

"Oh, no! Then it's already . . ."

Feeling drained, Rikka limply dropped the sheet. "Over. The auction is long over and finished."

CHAPTER SEVEN

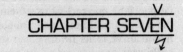

ARCING UP OVER the snowy white orb of frigid Uranus, the QSNT shuttle rocketed in toward the appointed section of the planetary rings. Okay, they were seriously late for the auction. But that was normal for them. Years ago, working under-cover, they had actually missed their own fake funeral. How-ever they did get to witness Maria Valdez dancing on their graves. A favor they happily planned to return someday, with tap shoes and a mariachi band.

As Uranus dropped below the view screen, a dark speckled band swelled to fill their view of space. The scene reminded Rikka of an old documentary she had done in college. Oddly enough, it was only in the later half of the twentieth century that humanity had discovered Uranus possessed rings, about a dozen small ones, four major bands, and a hundred assorted tiny moons. A regular cornucopia of cosmic jetsam. The bands were difficult to see using primitive optical telescopes because they were made of dark, reflectionless rock. The glorious rings of Saturn were such a spectacle because they were almost entirely composed of ice and frozen gases. It was as if poor Uranus was the janitor of the solar system, collecting the little fiddley bits left over after all the interesting planets were built.

And while the slush-ball mother world could only offer fabulous, slightly overpriced ski resorts, a thriving mining op-eration in the bands employed thousands of workers, and sev-eral hundred colonial UP outposts dotted the wild assortment of moons, moonlets, and moonoids. Settlers, scientists, and sightseers living together in peaceful subzero harmony. Just like it said in the travel brochures.

94

But the specific area of the rock rings that the SNT reporters were rapidly diving into was a dead zone; no spaceborne
mineral wealth or satellites large enough or suitable for colo-
nization. And the view was hardly awe-inspiring. However,
despite this sincere lack of commercial and intrinsic values,
the barren tumbling expanse of sterile boulders did have one
major factor in its favor.

Privacy.

"We're approaching the zone," said Deitrich, nimbly working the controls from the pilot's chair. Clothed once more, the
somber hologram was sporting his old "Space For Hire" uniform from when he was an independent rocket jockey. A
happy period before the Wilkes Corporation saved his hide
and then lost it permanently.

"On-line," said Jhonny, his pet cameras pointed out every
available window just in case anything interesting happened.
Like, say, if they were attacked by any of the incredible hordes
of criminals who had supposedly converged in this area.

"Communications bands are clear," said Harry, a hand to
his ear. "A traveling salesman for Ponticlift Industries spotted
us earlier, but I convinced him we were condom smugglers so
he didn't report the incident to the Space Police."

Who? Oh, yes, that new law enforcement agency patrolling
the rings and moons of Uranus. It was an amazingly original
name that nobody had ever used before. And such a natural!

"Way to go, Mr. Snyder," chuckled the ceiling.

"Engines are fine," puffed Michelangelo, smoking a bor-
rowed cigar. Gods above, below, and in-between was life
ever fine. The ship was fine. The engines fine. They were
above a fine planet. After a fine story and searching for
some really fine bombs.

"Hey, buddy," asked Jhonny in concern, watching the alien
wiggle his pointed ears and twitch. "How you feeling?"

"Fine," sighed the alien, blowing a blue smoke ring in the
shape of two hearts intertwined.

HA! I KNOW THE FEELING, scrolled Deitrich privately. His Si-
amese Twin MainBrain fiancées often had the cyborg blasting
cupids of flame out of the aft rocket array.

"Hey!" shouted Rikka with a start, both hands poised

above her console. "WatchDog scanners have found something! I can't quite recognize the signal . . ."

"The stolen bombs?"

"A Free Police corsair?"

"Hassan?"

"It's a giant, floating, stone . . ." Her voice faded away and
then came back strong. "Banana?!"

"Eh?"

"G'hshf?"

Snyder wiggled a finger in his ear. "Give me that again,
please?"

"A banana," confirmed Jhonny, fine-tuning his sensors and
staring at the glowing screen. "A half-peeled banana about
sixty meters in length, and it's alongside a stone ball and a
stone cube of equal dimensions."

Mentally relaying commands, Deitrich ordered the midsection of the bow window into magnification mode. The view
zoomed out and soon clearly discernible were a ball, box, and
banana.

"And what the prack are these things?" the Brain demanded, a bit bewildered. "Freak natural formations? Avant-
garde meteors? The paperweights of God?"

"They're samples," said Collins, tightening her jaw. "Or,
perhaps more correctly, tests."

A humming camera in each hand, Jhonny tilted his head.
"Tests?"

"Yep, without a doubt."

"Yeah? A test or sample of what?" snorted Harry in con-
tempt. Then his expression brightened and he smacked himself on the forehead. "Of the bombs!"

"Obviously," said Michelangelo, nimble talons typing a request for readings from scanner and navigation consoles. As
the gauges flicked into action he studied the results, steadily
chewing on the cigar stub jutting from a corner of his snout.
"Actually, it makes sense. The thieves wanted to be sure they
could control the weapons, so they started with a simple globe
statue. The most elemental geometric form. Then they tried
the much more difficult cube, and yes, it's a perfect square on
each side."

"Then they got fancy and did the half-peeled banana," postulated Collins, chewing a lip.

"As proof they could do anything," finished Snyder. "But proof to whom?"

"Full 360-degree scan, all frequencies," snapped Deitrich, both hands and his mind relaying orders to the shuttle equipment.

"And what are we looking for? More statues?"

"Possibly," offered Rikka, craning her neck to try to see above their vessel. Unfortunately, there was nothing visible but nothing. "But more likely some kind of a convention center."

"For the auction to be held in. Check."

"Maybe a class-two asteroid," suggested Harry, tripping switches and twirling dials. "Mostly composed of iron, nickel, and cobalt ore. Perhaps hollowed out with lasers and then fronted with triple-thick Armorlite windows so the bidders could sit in their double row of LazyBum recliners and watch the bombs in action."

Swiveling their seats, Jhonny and Rikka viewed the busy anchor with amusement.

"A guess?" asked Michelangelo curiously.

"Nope. There it is," said Deitrich, changing their course with a controlled burst of flame from the bow jets.

Swinging about, the shuttle dodged several minor mountains and swooped down toward a relatively open area in the ring. There among a cluster of stationary boulders was a fairly large asteroid, about twice the dimensions of the shuttle. The side facing them appeared to be flat and shiny, and when their searchlights swept across the rock, the reporters could plainly see a huge glass window. Bingo!

"How'd you know about the triple thickness?" inquired Jhonny, taking endless photographs.

Snyder shrugged. "Just common sense. Nobody but an idiot is going to watch a nuclear explosion behind one sheet of Armorlite, no matter what grade of toughness it boasts."

"They built a bloody observation booth," realized Collins, squinting against the reflected light of Uranus. "Damn place probably has carpeting, a wet bar, and a popcorn stand! The perps couldn't just test the bombs and claim the devices could do anything. The customers would want a live demonstration."

"These folk sure got guts," noted Snyder, in professional admiration. "I'm really getting a feeling that Hassan was here only as a bidder. Our friendly foe has class, but no style. Not like this."

Keeping a close watch on the ever-moving rocks near them, Michelangelo blandly accepted the deductive observations. Such permutations were purely human observations. When the news team had been in hot pursuit of Sir Deuteronomy (chainsaw opening a can of marbles) Jr., the first crooked Gremlin politician in human space, the reporters had followed his alien interpretations of the meager clues available. And they got the fuzzy bastard too. That would teach him to spartune without asking permission.

"Are there any other ships in the area?" asked Jhonny, logging their position into the navigation computer. "Disgruntled losers in the auction still moping about, anything like that?"

"Checking," said the pilot, and without touching the controls, the lights and indicators on the console took on distinctive patterns.

"Holy prack!" cried Collins at the top of her lungs, staring out the port window. "Deitrich, do a Deadman! Now!"

Instantly, the hull of the shuttle went solid black, the running lights clicked off, and every nonvital machine and powered circuit was killed. Even life support was lowered to bare minimum. Jhonny turned off everything but his shoulder camcorder and Mike extinguished the cigar.

Silent, powerless, the vessel drifted aimlessly onward in absolute blackness of empty space. Then a rock bounced off them and everybody squawked in shock. Damn, they hated it when that happened!

Arising from his chair, Harry got a pair of Wilkes Corporation trinoculars from the wall equipment rack and tiptoed over to join his friends at the bow windows. Following the direction of Rikka's pointing finger, Snyder focused just aft of the observation asteroid. In stationary orbit there were two commercial shuttles identical to their own, except that one bore the logo: QBBC, "Nightly Entertainment, Weather and

Sports" and the other proclaimed: QCNN, "Wherever there's news, you'll find CNN!"

"Oh, poop," growled the anchor. "Anybody got a bright idea of what to do with these uninvited yahoos?"

"Fake distress call?"

"Glue their airlocks shut?"

"Join forces and share . . . oh, never mind," relented the alien under the stern stares of his companions. Sheesh, it was only a suggestion.

"Lure them away with the bombs," grinned Rikka, rubbing her hands together. "Deitrich, using our big Z-band transmitter and booster relays, could you and Jhonny project a hologram outside the shuttle?"

The MainBrain pilot and android exchanged uneasy glances.

"Well, yes," admitted Jhonny hesitantly. "But the farther the distance the more difficult control is to maintain, and the greater drain it is on the restored circuits. They might easily blow."

"Besides, what do you want them to see?" asked Deitrich grumpily. "Another banana? Or maybe a nice pineapple?"

"No," said Collins evilly, "a nuclear blast."

"Great idea!" praised Harry.

"Thank you."

"Whoa there Nellie," said the pilot, raising a translucent hand. "I can make a big light flash, but there'll be no shock wave, or radiation . . . oh, wait. We're in space. Therefore, no shock wave and these are clean bombs."

"So, no radiation," agreed Collins. "Well?"

Jhonny looked up from the math equations scrolling on his wrist secretary. "It's a fifty-fifty shot, but I say let's go for it. Deitrich?"

Deep within the bowels of the shuttle, the MainBrain increased the flow of nutrients and oxygen to himself as a bit of liquid courage. "Oh, what the hell, let's give it the old college try."

"Fair enough. Which is your old college anyway?"

"Nuke U."

"Hardy-har-har."

Stepping out of Engineering and back onto the bridge,

Michelangelo uncoiled the cable around his arm and plugged
the pronged end into a shielded socket in the cockpit.

"Unless they are both asleep, their Dogs will register our
accumulation of energy for the fake blast," said Jhonny, typing commands with one hand and adjusting dials and slides
with the other. "So, as soon as we have sufficient power—"

Their two shuttles side by side with the asteroid, the
friendly reporters continued their conversation on a private
scrambled channel.

"Damn, the airlock is sealed, and the door configuration
doesn't match our smaller civilian ship design," noted Hanna,
clearly perturbed. In spacesuit and bowler, Lord Hyde-White
lifted a small bag of tools into view. "So we'll pick the lock.
It's slow work, but as we're the only people here, who cares?"

But just then, on both the control boards, meters ticked and
began to steadily climb upward, swinging well past danger
and starting inexorably toward "Run, don't walk."

"Hey," said O'Toole. "My WatchDog is indicating a really
tremendous power surge building somewhere near."

"Mine too. Let's triangulate for a direction."

"Now!" cried Mike.

With a sigh, Deitrich hit the button and vanished.

Suddenly the shuttles and asteroid were lost in deep shadows as blinding light flashed into existence a few kilometers
deeper in the rocky rings. The illumination overwhelmed Uranus and built to intolerable levels but then faded completely
away.

"Holy Hanna!" cried O'Toole, removing her sunglasses.
"Somebody is still testing those bombs!"

Jumping into the pilot seat, Lord Hyde-White stomped on
the accelerator pedal. "Let's go!"

As Deitrich rematerialized, the two shuttles streaked off
into the distance on double columns of chemical flames.

"Hello!" said the pilot cheerfully. "I do think it worked."

In the QSNT craft, Jhonny watched their departure closely

and carefully. This had been a critical decision; he needed to place the illusionary blast close enough for the others to see, but far enough away to keep them busy. The droid only hoped he figured this correctly.

"They're out of range," announced Harry, bent over a console, temporarily on WatchDog duty.

"Let's go-go-go!" shouted Rikka, and the SNT shuttle streaked in fast.

By careful balancing of aft and belly jets, Deitrich slid the shuttle right up to the observation window.

"Hey look, inside on the floor!" cried Michelangelo.

Everybody peered inside but could see nothing through the tinted Armorlite glass.

"What do you see?" asked Harry eagerly. "People? Hassan himself? Some guys wearing domino masks and holding a large bag marked SWAG? Great!" On his board, the scanner swept a green arm about on a clear screen. Nearby space was empty—for the moment.

"Well, almost as good," conceded the squinting alien. "There's little pieces of paper scattered over the floor."

"Auction slips!" rationalized Rikka, madly typing notes into her secretary. "Exactly what we need! That will tell us who, where, and even how much!"

"Perfect!" agreed Snyder, boosting the gain on the Dogs. "Deitrich, do your stuff!"

"Yawsa, *NASA!*"

Tiny flames spurted everywhere on the SNT shuttle and the craft pirouetted gracefully to slide sideways against the oval metal ring of the asteroid's airlock. But the telltale thud-double-click-hiss of contact and a lock did not occur.

"Trouble," said the MainBrain, frowning. "Damn, the airlock is sealed against unauthorized external tampering."

"Locked," translated Mike for clarification.

The cyborg ignored the heckling. "And the configuration is different from our civilian design. A match is impossible," he finished smoothly.

Reaching to the low ceiling, Collins pulled on her spacesuit helmet. "Okay, then I'll use a hand laser to detonate the explosive bolts on the rim of the doors and catch the papers as they come hurtling out in the escaping air."

There was a group pause.

"Give me that again?" requested Harry, cupping a hand to his ear. "Catch 'em, how?"

"We place our open airlock directly before the asteroid's closed airlock," she explained, pulling on gauntlets. "We then evacuate our ship, and when we're at zero pressure, we blast open the asteroid."

Ah! "And as the air rushes out, it'll carry everything loose inside the observation booth directly into our ship. We then slam our airlock doors closed, repressurize, and scram!"

A grin. "Yep. Child's play."

QUICK, FIND ME A CHILD. Damn, scrolling again. Old habits were so hard to break. Ask any nun.

"Timing is going to be very tight on this," stated Jhonny, assisting his friend don her life-support backpack. "One wrong move and those papers get scattered to the stars."

"And me too," added Collins.

Snyder waved that trifle aside. "We can find you with a transponder."

Tramping onto the middeck area of the shuttle, Collins started to ask for all interior hatches to be sealed when a series of muffled thuds told her the request was already in progress.

"Leave the emergency stairwell to the storage deck open at both ends," she instructed over her helmet radio. "That will give the papers additional yardage to cover and me an extra few seconds."

"Gotcha," said Harry.

She took a breath. "Okay, start the evac procedure."

"Acknowledged," said Deitrich formally.

Through her helmet earphones Collins heard a steady sucking sound that soon diminished into a whisper and then was gone. After another minute, Mike informed her they had an internal vacuum.

"Then open both doors of the cargo level airlocks, and open both on the main airlock."

"Confirmed," said Jhonny, giving a thumbs-up. "Luck, chief."

"If anything goes wrong, we'll try and save your brain."

"Oh, shut up, Deitrich. Good hunting, kid."

"Ditto!"

It was an eerie sensation to the reporter to see the airlocks open silently. The airlock of the observation asteroid was less than a foot away from the shuttle. Which was probably as close as Deitrich could get them without denting their vestal wings.

Taking a regulation stance, Rikka aimed the laser at the oval rim of the closed doors and touched the trigger. Instantly, the tracking laser dot appeared on the burnished metal framework. Getting a feel for the job, she rotated the beam round and round the frame, going faster each pass until she had the rhythm mastered, and then pulled the trigger.

A shimmering beam of light lanced from the muzzle and molten metal exploded outward from where it touched. Repeating her earlier motions, Collins managed to traverse the oval only once when the explosive bolts inside the frame did what they liked to do best and a soundless blast filled the shuttle.

In a silent explosion, the door flew into the shuttle and before Rikka could react the two-ton mechanism slammed into her with triphammer force. Flying backward, the reporter hit the bulkhead, smashed between door and the wall. The resulting clang nearly deafened her, but Rikka still clearly heard the crack of her faceplate as it spiderwebbed into a jagged pattern. Out of the corner of her helmet, the terrified reporter saw the papers hurricane into the shuttle and then darted down into the cargo hold.

"Doors!" she screamed, that dreaded whistle filling her ears with its carrion call of death. Crap on toast, had this ever been a bad idea! Almost worse than her marriage!

With a bang felt through the deck and bulkhead, every airlock slammed shut-shut and the winds died. Suddenly lacking impetus, the papers whirled madly about inside the chilly environment of the spacecraft for a few moments before settling into corners and on top of things.

"Emergency repressurization," said Deitrich.

Gasping from adrenaline fatigue more than a lack of air, Rikka didn't bother telling them to hurry. In ragged stages, the whistle slowed, then topped, and she allowed herself to release that death grip on the doors atop her. Hadn't done much good anyway.

Another minute passed and then the doors toppled over to the deck with a strident crash that was music to her ears.

"Hi," she panted at a scowling Michelangelo.

Although of alien origin, the technician's expression was plainly of mixed fury, concern, outrage, and somehow it made Collins feel like a mentally retarded two-year-old. Which was the desired effect.

"Agreed! I'm a total pracking idiot and promise to never do anything like this damn-fool stunt again. Pax?"

His stern features softened into a bearable grin. "Pax, bozo."

"Alert!" cried Jhonny's voice. "They're coming back!"

Harry chimed in fast, "Deitrich, another nuke!"

Another? "Well, I'll try," said the pilot hesitantly.

Kilometers away, another tremendous light burst occurred.

Executing a perfect 180, the two shuttles flipped over backward and raced away again into the planetary belt.

"Good work, Deitrich," complimented Harry on the bridge, but the pilot's seat was empty. "Deitrich?"

"Here," sighed the ceiling speaker listlessly.

"I said the circuits would blow," said Jhonny's voice from under his console. Wisps of smoke trailed up around his bulk and there came the crackle of laser welding and the brief stink of burning plastic. "Ow!"

"You okay?"

The android rose into view, a wounded digit in his mouth. The action didn't ease the pain, he just liked the flavor. "Sure, no serious damage to me. But the projector is dead."

"Nobody home," sighed the ceiling. "Ah well, it was fun while it lasted."

"We'll get you a replacement circuit ASAP, promise!"

That's what they had told him when the original had blown six years ago! Refraining from comment, the MainBrain activated his virtual reality circuits and formed a mansion inside his mind, then made himself a body clothed in slippers and bathrobe, an easy chair, gave himself a beer, and added

Raquel Welch to give him a shoulder massage while Dolly Parton appeared to sing and dance for him.

God, it was pure hell being a bodiless Brain.

Back in the middeck area, Rikka finished removing her spacesuit and shoved it unceremoniously into a storage locker.

"Come on, let's blow this popstand," she said into her throat microphone. "And get your butts back here to help, guys!"

Ms. Parton stopped in midnote and Deitrich mentally ordered the shuttle to head for Media.

Using tweezers and whisk brooms, the reporters lovingly gathered the crumbling papers and laid them carefully on top of an editing table. Gleaming white paper only minutes ago, the material was now brownish-black and disintegrated at the slightest touch. Plus, they were quite unreadable.

"The paper is freeze-dried from exposure to space," explained Michelangelo, anointing an order for a pastrami sandwich with a stabilizing solution. If they could experiment on anything, lunch seemed safe. But even the gentle moistening spray of the atomizer bottle caused the desiccated material to become sodden and melt into worthless mud.

"God damn it, hadn't considered cheap paper," complained Snyder, using a Wilkes pocket antigravity ladder to try to levitate a brittle square with numbers written on both sides. But even the slight lifting motion destroyed the page utterly. Crap!

"We're so used to dealing with computer flimsies made out of plastic, the possibility of organic matter simply hadn't occurred," noted Michelangelo sourly.

"Who still manufactures paper like this?" asked Rikka curiously.

Walking to the library, Jhonny flipped through a few books on Supply and Requisitions. "Too many," he reported glumly. "Any visible watermarks?"

"Hardly."

"X rays," said the alien resolutely. Logic demanded that a technical problem must have a technical solution. Or, at least, that's what it said on the inside cover of the *Don't Call Us, Go Fix It Yourself* shuttle maintenance handbook.

"Might work," said Deitrich from a wall speaker. "Conventional space pens use ink with a high composition of clay to keep the fluid from fragmenting and drifting about freely in zero G. This should give the printing a slightly denser molecular structure than normal organic paper. A medical X ray could possibly read the messages."

Harry snorted. Whew, what a list of ifs and maybes. Hadn't heard a lineup this questionable since the last group appointment to the Supreme Court.

"Would a CAT Scan, mass spectrograph, electron microscope, or a sonic probe do any better?" asked Rikka, struggling to remember her high school journalism classes in basic sneakiness.

"Nope. Good old-fashioned X rays are our best bet."

"And how do we get the Closet-Doc to do this?" asked Harry skeptically. "Tape them to our body?"

"No, we'll use pocket-docs," said Jhonny and pulling a white box marked with a plain red cross from his belt, the android laid it tenderly on top of a square of paper. The pocket-doc immediately flashed a warning to notify the insurance company and next of kin. Sorry, but this patient was incredibly dead.

"Docs don't give specifics, just a diagnosis," said Deitrich. "We'll need to create an interface."

"That I can handle," said Michelangelo, pulling tools from his vest. This situation was direct from Chapter Fourteen: How to Makes Things Talk to Each Other Even When They Don't Want To, Without Using a Hammer.

As the two news shuttles coasted to a stop beside the remains of the observation asteroid, their searchlights clearly showed its present state of violent reorganization.

"Oh, I say," sighed Hyde-White into his spacesuit helmet. "It certainly appears that we, as the criminal classes say, have been hoodwinked!"

"The damn crooks must have faked those explosions and returned to blow the observation booth," added O'Toole furiously, staring at the dark empty rock. Nothing remained inside, not even a scrap of paper. Even oily fingerprints would have boiled away in the explosive decompression. Prack!

"Royally screwed is the term I would have used," she added.

"Vulgar, but acceptable," said Alexander, slumping in his cockpit chair and removing his cap from a silver BBC hip flask. "But at least we have one consolation."

And O'Toole knew what that nebulous item was. "We're still ahead of the competition on this story," she smirked triumphantly brandishing a CNN thermos.

"Raw-ther," drawled the British Lord in droll agreement.

And the two reporters clinked the drink containers against their respective video monitors in ritual consolation.

Stepping back from the cluttered worktable, a sweaty Harry rolled down his sleeves and decided that Rube Goldberg would have been proud of their rude Frankenstein.

Hardwired to the laptop computer terminal, linked to the shuttle's transmodem via a coin-operated foot massager, attached to a briefcase WatchDog scanner monitoring the mixed array of pocket-docs, the laser printer began humming loudly and extruding discolored sheets of blurred writing.

"You know, love is like a butterfly," said the ceiling wistfully.

"What?" demanded Collins.

"Eh? Ah! Oh. Nothing. Sorry," apologized Deitrich. Country music later, work now.

Blowing on a fax to cool the plastic, Mike taloned a sheet curiously. "Say, what is wrong with this writing? Is it backward?"

"Maybe it's upside down," offered Jhonny skeptically, twisting his head about. "Or shorthand."

"No, some of it is unreadable, but most resembles Arabic," said Harry, holding a stat to the light. "I think."

"Me too," added Rikka, scowling angrily. "And there's only one master criminal in space who happens to read and write that ancient tongue."

"Hassan,' they chorused in loose harmony.

Politely, Mike bit his tongue. To him the wild lines looked like a bunch of drunk worms had been dipped in ink and played a game of Twister. Which was a swell way to spend an

evening, but hardly something conducive to the dissemination
of data. Body language had its limitations.

"There's something else strange about these slips," announced Jhonny, using the magnifying viewfinder of his
Toshiba camcorder as a microscope. "All of the writing is the
same."

"How could that be?" asked Michelangelo, doing an impersonation of a trombone player with his glasses. How could
anybody tell which was the words and which the squiggles?

"What it means is they used a stenographer," answered
Collins with a snap. A steno expert who knew Arabic? Wow.
They were dealing with real pros here. Her group would get
no fresh clues from these addled scraps. Without a doubt, they
were totally stalled at their present layer in this onion of truth
. . . hey, waitaminute. Layers of truth. Could it be that simple?

Lifting a sheet, Rikka laid it on atop another and turned on
the lamp inside the editing table. Shining from underneath,
the two sets of squiggles made even less sense. But her teammates got the general idea and began a fast game of mix and
match. Slowly, a few of the unreadable mess of irregular lines
began to form recognizable patterns when placed in overlapping positions, and soon a very definite pattern emerged.

"This isn't Arabic, these are floor plans to buildings!" cried
Harry in delight.

Sitting down, Rikka exhaled. "Structural designs to show
where the places can be easily destroyed?" she asked, feeling
ice form in her veins. Oh, no, had the terrible Terra Terrorists
returned?

"Not likely," said Michelangelo, studying the overlays.
"These are the wrong type of plans for destructive action."

Whew.

"But why would they have blueprints at an auction?" asked
Deitrich from above. Softly in the background could be heard
crowd applause, neighing horses, fiddles, and whooping Indi-
ans. Sounded like a heck of a party. Or a medium-sized war.

"Who says there was an auction?" replied Jhonny, recording everything on the table in triplicate. "Upon reconsidera-
tion these figures under the squiggles may not be
astronomical amounts for bids, but instead, engineering de-

tails involving building dynamics, real and tensile strength of the construction materials, and vector torque wave analysis patterns."

"Ah!" said Deitrich sagely. Whatever that meant.

"Try it in plain Esperanto," prompted Snyder. If there was no auction, then what the hell were Hassan and Mr. Nobody doing? Or were they even involved?

A pink plastic finger trailed along dotted lines and parallel grids. "It's a map showing where the structural weak points are."

"For ease of entry?"

"Exactly."

"Can we tell which buildings?" insisted Collins, leaning forward eagerly. "The White House? Not-Uncle-Bob's Castle? Koop Medical Hospital? Geneva L5? SnowBall Hell Prison?"

Calmly, Michelangelo speared a sheet with a talon tip. "No problem. See down here in this corner? The inspection seal tells the world code and government department, branch, everything."

"I'll access the files of the UP building inspector," said Jhonny, sitting down at the computer and cracking his knuckles. "Since we already have the official secrecy codes, this will only take a moment. Not even much of a challenge."

Nearly bursting with excitement, Rikka and Harry gazed at each other and tried not to hug or faint. At last they were getting close to the core of this weird story. They still didn't have a who, but with a what and a where in their hands, when and why were soon to follow and then they would have everything!

Under the android's adroit ministrations, the screen of the computer soon flashed a series of official seals and government codes, then began scrolling file names and menu items.

Here it comes, any moment . . .

The list was short, and anything but sweet: the Imperial Bank of Mars, First Lunar Security, and Fort Knox on Earth. The three most legendary, most impregnable repositories in existence, each was surrounded by a private graveyard as a visual aid to deter hopeful bandits. However, the QSNT re-

porters had a bad feeling that these vaunted claims of adamantine invulnerability were primed to become historical
footnotes. And real soon now.

Then the computer scrolled to a new screen.

"Hey, there's a fourth place on the list!" cried Jhonny, a bit
surprised at the slow response. Must have been a really ob-
scure file. Or very heavily guarded.

Eagerly, the reporters gathered round.

"What's this one? The Maharajah's temple on New Deli?"

"The location of the lockbox where Wilkes hides our pay-
checks?"

"The number ten hole on the second leg of the Miami golf
course?"

In unison, his teammates turned to stare at the anchor.

"It's a really tough bank to break," explained the golfing
enthusiast.

"No, it's . . . The Spot?" squeaked Rikka, almost stunned
speechless. It was a rare and unpleasant experience for her.
"Isn't that a space-based observatory for studying the sun?"

"Yes, it is," said Michelangelo, thoughtfully raking his face
with a paw. "Curious. Most curious."

Harry stuck a cigar in his mouth, took it out, and then put it
back in again. "What in the worlds do three armored government banks and a scientific L5 that could be taken by a kinder-
garten class armed with spoons possibly have in common?"

"Nothing," stated Deitrich flatly. "I've done a review of
their locations, political affiliations, listed contents, theoretical
contents, known enemies, stockholders, and beer consump-
tion. They haven't got one single thing in common. Nada.
Zero. Bupkis."

"Absolutely nothing?"

"Ab-so-lutely."

"And that," Rikka mumbled under her breath, her vision
unfocused in deep rumination. "Is damn significant!"

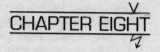

CHAPTER EIGHT

THE REVERBERATION OF the titanic blast were still echoing in the darkness of First Lunar Security when a bedroom door slammed open and there stood a furious figure in pajamas, fuzzy slippers, and laser pistol. Okay, now he was pissed!

Colonel Derek O'Malley fumbled his way along the unlit corridor and into the gaping doorway of the Base Command. Filled with angry, cursing soldiers, the room was badly illuminated by a scattering of pencil flashlights, some glow-in-the-dark superhero underoos, and a few cigarette lighter flames. The damn place resembled the audience of a rock concert! The circular bank of video monitors above the control panels formed a staggered series of phosphorescent gray squares that seemed to float in the air like the ghosts of so many dead television sets.

"Halt! Advance and be recognized!" ordered a soldier, appearing out of the blackness, the multiple barrels of his Hiroshima 99 assault rifle only a faint impression of one-way death.

"At ease, Private," barked O'Malley, attempting to walk by the shadow, but the pitted muzzle of the patented spleen imploder did not move an inch.

"Password."

"Winky dinkies, laughed the magic pink bunny," snarled the officer impatiently. Damn that idiotic security computer and its randomly generated passwords! Still, this was better than that incredibly depressing love sonnet by The Village People.

The deadly barrel of the rapid-fire weapon still did not lower, only shifted aside. "Enter, sir."

"Good man," complimented Colonel O'Malley, stepping closer. "Private Johnson, correct?"

"Ah . . . yes, sir."

"Summon assistance and get that damn doorway blocked off. I hate standing around with my ass exposed."

A dimly seen salute. "Affirmative, Colonel."

"Major Blake!" bellowed O'Malley in his best top sergeant voice as he pivoted and strode into the stygian control room.

In the flickering blackness, a tall figure stirred in the milling crowd. "Colonel? Glad you're here."

"I'm not," snorted the bird officer, striding through the mass of personnel. He had been pleasantly asleep, dreaming about winning the Solar lottery and committing suicide by splurging his entire winnings on a single lustful weekend at the Pleasure Palace brothel. It was a repeat fantasy, but a treasured favorite. "Okay, what the hell is going on in my bank?"

"Unknown at present, sir," reported the Major calmly. "The explosive bolts on the door seals blew just before the reactor went off-line. We have no power, sir. Both of the auxiliary generators have failed to come on-line, the emergency battery lights won't operate, and even though we have manually thrown the switch to connect the base to the Starlite City power grid, nothing has happened."

"Is the monthly bill paid?" asked a young voice, and he was given a group yes.

"Chemical lights," ordered O'Malley and soon a soft green glow filled the control room. "Okay, what's the trouble, Crabtree? Is Luna at war? What was that explosion?"

With a sigh, the Damage Control Officer removed his cap and brushed a hand across his crew cut. "Details are unclear, sir," reported the man sadly. "However, unless I'm seriously mistaken, we've been hit by an EMP blast which fried all of our transistors. It's the only thing that makes sense!"

Bank Command became deathly quiet. An electromagnetic pulse of that strength could only be generated by a hydrogen bomb blast. Or something ever stronger. Geez, maybe it *was* war.

"Shitfire," whispered O'Malley. "What's our Def-Con status, Lt. Sczesny?"

Twisting about, the Chief Communications Officer looked up from the inside of her inactive board. "At last report, Luna and Terra were both at Defense Condition 5, sir."

"Five is a long way from one," muttered Colonel O'Malley aloud. "But for an electromagnetic pulse of that level to effect us down here, somebody must have aimed a nuke at Green Cheese City, missed, and the damn thing detonated directly on top of us."

"But if that's correct, then why haven't we been hit by the shock wave? And where's the radiation?"

"Sir? Colonel?"

"Yes, Dupont?"

"What if a miniature nuclear bomb had been detonated inside the civilian parking lot directly outside the bank?"

"Oh, don't be an idiot, Lieutenant," scolded a brother officer. "The radiation wave would have automatically tripped our defensive shields long before the EM pulse could have done us any damage. And that shaking may have only been a moonquake. Besides, there's no such thing as a shaped nuclear charge."

The officer hung his head. Yes, that was true. It was as mythical as the hoop snake and a comfortable watch band.

"No, I think Dupont is right," said Crabtree hesitantly. "It seems impossible, but the bank may be compromised."

"Maybe it was a meteor strike," offered a corporal, still in curlers and leather bikini. "Or a power surge from the Gagarin tokamac plant?"

"That makes a lot more sense than a shaped nuke," snapped the Colonel. "But we can't take the chance. Hannigan!"

A tall, lanky woman rose to attention. "Sir!"

"Form a squad and physically secure the elevator. If anybody tries to enter or leave without my permission, blow the sack."

The Lieutenant swallowed hard. When opened, the half-ton bag of organic sealant atop the elevator would stiffen into a rock-hard plug, permanently preventing anything from leaving the base. Ever. Unless they got eventually reincarnated as civilians.

"Yes, sir," replied the soldier, her pasty face glowing in the darkness. With a salute, she turned and departed. But very slowly.

Just then, another muffled explosion was heard. And for a split second the power returned, every light and machine coming back on-line full force. The doors slammed closed and blackness descended again.

"What the ... hey, we're locked in!" noted a stocky sergeant, tugging on the handle of the fifty-ton portal.

Colonel O'Malley tightened his jaw. That did it. They were under attack! Unless the Gagarin tokamac had suddenly developed intelligence and was trying to communicate to them with Morse code, or this was the world's first orchestrated meteor shower. A quick glance at his wrist secretary listed both events as highly unlikely. Right up there with finding a comfortable watchband. Good enough.

"Security, I want the entire base swept! Every stinking level! Shoot any intruders on sight!"

"And how do we do that, sir?" asked a lieutenant, tapping the armored slab of the door with the barrel of her rifle.

"Your problem!"

Obediently, the noncom removed a hairpin from the coiffure of a sister officer and diligently went to work on the lock. What the hell, it always worked in the movies!

O'Malley chose his next target. "Crabby, make a team to try and repair the Luna Moth Hotline. We need to speak to HQ now!"

"Aye, aye, sir."

"And order a ton of fresh batteries," softly said a private from the blackness.

Taking in a lungful of air, the Colonel let it out slowly. "Carol, prepare for self-destruct."

Major Manohan had been expecting that command. "I'll do my best, sir," she said. Snatching a tool kit and a flashlight, the officer clambered into the air vent and began wiggling toward the Dinner Reclamation Arsenal, where a tactical nuke was cleverly disguised as an industrial-sized barrel of

creamed chipped psuedospam on toast. Something no experienced soldier would ever touch except under direct orders.
And maybe not even then.

Another muffled blast shook the building to its very foun-
dations. And beyond.

"Hey, that was from the direction of the vault!" cried a private. "This ain't a war, but a robbery! Somebody is after the
bloody vault!"

"No, sir," replied a major, studying a mechanical dial on
the control board. He didn't recognize the voice, but only an
officer would have shouted like that. "Somebody is already in
the bloody vault."

Furious, Colonel O'Malley grabbed a Hiroshima 99 rifle
from the hands of a startled private and turned its chattering
fury on the door to the control room. The electrostatic dis-
charge from the muzzle formed a wild strobe effect in the enclosed space. Ricochets filled the air, coffee mugs exploded,
papers formed a punctuated blizzard, and everybody dove for
cover.

However, the thick door was only slightly marred from the
fusillade of armor-piercing military rounds, which apparently
weren't quite armor-piercing enough.

"Oh, prack," sighed the Colonel, throwing down the exhausted weapon. Damnation, this always worked in the movies!

"Sir!" barked a lieutenant, his salute as crisp as the seams
on his pants. "What are our present options?"

Sensing the tension in the air, O'Malley gave the dire matter a full second before declaring their sole realistic course of
intelligent action.

"Early retirement?" groaned the soldiers, aghast. Oh, no!

Less than a minute later, a heavily laden freighter blasted
off from the underground parking lot of First Lunar Security
and started zigzagging its way across space at Fatal speeds.

Directly toward Mars.

"What?" cried Paul Ambocksky, rising from his chair by
the sheer volume of his shout.

Removing her protective earmuffs, Mrs. Seigling repeated her earlier statement about the robbery.

"First Lunar Security? Holy prack! Where's the SNT?"

The human secretary checked the computer clipboard in her hands. "Their last reported position was near Jupiter."

Well, that certainly 86'd any possible 66 for his #1s!

"Okay," he said aloud, reverting from slang to Esperanto. "Then send Lois Kent, with a backup team of whoever is available. Alert the Legal Department and notify the editors on Crime and Financial. I want a hotshot ready within the hour and full coverage for the morning six. And with pictures, damn it. Oh, yes, and wake Ms. Valdez."

"Good Lord, why?"

"Because she isn't needed and it'll honk her off no end."

What a splendid idea.

"By the way, what did the criminals get?" the News Producer asked, sitting down again and reaching for the antacids.

A quick look at the clipboard. "Umm . . . everything."

Unable to restrain himself, Box whistled long and hard.

"Anything else, chiefy?" asked Mrs. Seigling, poised to replace the earmuffs.

Chew, swallow, grimace. "Yeah. Sure. Find me the SNT!"

CHAPTER NINE

MARS, THE PURPLE planet.

Already partially terraformed, the atmosphere contained enough free water vapor to give the air a definite bluish hue. Azure was a long way off, but purple was a lot better than the original dreary color. Better dead than red.

"Warning," announced the PA speaker set in the control board of the QSNT shuttle. "You are entering the atmosphere of Imperial Mars. Local laws and regulations apply. Lizards are strictly forbidden from this point onward. This is a fire free zone. The unrestricted use of chemical flame is a felony and punishable by twenty years as a public lavatory attendant, second class. Have a pleasant stay. Long live the King and Queen."

"What a world," muttered Rikka, adjusting their trim and tapping figures onto the keypad of the minicomputer in her spacesuit forearm. The reporters had been on their way to Luna, when a notice came over the Media scrambler that the Imperial Bank of Mars had just been robbed by perps using the same MO as on the Earth moon. And since IBM was closer, they came here directly. The Nuclear Gang was moving fast and if the reporters wanted to even stay abreast of the crooks they had better do a bran muffin and really get moving.

Swiveling his head, Michelangelo compared the meters to the vector graphic monitor and the scanner screen. Night blanketed the hemisphere below, and only a handful of lights scattered in the darkness. Mostly because there was a classic movie on cable: *Debbie Does Deimos*.

Attentive to the radar, the sensors, and taping the local TV channel, Deitrich angled the flight of the shuttle into a lower orbit. "Okay, folks, we're going dayside."

At maximum velocity, the QSNT shuttle streaked through the rarefied atmosphere, the thin contrails from their wings scratching white lines across the black sky. Night, evening, twilight, and dawn passed in amazing swiftness. Then rosy morning exploded across their windshield as the huge sun crested the planetary horizon.

The Toshiba never stopped clicking.

The sky turned a lovely magenta, and below the fluffy cloud layer, irregular continents could be glimpsed. Oceans were few and far between. The bodies of carefully gathered water were more inland lakes than anything else.

There was a beep from the dashboard, and Harry touched his ear. "We have company," announced the anchor.

And from out of the clouds, flying in tight harmony, came the four sleek black shadows. Winged needles bristling with ebony slivers of deadly "Gotcha!" missiles. Tarantula fighters, the second fastest attack vehicle in existence. The fastest was the Tarantula Manufacturing Company repossession tow trucks.

"These are our quote, escorts, end quote," said Snyder, listening to the military speech. "Translation: get out of line and they blast us into pyrotechnic sushi."

Michelangelo snorted amusement. This sort of thing was fairly standard when reporters arrived after a major robbery. The locals had to show how tough they were, and how it couldn't be held against them that the robbery occurred in the first place. The police, college students, and business executives did the same on his own homeworld. Covering your ass was obviously a basic instinct in every sentient being.

"Thank the officers for their concern and please inform them that we're going in for a low-level sweep," said Deitrich.

"Acknowledged, sir," said Snyder formally, then he lifted the hand mike to his mouth. "Hey, clowns, try and keep up with us, okay?"

"Thank you, Captain Tact of the Couth Patrol," snarled

Deitrich as the Tarantulas moved in even closer to the shuttle and began rotating about it sideways and spinning on their axis. Bunch of damn military show-offs! Phooey.

Collins glanced out her window, at the world below and space above. "Are we going to do a strafing run?" she asked.

"Yep."

Consulting the altimeter, Michelangelo made a mark on the glass cover with the stub of a wax pencil. "Excellent!" He had wanted to check their trans-atmospheric stabilizer under a stress situation. This was the perfect opportunity.

"Ah, just how low do you plan to go?" asked Rikka nervously.

Deitrich said, "Remembering the recon we did on the Neptune?"

"Geez, do I ever! We almost got an icicle caught in the manifold!"

A fiendish chuckle. "That, my friend, was a deep-space orbit."

"I quit," announced Jhonny, reaching for the ejector handle of his chair. "Just let me off here."

"Too late," cried the pilot. "We're going in!"

Gleefully, the MainBrain pushed the throttles to the stopping bar and the aft engines thundered in response. Now those military slugs would see some real flying! A crushing wave of acceleration pushed the reporters hard into their seats. Automatically, the Wilkes Corp. spacesuits inflated their inner cushion lining in an effort to compensate and soft Muzak began playing to soothe addled nerves.

Screaming in toward the planet, the bucking shuttle forced a path through the thickening air, until it boomed past Mach One, Mach Two, Three, and then knifed into the cloud layer. Dropping even lower, the sleek white arrow and its entourage of black shadows zoomed downward, the ground approaching with alarming speed. Individual structures, such as major rivers and mountain ranges, became discernible. Everywhere there were cities, giant sprawling metropolises of stone, steel, and cable TV dishes.

Targeting the largest, soon the SNT shuttle was zooming over the outlying Edgar Rice boroughs of the mighty H. G.

Wellsville. In the distance its oversize sister city of Orson Wellesburg. The mighty Grover's Mill Bridge connected the two, but nobody knew who that was named after. Perhaps a mutual friend.

"Video discs spinning," announced Jhonny, sweaty but happy. This was some great footage. As long as he survived to use it. "Cameras on auto-focus. Watch out for that mountain. Scanners doing a prelim record. I said watch out for that mountain!"

Wings dipping, the shuttle rocketed past a snowcapped outcropping of jagged rock. Streaking past the tree line, the scanners found a nest of twigs and mud on a ledge. The feathered occupants squawked in resentment, but when the sound waves reached where the shuttle had been, the craft was already kilometers away.

"How's the chemical fuel?" asked Rikka, unwilling to release her grip on the armrest of her seat. When Deitrich was in this mood, all you could do was pray and hang on for dear life.

Enjoying the ride, Mike gave the gauge a fast glance and then a soft thump to make sure the needle wasn't stuck. "We've barely touched the mains. Fifteen thousand gallons of HyLox in reserve."

"No chance of a repeat of our earlier crash at Media?" asked Harry bluntly, his face pale but still photogenic.

Rocketing over a wild forest, the shuttle leveled its flight path parallel to the ground. "Criminey, you guys never let a fellow forget the past, do you?" retorted Deitrich.

"It happened only twenty-eight hours ago!"

"That's what I said, the distant past."

Streaking past kilometers of fallow farmland, they saw in the far distance a city of skyscrapers and arching bridges. Rapidly approaching, the shuttle dropped still lower until the buildings towered above them.

This close to home base, the Tarantulas stopped showboating and rigidly assumed a proper military formation.

Moments later, they were directly above H. G. Wellsville: buildings, towers, and structures flashing by in a blur. The air was so thick this close to the ground that it felt as if the shuttle was underwater. Gusts of wind blowing along the canyons of the city streets tried to flip them over, or smash the spacecraft into the strange arches. But Deitrich fought the expected turbulence and tried his best to keep the shuttle flight flat and level, allowing Jhonny's cameras to take clear photos.

A swirling tornado of dust and trash followed their wake along the wide boulevard. Suddenly a gigantic IBM skyscraper was directly ahead of them and the engines died.

"Aiyee!" screamed somebody on the bridge.

With a gentle hiss, the shuttle came to a complete halt in midair and floated gently onto the roof of a skyscraper.

"How was that, Oh ye of little faith?" smirked the ceiling.

In tight formation, the Tarantulas circled the skyscraper once as a compliment to Deitrich, then streaked off to find additional visitors to escort. Maybe the next group would be more appreciative of their flying skills, or at least not so darn sarcastic.

"Little faith? Not anymore," panted Collins, forcing her hands free from their death grip. "I just saw God."

"And he was an android," added Jhonny with a grin.

"Gremlin," corrected Michelangelo, gesturing with his glasses.

"A fan of QSNT," amended Snyder, and everybody agreed on that point.

Outside the shuttle on the flat floor, the crowd of police officers and military personnel who had scattered wildly at the landing proudly marched back toward the shuttle as the engines turned off.

With a dramatically loud bang calculated to unnerve anything with hearing, the airlock door slammed open and out popped Harry, microphone in hand. The stunned delegates blinked their watery eyes and waited for sound to return.

"Hi there!" smiled Snyder as Jhonny appeared behind in the airlock, his camcorder flashing steadily. "I'm Harry Snyder, QSNT. What did they steal?"

"Well, Mr. Snyder," started a plump official, tugging his robes of state to better cover his stomach of fat. "Until there has been a full and complete investigation into this matter, it would be unwise and imprudent to speculate on such details as amounts taken, or even if there has, or has not, been a robbery and/or attempted robbery, instigated and/or planned."

As Harry pretended to take notes on the volumes of nothing said by the pontificating politician, Rikka hopped out of the spacecraft, took an elderly Imperial chamberlain by the elbow, and hustled him off to one side.

"Lord Frederick, remember when there was a drastic shortage in the funds of the Not-Uncle-Bob's Castle servants' pension?" she said low and fast. Which was the only way to play hardball. "And I helped find the embezzlers and clear you of the charges." She paused. "Even though you weren't innocent on every charge?"

Glumly, the man nodded. Okay, it was payback day.

"What did they get?"

"The Youth Drug," sighed the man, placing a pocket-doc to his aching head. "Roughly two tons."

Tons? Yikes! "You store Youth Drug here?"

"Not anymore!" said the chamberlain sullenly.

Rude, but understandable. "But how did the thieves overcome the army of guards?" asked Rikka, pressuring for an answer.

"The Youth Drug," sighed the man.

The reporter started to complain, but then realized the truth. She had asked a simple question and gotten an astounding answer. How had the criminals stolen the Youth Drug? They used Youth Drug. The Imperial Bank of Mars was proofed against poison gas, viral, or bacteriological infection, any airborne agent that might allow a thief to subjugate the whole complex.

But nowhere in any of the building's specifications had anybody ever asked for the place to be protected from the Youth Drug, a wholly medicinal substance. Should there be a leak from the vault, the guards would only be too happy to have thirty or forty years added to their lives.

"And they blew a hole in the vault door?" she ventured for a guess.

Where had she gotten that information? "Yes, but we have no idea how they made that tremendous rose," said the man, using the doc to mop his brow.

Collins nodded to herself. A rose-shaped hole in a bank vault door. Yep, that was her perps, sure enough. Reaching out, she shook the man's hand, palming her business card into his—a tightly folded hundred sanddollar bill.

"Thank you very much for your valuable consideration," she said loud enough for the others on the roof to hear. "And you're quite correct. We should go get clearance from the Royal Censor before asking questions involving a sensitive Imperial installation."

"Always glad to assist a member of the press," said the pale chamberlain, taking his cue and her card.

Looking glum the reporter piled back into the shuttle, closed the doors, and turned on the scrambling systems. Keeping to the pertinent details, Rikka recounted her brief interview with the High Lord Chamberlain.

"These people are good," muttered Harry in grudging appreciation.

IN SPADES.

"Our perps are trading up," thought Rikka aloud. "They steal the Venus bombs, to steal a million dollars of Luna currency, to parlay both into obtaining a billion dollars' worth of the Martian Youth Drug."

A billion sanddollars' worth. Which made it a lot more considering the current exchange rate. The worst rate was between England and the Independent Asteroid Belt, where the exchange was four pounds to the rock.

"From bums to billionaires in twenty-four hours," said Michelangelo whimsically.

"Hey, that's good," complimented Collins and she quickly jotted down the remark.

"Feather my props," cursed Deitrich in ancient aviation slang. "But with those bombs and the Youth Drug, what the prack is the final goal? What else could these people possibly want? Or need?"

"They could buy a world with what they have," whispered Rikka, stopping her typing.

A stunned silence filled the spacecraft as everybody wondered if the pilot had just impetuously answered the big question.

Humming softly, the main engines of the shuttle came to life.

"Next stop, Fort Knox!" said Deitrich.

"Which one?" muttered Snyder, climbing onto the bridge.

Paw on the lintel to guard against banging his head, Mike halted in the act of taking his oversize chair.

"Beg pardon?" the alien asked, surprised. "What do you mean, which?"

Each independently, the SNT turned to face their giant friend.

"Mike," said Rikka, wetting her lips. "Did the floor plans we found say Fort Knox, Kentucky, North America, Earth?"

"Or just Fort Knox?" finished Harry, resting an arm on the back of his chair.

"Is there another?" asked the technician innocently.

Jhonny hit himself in the forehead with a metallic clang. "Prack! It's not Fort Knox, Earth, it's Fort Knox Arsenal on Mercury!"

"Why would these people need more weapons?" asked Michelangelo, trying to salvage some part of his wounded pride.

"Who cares? But we better tell the cops," said Rikka. "There are instances when even we should obey the law, and this is one of them."

"But we can't," countered Harry, worrying his mustache. "I already informed InterPlanetPol that the next attack should be at Fort Knox, Earth! If we now tell them it's Mercury, they'll only think we're trying to lure them away from the crime scene so that we can get an exclusive scoop."

CAN'T BLAME THEM, scrolled Deitrich. WE'VE DONE IT BEFORE.

"But never on anything this serious or potentially lethal," stated Mike, nervously sharpening his claws on the back of his chair. Skratch. Skratch. "What should we do?"

"We go to Mercury for an exclusive scoop," Collins replied, strapping herself into the copilot's chair. "And with any luck we get pictures of the crooks in the act, then notify the police, they make an arrest, we serve as witnesses in the trial, and Wilkes rewards us with a two-week paid vacation on the Hedonism World asteroid theme park!"

"I can live with that," smirked Snyder, activating the police radar scrambler and requesting launch clearance at the same time.

In a rumble of controlled thunder, the QSNT spacecraft lanced into the purple sky of Mars. On the skyscraper rooftop, the guards and politicians scurried about retrieving their hats.

"Mercury, here we come!" announced Deitrich in his most stalwart voice. "And we're going to be there before the crooks strike!"

The SNT loudly cheered the bold sentiment.

"Oh, by the way," said Michelangelo, busy at his engineering console with his gleaming talons. "There doesn't happen to be a third place named Fort Knox, is there?"

And even before it properly accelerated, the spacecraft slowed to a halt.

Oh, hell. Yes, there was.

CHAPTER TEN

THE FIRST SHAPED nuclear detonation annihilated every security satellite orbiting above the Fort Knox Refinery on the western peninsula of the Republic of Titan. The blast was so bright that the fireball eclipsed the mother planet of Saturn from the sky for the duration of its dramatic existence. Seconds later, the next explosion cut loose a full spectrum EMP blast inside the cool atmosphere, frying every working transmitter within a thousand kilometers. Which allowed half the planet to sleep late as their clock radios no longer worked. The third ignited directly above the refinery's storehouse, smashing the robotic missile batteries and automatic Bedlow laser cannons into wafer-thin wall decorations. And the next punched a twenty-meter-wide tunnel clean through the armored roof, and the next ten floors, reaching straight to the sub-sub-sub-basement. And beyond.

Staring aghast at the half a coffee cup spilling decaf onto his shoes, the head of security screamed nearly as loud as the alarm, only he also dashed for the nearest exit. Scrambling out the laundry chute, the man made a mental note to mail in his resignation from the nearest open bar.

As the rest of the staff dove out of assorted windows and scattered for their lives through the parking lot, a bulky freighter nosed directly into the gaping hole and proceeded downward at a leisurely pace. In its wake, the random pieces of furniture would tumble down after the space vehicle, bouncing off its hull and doing little to impede its progress. But this was not unexpected, as the poor tactical defense factor of a cushioned divan was well researched by the military.

However, as advertised, the patented "Mother-in-Law" Klaxon never shut up, even when the power was cut off and masked invaders in spacesuits shot the control panels to sparkling trash. Whew. Good design. No wonder Gardner Wilkes was a billionaire. The man must be a genius!

Nine hundred fifty million kilometers away, a pair of legs extended through the shiny hull of the Media Space Station and then drifted along walking through the starry vacuum as the owner of the structure heroically tried to master his Wilkes Corp. Handy Home Hologramphone—Be There and Be Square!

Thank goodness he only had it on the Beginner setting.

"Mulligan," replied the young Titan police lieutenant, coming to attention and saluting the video monitor on his desk. "Lt. Joseph Mulligan."

"Where's Heisenford?" demanded a gruff voice from the speaker.

A polished shoe eased a copy of his *ParanoiaMan: the archenemy of everybody*! comic book under the desk where it could not be seen. "The Captain's at home with the flu, Mayor. I'm in charge this afternoon."

The elderly woman on the screen kept her feelings from showing and spoke positively. "Okay, then it's your problem, Joe. Call in every officer you have and alert the SWAT team."

The acting watch commander swallowed hard and touched the service automatic at his hip, never before fired except at the target range. "What is it, Mayor Higgins? A riot? An attack of the Free Police? Another Bombs-and-Roses concert?"

"Worse. Fort Knox is under attack by masked raiders. I want every available cop there immediately. Fill that building with police!"

The tension drained from the Lieutenant and he dropped back in his swivel chair. Ho-ho, so it was only a damn joke. Should have expected something like this on his first tour of command. Hazing the fresh kid. Didn't the Mayor have anything more important to do?

"Come off it, Your Honor," said the man as rudely as he

dared to the leading politico of his city. "That refinery is impregnable. It says so on the billboard."

The speaker almost jumped off the desk. "MULLIGAN, YOU IDIOT! DO YOU THINK I WOULD ORDER A GODDAMN POLICE RAID ON GODDAMN FORT KNOX AS A JOKE? YOU GET YOUR GODDAMN MEN THERE YESTERDAY, LIEUTENANT, OR I'LL HAVE YOUR BALLS FOR GODDAMN BREAKFAST!"

As the video monitor faded to black, Mulligan scrambled from his swivel chair and started flipping every alarm switch there was on the desktop control panel.

Oh, dear, this was going to look very bad in the daily reports.

"Found 'em!" cried Snyder, hand to his earphone.

"Where?" demanded Rikka's voice from the lavatory.

"Titan!"

"Coordinates locked!" mumbled Jhonny, a silicon vindaloo flavor stick extending from the corner of his mouth. Pungent wisps of spicy steam rose from the end of the android confection.

"Safety stops removed," stated Michelangelo, a pawful of wires hanging limply from his grip. Sniff. What was that awful smell?

"Poof, we're gone," announced Deitrich, and the stars blurred as the shuttle streaked off at its absolute top velocity of Fatal Five.

On Titan, two thousand horribly beweaponed Leviathans rose over the mountain peaks that surrounded Fort Knox Valley. The monstrous flying tanks maintained a tight formation of concentric circles while the floating missile platforms took advantage of the natural protection of the rocky Stiliveski cliffs. Tagging behind the armanda were hundreds of support vehicles from the Titan Interplanetary Tank Squadron: armored medical ships, armed troop transports, Artificial Army Intelligence hovercraft, and a massive, multiple propeller, mobile command center helicopter. As with many military groups, TITS heartily believed that size was important, and this philosophy had never been more evident than today.

Unnoticed on the ground, waddling through the forest and streams, came two young Space Marines in Samson powersuits, fresh from the experimental labs at the Arsenal of Strategic Security. The soldiers possessed no implements of destruction save their armored limbs, but those were enough. If the flying tanks failed, then the powersuits would step in and tear the thieves apart by hand. Actually, the boys were quite looking forward to the experience. But then, that's why they had the job.

As everybody across the solar system knew, TITS and ASS were a powerful combination.

In perfect unison, the Leviathans fired a warning shot with their particle beams; a blinding spiderweb of ultra-hard radiation converging on the refinery building. But the shimmering blister of a colossal forcefield dome met and repelled those terrible rays. The valley contained the reflected heat flash and the surrounding forest ignited into a raging inferno. Hungry flames licked at the belly armor of the tanks as they swooped along the mountain slopes coming in for the kill.

"SURRENDER!" thundered the voice of the commander from the PA speaker on every tank. "OR ELSE NO MORE MR. NICE ARMY!"

The back seat from the particle beams had created a zone of hellish intensity in the center of the valley, grass and shrubs long since atomized from temperatures rivaling those at the surface of the sun. The rocky earth itself was slagging into a molten ring of bubbling lava that lapped at the immaterial boundary surrounding the buildings. The very heat that coverted the stone into a powerful offensive weapon was also the dominant factor in holding the lava at bay.

"Can we have a minute to think about it?" weakly called out a voice from the refinery parking lot loudspeakers.

In response, the Leviathans poured out gigawatts of subatomic death. With the same results as before. Only more so.

"We'll take that as a no," crackled a burning loudspeaker.

* * *

In the hovering command ship, an aghast major turned to her CO. The commanding officer seemed to be suffering a mild heart attack.

"Stop lasers," subvocalized the General bitterly. "We're only expending vital energy. Attention, all tanks, advance while firing your main cannons. Everyone else go to Vulcan miniguns, Gatlings, and Gibraltars. We'll nickel-and-dime the bastards to death."

"B-but what about the refinery, sir?"

"We'll build a replacement," grunted the CO, touching his throat mike. Ah, this was more like it. No finesse, complex battle strategies, or politicians. Just raw unbridled brute force. War the way God meant it to be. "All units . . . FIRE!"

The order was relayed and the tanks charged. Spent brass casings from the machine guns and Gatlings arced into the sky, making golden streams as the assault force spewed out a million rounds a minute.

Large chunks of the refinery started disappearing. But at that exact moment, from the exhaust vents of the refinery came billowing pink clouds. Carried onward by the raging thermals of the lava, the vapor soon filled the valley.

Instantly, the Youth Drug penetrated the airlock seals and every soldier slumped over at their controls and immediately proceeded to stop aging. With only youthful sleepers at the controls, the Leviathans ambled about uncertainly in the sky and for a few moments and then tumbled downward like a rain of ten-ton metal bricks.

Of the entire assault force, only the command ship helicopter remained airborne, the backwash of the rotating blades keeping the stupefying medicine from inhibiting the crew.

But then the chopper shuddered as its thin hull was clipped by a dropping missile carrier. Delicate controls blew up and short circuits abounded. Fat sparks crawled like mad insects across the navigation console. In a brilliant flash, the main computer fried like bacon in a microwave oven, sizzling and popping. Then the conked, cooked chopper plummeted.

These events went mostly unseen by the pilot and copilot, as the destruction of the computer had made them temporarily

blind, wild spots and pinwheels dancing before their eyes. However, the soldiers could hear and feel the assorted destruction. It
sounded worse than the time they had accidentally plugged the
self-destruct unit into the laundry and blown their own socks off.

With a loud yelp, the pilot jerked her hand away from the
dashboard and stuffed a burned finger into her mouth.

"What is it, Sarge?" demanded the copilot, painfully rubbing his teary eyes. His nose told him smoke was everywhere.

"Even the damn reserve boards have shorted out," she
mumbled around the wounded digit. "Switch to manual and
brace yourself. We're doing our impersonation of Wall Street,
1929."

"Eh?"

"We're gonna crash."

Pulling on his gloves, the youth flipped the appropriate
switches. "Maybe the automatic backup systems will kick in
and save us," he said, hope and fear mixing in his voice.

Holding on to the joystick with both hands, the blind
woman snorted. "Right, and maybe your mother is still a vir-
gin, but don't count on it." Skillfully, she elbowed the intercom button. "Attention! This is the pilot. Prepare for crash
landing! Repeat, prepare for crash landing!"

Everybody scrambled for safety and three awful,
heartstopping seconds later there came a thump from beneath
them and the whooshing rotors above slowed to a gentle halt.

Using considerable force, the copilot swallowed his heart,
returning it to the accustomed position. "Jumping Jesus,
Sarge, how'd you do that?"

Wearily, the Army pilot slumped in her seat. "Years of experience falling off bar stools, kid. And don't you forget it."

Sensing their presence would no longer hinder the pilots, a
pair of pocket-docs mounted on spider legs crawled out of
hiding and proceeded to make medical repairs.

"What should we do?" asked the kid.

"Nothing," replied the woman, pulling her aviator's cap
low over her face. "What can a couple of blind pilots do?"

Inactivity, the goal of every serviceman, just didn't seem
proper in the midst of battle. "So we just sit here?" As a
trained professional soldier, the youth would willingly try

anything at least once. Twice if it didn't scar and three times
if it made money.

She grunted at him. "No, moron, we fervently pray to
Christ that the crooks don't blow our ass off while we wait
for the brass hats upstairs to do something clever."

Hovering above the craggy peaks of the Titan hills on their
belly jets, the QSNT shuttle was positioned directly between
two outcroppings of mountain rock, giving them maximum
visibility and minimum exposure. Dying was not an accepted
method of bringing in a hot story, and if it was, they would
have negotiated their contracts.

"Jhonny, baby, bubby, tell me you're getting this," begged
Rikka, her face pressed against the glass of the shuttle window.

"I'm getting it! I'm getting it!" cried a voice from within
a whirring cocoon of cameras and recorders.

"Wow, what a show," extolled Deitrich from above.
"Haven't seen anything like this since that soccer game in
England!"

Whiskey glass in hand, Snyder agreed, "If only we had
even one scantily clad babe in the scene, we'd be winning
awards for the next ten years!"

There was a pause.

Everybody turned toward Rikka.

"Don't even think about it," she muttered, not even looking
their way.

Everybody turned to the window. Ah well, it never hurt to
ask.

Meanwhile, in the uppermost level of the crashed helicopter, the CO of the decimated assault force pulled himself off
the floor and resumed his seat in front of the 3-D computer
simulation of Fort Knox Valley. The environmental scanners
told him what had happened. So, hit us with some Youth
Drug, eh? What a dirty trick. And well played too, he might
add.

"Damn it to hell in a handbasket," growled the General,
staring at the hologram display as if it were something un-

pleasant found in a sandwich. "We're up shit creek without a paddle, aren't we, Major?"

Once scandalized by her CO's constant use of profanity, his aide was long immune to it. "Yes, sir, its pretty bad," she agreed. "Well over half of our armored units are disabled. Crews unconscious, or the vehicles are not able to employ their emergency rotating armored land belts."

"Treads, Major. Call them treads, damn it. And what do you mean unable to employ them. Why in bloody hell not?"

She offered him a hastily scribbled report. "Two hundred tanks have broken ... treads, sir, with no spare shoes aboard to effect repairs. Eighty-five are sideways, and twenty are up-side down."

"What about the powersuits?" he asked, trying to decipher his aide's handwriting.

"Are currently located in Sector 4, approximately thirty meters underground playing Scrabble."

Rendered temporarily speechless, the General dropped his jaw, closed it, looked at the report, her, and the report again until he could bellow, "What!!"

"Apparently, sir, they were each directly under a tank when the crash came," hurriedly explained the Major in detail. "The force of the blow must have driven them deep into the ground."

Another curse. "Scrabble?"

The Major shrugged her shoulders. "They're trapped in solid rock, sir, and it will take an excavation team days to free them."

Doffing his helmet, the General used a handkerchief to mop his brow. Oh, well, literacy was also important to the modern military.

Viciously, he stabbed a finger at the full-color hologram of the valley. "Call Divisional and request any additional support they can send us. Heavily armed, wide awake, and sealed in-side spacesuits, God damn it!"

The aide-de-camp saluted. "Affirmative, sir."

High in a corner of the tactical bridge, an automatic video recorder continued to relay every action and word back to the Titan Unilateral Supreme Headquarters, and before the Major

had covered the six paces to the hotline phone, it bleeped at
her with an incoming transmission. With a surprised expression, the aide watched the telecommunications device closely
as it decoded the signal and a laser printer whined out a hard
copy of the message on edible security paper.

"Sir," gasped the Major, clutching the front of her combat
fatigues. "It's confirmation from HQ on your request for more
troops!"

Stunned, the General nearly fell out of his chair. "Jesus H.
Tap-Dancing Christ! You mean those nitwits were actually
paying attention for once and not playing hide-the-salami
with their secretaries? Great! What are they sending us?"

The Major read the paper again just to make sure she had
the message correct. "The entire available reserves of the Republic of Titan. Starting with fifty thousand troops, five tank
battalions, two destroyers, and a hundred dreadnoughts.

"And one person named Lulu," she finished, slightly puzzled. Eh?

Eagerly, the soldier rubbed his hands together. "Hot spit,
now they're talking! ETA?"

"Twenty minutes, sir," stated the woman, feeling slightly
groggy from the magnitude of what was happening. Somebody at HQ was really honked off about this fiasco. "They'll
be transported in on helicopters and ground cars armed with
electric fans."

"Ha!" cried the General, snapping a finger in the direction
of the base.

Finished with the report, the Major stuffed the paper into
her mouth and started diligently chewing. Hmm, not bad actually. Mocha pistachio. Much better than those nasty prune
memos from the rear echelon.

"Okay, Major, let's see how much damage we can inflict
upon these bastards before the cavalry arrives. Activate the
emergency override on the tanks and have the computers con-
tinue the attack. That will buy us some time as a diversion.
Have every Leviathan immediately proceed to the edge of
that lava pool and prepare to open fire on my signal."

Chewing, his aide saluted. "Oye, Oye, shar."

. . . and a staggering fireball engulfed the entire refinery.

Brutal winds screaming in unrestrained fury, a strident rumble of nuclear destruction shook the valley, rattling the tanks and the stupefied soldiers inside like Vegas dice. And from the blast crater there arose the classic mushroom cloud of layered thermal currents battling for supremacy above the white-hot blast crater. And while it is true that "Tactical Mushrooms! The snack that assaults your tastebuds!" also used the design, even they admitted that the atom bomb had created the symbol first. However, the food manufacturer did insist that theirs was prettier and caused only half as many mutations.

Wind and lightning cleared the air of the valley. Soon there was nothing remaining but a gaping hole in the ground where the building had once stood, and wisps of vaporized rock wafting about in the breeze of utter annihilation.

Awakened from their nap by the noise and heat, the incredibly healthy crews of the Leviathans yawned and stretched and scratched and wiggled about in their loose uniforms. A trick that should have taken them years to perfect. On the deck of each tank was a littering of robotic limbs, bionic parts, glass eyes, dentures, toupees, and falsies, each replaced with fresh new living tissue. Much to the delight of the soldiers and the chagrin of one lone private who would now have to go back to Sweden for that special operation all over again.

How very inconvenient.

A passing scout for the Bombs-and-Roses "Titan Your Grip" tour noted the explosion and casually dismissed the event. Expensive, old hat, and, most importantly, much too loud. Nothing was allowed to be louder than the band. It said so on their T-shirts. Unfortunate, really. The scene would have made a splendid glow-in-the-dark poster.

"What was that?" stormed the General furiously, oogling the hologram screen. "A nuke?"

Standing at the WatchDog control panel, the Major confirmed the observation. "Yes, sir. Apparently the thieves blew up the building."

"The pracking bastards preferred death rather than be captured alive," he sneered contemptuously. "Cowards!"

"Or loonies," agreed the Major. Damn strange though. Could it be a trick of some kind?

Dragging his shoe heels to slow the motorcycle, Lt. Mulligan came to a skidding halt directly in front of the dilapidated chain-link fence partitioning Fort Knox Refinery from the public access road.

"Okay, enough of that already," said the cop, pushing his hat onto the back of his head and placing arms akimbo. "You there! In the tank! Yes, you buddy! You're all under arrest!"

On the QSNT shuttle, Michelangelo had trouble swallowing and speaking. "No, that's not what I said."

Harry spun his head from the amusing view of the police officer lecturing the youthful, but literally steaming soldiers. "Eh? They nuked the building, correct?"

"Well, yes and no."

"Explain, please," demanded Rikka, starting to get that old trouble tingle in her gut again. Or maybe it was just Jhonny's flavor stick. Flecks of paint were crumbling off the wall near him.

"That blast was . . . controlled, shaped," the alien reminded them.

"And?" chewed Jhonny, happily rewinding a videotape of the blast.

The huge technician looked toward the ceiling. "And the bomb didn't blow up the building," he reiterated. "It blew the building up!"

CHAPTER ELEVEN

UNCARING OF ECONOMY, Deitrich wastefully blew kilos of raw fuel out the belly jets, flipping the SNT shuttle upright on its end, and punched for full power. In a thunderous roar, the craft lifted into the clear sky on a column of fire. The sonic boom of its departure rattled the teeth of every exposed person in the Titan valley and loosened the rocky soil around the powersuits, allowing them to crawl to freedom. Whew. They would never be mean to a nail again!

Mach Two ... Mach Three ... the sky before the hurtling shuttle was distorted by the sheer speed of the craft. Retractable launch covers protected the windshield, but through the pinhead video cameras, the reporters could see clear air in front of the vessel, a calm tunnel surrounded by misty turbulence. A velocity tube. Quite pretty, actually. It was one of the benefits of having their own private shuttle. Aside from never having to hunt for their luggage at a spaceport baggage claim carousel.

"How come we saw something the T.I.T.S. didn't?" demanded Rikka hotly. If there was anything the reporter hated it was believing a story was over, only to discover she hadn't even scratched the surface yet. A mystery that concludes with the bad guys dying was quite acceptable, made good copy actually, but an open-ended story that simply stopped cold with the participants escaping capture was intolerable! She had a right to know! Ah ... and the public did too.

"The Titan military was too close, the flash blinded them," explained Michelangelo, regulating the flow of liquid hydrogen and liquid oxygen to their chemical engines. "Plus, we had elevation and were above the event plane of the tachyon secondary wave front emission perimeter."

Harry removed the cigar from his mouth and raised an eyebrow at the pontificating technician. "Excuse me, Michelangelo, no offense meant, but are you making this stuff up as you go along?"

Standing to his full towering height, the huge alien looked down at the tiny gray-haired human and scowled through his pince-nez glasses. "No."

Snyder shrugged. Still sounded like techno-babble to him. But then, so did the instructions for his VCR. Had anybody in history ever clearly understood how those things worked?

Blue sky changed to soft gray, then starry black, and raw sunlight suddenly bathed the spacecraft as it erupted from the atmosphere. Free at last from the clinging drag of Titan's dense air, Deitrich kicked in the thrusters full force and the shuttle blasted forward with renewed velocity. Off to the side was the silver-ringed glory of Saturn, its colossal red-and-yellow bulk filling the visible horizon as if it were the mighty sun itself, drunk and slightly overdressed at a bad Mexican costume party.

Jhonny quickly located the refinery floating serenely in space. At its base was a perfectly round mound of concrete and rock from the valley floor. Wow. The controlled nuclear blast had thrown the building into space just like an old-fashioned chemical rocket! Hopefully, the thieves inside had been protected from the crushing G forces by antigravity nets or else all anybody would find would be some rather disgusting criminal ooze. Yuck. And it was a definite tribute to the Titan construction company that the building survived in such good condition. But then, it was a maximum security military fortification designed to withstand a wide spectrum of brutal poundings, ranging from enemy sneak attacks of Marines on shore leave.

"Get ready to do a sensor lock with the WatchDog in case anybody tries to escape," said Rikka as the shuttle maneuvered closer on its rumbling engines.

But then, without warning, there was a blinding flash of light that filled the universe. It seemed to last for eternity, eventually fading away into nothingness. When their eyes cleared, the reporters could plainly see that the Titan building was completely gone.

"Scanners!" snapped Deitrich, bringing the craft to a complete halt.

"WatchDog is clear. Sensors same," reported Jhonny glumly.

"They went Fatal," sighed Snyder, his cigar drooping. "Or rather, they tried too."

Rikka slumped in her seat. Dead. The thieves were dead and so was the story.

"Farewell," intoned Michelangelo, placing both palms together and then turning them outward in a ritual good-bye. "This is why we cannot travel to the stars. The induction field of an FTL engine triggers the quantum irregularities of our denatured tin elements. If there is any loose tin on board, it can fuse into fission and ignite. We have only four grams total of the metal on board. They were inside a warehouse full. Maybe ten tons!"

"Just slightly a tad over the critical limit," observed Jhonny coldly. This was most definitely a prime example of cleaning the gene pool.

"How could anybody be so stupid as to try and escape from a refinery of tin by going FTL?" demanded Snyder, also annoyed.

"Suicide?" asked Deitrich from above. "The Titan military was hot on their trail . . . but no. The surface blast sent them free. We were still in pursuit, but we had no intention of trying to arrest them. We're reporters, not cops."

"This is bullshit," stated Rikka, rising from her chair and starting to pace about the bridge.

Harry pulled in his legs to give her thinking room. They had all seen this act before.

"Agreed," he said, trying to prime her mental pump. "These folks have been sharper than a Ginsu for the whole caper. They steal the bombs, to steal the Youth Drug, getting the tin. Going up, up, up, and then. Blam! They do the single most stupid trick anybody has heard of since the invention of the yo-yo grenade."

Standing still, Rikka folded her arms and closed her eyes. Her mind launched into a cosmic maelstrom of thoughts and possibilities. The rest of the team went silent, letting the boss cook in private. Deitrich even killed the standard beep-beep from the cockpit that told them they hadn't crashed into an asteroid.

Minutes passed. Collins's shirt became damp with sweat. Her face went from livid to pale as she struggled with the emotional content of proposals and schemes.

"Ha!" she barked, startling everybody.

GEEZ, DON'T DO THAT! scrolled Deitrich. NOW I HAVE TO GO CHANGE MY HOLOGRAM SHORTS.

"Did we video the explosion of the refinery building?" asked Rikka, staring out the bow windows, her back to the team.

"Sure, SOP," said Jhonny, pulling a disk from his console.

"Give it to Mike, please."

The alien accepted the disk and wondered what he was supposed to do with it? Make a duplicate? Play Frisbee?

"Mike, would you run a mass spectrograph analysis of the blast, please," asked the reporter, her mind busy playing with ramifications.

Wordlessly, the alien slid the disk into his engineering console and started the test. Ah, clever.

"Brilliant!" smiled Harry. "The explosion generated a light flash in a vacuum, near perfect conditions for conducting an examination of the wavelengths of the light emitted to determine the molecular formation of the elements involved."

"Thank you, Mr. Wizard," scoffed Jhonny. "But this is not PBS. We know basic science, thank you."

A nod. "Sorry."

"What exactly am I looking for?" asked the technician, his face illuminated by winking lights and flashing LEDS.

Collins placed a palm against the insulated Armorlite window. Stars framed her fingers like diamond rings. "There should be a lot of steel, glass, copper, iron, all the usual expected stuff. Plus a lot of organic compounds."

"And?" prompted the alien.

"I'm betting there won't be any complex carbon molecules.

Just the simple ones from furniture and rugs. But nothing complex. No living molecules.

"Not a single solitary pracking one."

Hunched over his flashing console, Michelangelo concentrated on the work at paw. Hadn't done anything like this since his stint as a fry cook for Burger-Mania restaurant chain before he got his degree and QSNT hired him. They weren't real hamburgers, just an incredible simulation. Diligently he would search for any impurities and have them ruthlessly removed, such as vitamins, texture, and flavor.

"Watch for any of the higher elements on the periodic table," instructed Rikka, fisting a palm.

"Higher elements?" prompted Harry, nervously chewing on a cigar. "Such as?"

"Such as thulium," said the alien, scrutinizing the meters and dials. "That would be money from the vault. And uranium, that would be from some depilatory cream or a mouse trap. Trace amounts of radium, probably a glow-in-the-dark clock, or a solar-powered condom. There's also some Einsteinium, titanium, Californium." Then the alien paused the double-checked the readouts. "And here's two interesting items. First, I am not getting much reading on tin! No more than fifty or sixty kilos I would guesstimate."

"I thought it was kind of a whimpy explosion for ten tons," observed Jhonny thoughtfully. "So they must have managed to jettison most out of the building before the big blast. Maybe in a lifeboat from their assault ship."

"What's the second interesting thing, Mike?" asked Snyder, tapping his ashes into a burn-scarred depression on his console. The anchor knew he was smoking too much on this story, a sure sign of nerves, but stolen bombs made him uneasy. Next chance he got, better load up on some flavor sticks.

The alien offered them a printed copy of a horizontal rainbow bar sliced by thin black thins. "The blast contained incredibly high amounts of palladium."

"Palladium?"

A nod. "Yes. Almost a ton of it."

There was only one answer for that.

"Robots," said Harry, crunching his cigar. "The freighter that blasted its way into the refinery was full of robots!"

Sudden understanding flashed across the bridge like a towel dropping in a co-ed sauna.

"That's why nobody has been hurt or killed so far in these robberies," shouted Collins excitedly. "And why the Youth Drug was used against the tanks and not the bombs. Robs can't kill!"

"Robots did the stealing and then deliberately killed themselves? Why?"

"To throw us off the trail!" declared Snyder, grinding his teeth. "The old 'gosh, we're dead now, so don't search for us anymore' trick."

"So whoever is really in charge could get off scot-free!" said Jhonny, cradling his camera and stroking it like a cat.

"Exactly."

Smiling broadly, Harry walked over and shook Rikka's hand. "Madam, you are a genius!"

"Thanks," she dimpled. "Took you long enough to realize it."

"It was the overwhelming modesty that hid your intelligence."

"Shaddup. Deitrich, what's the chance of tracking that lifeboat, escape pod, whatever, out here?" asked Collins excitedly. "The one that the real crooks escaped in." Eagerly, she watched the winking array of screens before her and the fluctuating meters in the overhead wraparound console.

"Ah . . . none," replied the ceiling. "Not after the interference created by the blast. I'm operating strictly on visual at present."

Damn.

"We can't track them at all? Impossible," snorted Harry, mimicking the sensor controls of his communications console. "By necessity, it had to be a small ship and they couldn't have gotten very far traveling at sublight speeds."

"Unfortunately, I concur with the sensor readings," growled Michelangelo, irritably clawing the controls. "WatchDog scanners show clear. The same with radar, sensors, EM, and proximity. We are alone in orbit."

"Are you sure?" asked Rikka, probing for flaws.

"Positive. No doubt whatsoever."

The fuming reporter frowned and made vague hand gestures. Then she went stock-still. "Wait a damn minute, who's got a list of what was stolen on Luna?"

I DO.

"Was there any superconductor cloth taken from the bank?"

CHECKING . . . YES, THERE WAS. NEARLY A SQUARE KILOMETER, ALMOST A WHOLE BOLT. HEY! THEY STOLE PRECISELY ENOUGH SUPERCONDUCTOR CLOTH TO COVER A DOZEN SHUTTLES LIKE PILLOWCASES!

"They're doing a Deadman maneuver!" roared Mike furiously.

"Draped in superconductor cloth, we'd have trouble locating a planet," stated Snyder, glaring hostilely out the windows at the black, but not empty space around them. Waylaid by one of their very own tricks. These guys were good. Almost too good to be mere thieves. Could they be smugglers? Or even fellow reporters?

"I want everybody to take a quadrant of space and manually search for any missing stars," ordered Collins, slaving her console to Navigation and accessing the chart files. "They have got to be moving away from Titan, and even though a lifeboat is damn small there's still a slim chance they will eclipse a star and betray their position. Let's move!"

The new team chorused in agreement and went eagerly to work.

Sipping mint juleps and yawning, a heavily armed battalion of soldiers were lounging about in lawn chairs or sunning themselves atop their tanks parked on the lush Kentucky blue grass surrounding the armored underground fortress of Fort Knox, Earth.

Suddenly a hologram flickered into existence next to a dozing general in flak jacket and Bermuda shorts.

"Sir!" called a messenger, startling the resting officer. "SitComTac reports the criminals have attacked the Fort Knox Refinery on Titan!"

Placing aside her drink, the General got to her feet and

stretched. "I thought it might be something like that after this long a wait," she admitted. "Is TITS on the job?"

"Yes, sir!"

A smile. "Then please relay to them my compliments, and ask if they wouldn't mind arresting the SNT for me?"

"Ah ... the charges, sir?"

"Mostly for wasting my Saturday," said the General, rubbing suntan lotion on her arms. "But there is also aiding and abetting known criminals, maybe some espionage. Inciting public unrest. Hey! Are you guys unhappy and ready to riot?"

A highball was raised into the air. "Absolutely, sir!"

She nodded. Good man. "See? Inciting mutiny, possibly treason, and ... anything else Titan can think of."

"Is this really a good idea, sir?" asked the messenger hesitantly. "They have helped us innumerable times in the past."

The local weather dropped fifty degrees fast.

"You aren't by any chance an accomplice of theirs, are you, Private?" growled the General in a threatening tone.

The Corporal glanced at his lone stripe, then went rigid and gave a fast salute. "Fry 'em in hell, sir!"

"Better," said the General, sitting down again and pulling her cap down over her eyes. And for this she canceled a skiing trip to Uranus? "Go get the bastards, son."

"Aye, aye, sir!"

"And still more nothing," sighed Michelangelo, placing aside his magnifying glass and straightening his back to the sound of creaking leather. "The four of us cannot properly watch in detail a full 360-degree globe of space."

Rubbing tired eyes with his elbows, Jhonny turned off his monitor. "I agree," sighed the android sadly. "Let's admit it, they beat us again."

"Prack!" cried Rikka, slamming a fist onto the arm of her copilot's chair, inadvertently activating the personal hygiene unit. On the sly, she disposed of the toothbrush in her mouth and hoped nobody noticed.

And as infuriating as the earlier statement was, there was no denying the painful truth. The reporters had been outmaneuvered like rank amateurs. Who the hell were these thieves? Master spies going into business for themselves? A cadre of MainBrains out on a lark? Clones of Prof. Ketter? All of the above?

"Any chance this could be the Free Police?" asked Deitrich.

Harry grimaced. "Lord, I hope not."

" 'Cause these weapons in the hands of the space pirates would be used for endless evil?" inquired Michelangelo curiously.

A snort. "Nyah. They have tons of guns already. No, I hope it isn't the Free Police because whoever is behind this scheme is a genius. And the only thing keeping the Freeps in line is a sincere lack of brains."

"Brains and guts," corrected Collins, busy reading a report.

"No, they got guts," said Jhonny and reaching into a pocket he withdrew a thick sheaf of photos. "Wanna see some?"

Respectfully, his teammates declined the kind offer.

In a muffled roar, the mains came on-line. "Come on, we've got to get to The Spot," announced Deitrich.

"Check," winked Harry. "Since that was the fourth set of plans, it must be the next place on their hit parade."

"Only this time, the crooks don't know that we're going to be there ahead of them!" said Jhonny, using this lull to climb on top of an inverted ceramic pot and water a small hanging plant suspended from the ceiling. A gift from a friend, Media regulations forbid having it on board, so the whole team assisted in its cultivation.

"Yeah, nothing can stop us now!" proudly agreed Collins, buckling her seat harness.

"Satellite News Team!" boomed a voice from every reflecting surface inside the shuttle, including Michelangelo's glasses and Deitrich's Armorlite jar. "This is Titan Security! You are under arrest!"

Instantly, Jhonny whipped out a minicamera and craned his neck to peek out the port window. Filling nearby space was more cruisers, patrol ships, and frigates than the manchine could possibly count. Momentarily stunned by the staggering array of armament outside, the camera-op dithered between taking a photo or getting back into his seat. Picture, seat. Picture-seat. Picture? Seat?

In all truth and honestly, Jhonny Smith was so startled by the unexpected arrival of the police, the android simply didn't know whether to shoot or get off the pot.

"Evasive maneuvers!" commanded Rikka, oblivious to her friend's internal dilemma.

The ship shuddered.

"Can't," answered Deitrich. "They have us with a tractor beam."

"Deadman?" asked Jhonny, regaining his seat while constantly snapping photographs. Compromise was the solution to most problems.

"Scramblers have been nullified," announced Mike calmly, snapping a switch on/off/on with zero results.

"Watergate!" snapped Harry, and with oft-trained speed, the team spun about in their seats and started deleting records and dumping files. A good story was always a matter of timing and luck.

And apparently they had just blown both.

CHAPTER TWELVE

IN STEELLOY HANDCUFFS and leg irons, the four SNT reporters shuffled into the office of the boss. They were bracketed by large burly officers of Titan Security who apparently had volunteered to have their humor glands surgically removed.

"Good God, Lieutenant," exhaled Ambocksky, rising from his chair. "What did the lunatics do now? Espionage?"

"Nothing quite that serious, sir," smoothly replied a Media lawyer from the back of the crowd. A Mr. Gildersleeves, if Box remembered correctly. He wasn't quite as good as his partner Rosenkranz, but that fellow was always losing his head.

"The matter is serious enough!" snapped a brevet major, slapping his leg with a swagger stick. The artificial limb rang like a perfectly tuned bell. "Trespassing on government property. Unauthorized photography of secret military installations. Aiding and abetting! And a dozen other important charges!"

"Purely misdemeanors," corrected the Wilkes Corporation lawyer, snaking his way through the doorjamb. "Or else the bail wouldn't have been so reasonable."

"How much?" sighed Box, reaching for the antacids. There went another season's budget.

The SNT reporters began studying the ceiling.

Mr. Gildersleeves knew the amount, but he consulted the receipt in his pocket as a professional show of not trusting anybody. Even himself. "Half a million."

The carafe was emptied in a shaking hand. And his pension.

"They even impounded Deitrich," mumbled Rikka, staring humbly at the floor.

AND THAT TOWING HOOK WAS COLD!

"But the papers are in order, the judge released them under their own recognizance," smiled Gidersleeves without exposing his teeth. That was a move saved for court and shark fishing.

"Sad, but true. They are free," said the Major, watching the reporters for any traitorous actions. "For the moment."

Box walked around the desk and shook the Titan officer's hard hand. "Sir, I would like to thank you for your courtesy in this awkward and confusing matter. And I can assure you these people will receive the stiffest possible punishment from the management of this station."

His trigger finger itching wildly, the soldier reluctantly accepted that. There would surely be another time.

"Then we will take our leave, sir," said the Major, saluting with the swagger stick. His hat also rang. "Platoon! Release. The. Prisoners!"

On command, the chains dropped to the floor and the reporters rubbed their chafed wrists. Six clever retorts leaped into Rikka's mind, six to Harry's, and an even twelve to Deitrich's. Mike calculated what it would take to make the soldiers' rifles unload in public and Jhonny finished his estimation of how much itching powder it would take to make them break formation, but nobody said or did anything. There would always be another chance. It was so easy to cut the strings of martinets.

A private gave the camera-op his Toshiba back. Checking inside, Jhonny saw the video disk was gone. As expected.

"H'bout face!" called the Major far too loudly for the enclosed office. "In formation! Double time! Harch!"

With machine precision, the soldiers marched from the room doing a cadence count about a lovely young lady from Venus.

As they disappeared into the ocean of desks, the lawyer waved good-bye to Box and tagged along behind them, watching for any infraction of the station's safety code he could bring against them in a tribunal and jotting down the mildly obscene military poem. It was a goody he hadn't heard before.

As the door cycled shut, Ambocksky slapped a section of his desk. Obediently, the walls darkened to opaqueness, the door locked-locked-locked, and a scrambler whined in action.

"Well?" asked the Producer anxiously.

A sly smile spread across the faces of the four reporters.

"We got a story, chief," said Rikka. "The stolen bombs were used on Luna, Mars, and Titan!"

"Wow! That's great!"

"There's more," said Harry, heading for the file cabinet.

Paul handed him a glass. But a small one. "Good Lord, what?"

"The perps didn't die on Titan; they escaped," announced Michelangelo.

"You're on drugs," admonished their friendly boss. "Or maybe the police hit you on the heads too often?"

Nobody spoke. Which said volumes.

"Seriously?" Ambocksky asked excitedly.

Reaching into a breast pocket, Jhonny tossed a disk toward the desk. Box made the catch one-handed. "Here's a complete report," said the camera-op. "With pictures."

Paul glanced from the disk to the empty camcorder he had seen the soldier give back. "And how did you smuggle this out?"

Jovially, the android opened a service panel in his forearm. Inside were several other disks and a bottle of insect repellant.

"Fabulous!" laughed the Executive Producer. "Good work, troops."

"Please!" said Collins, frowning.

"Good work, gang," corrected Box hastily.

The reporters nodded. Much better.

Just then their calm revelry was shattered by the red alert Klaxon atop the TV set in the corner. Lights flashing and horns blaring, it sounded louder than the end of the world. Which bothered the reporters tremendously, because it had once announced that very fact. Happily, erroneously.

"Silence," commanded Box and the alarm went quiet.

"Physical hard copy," he ordered, and from a paper-thin

slot on his desk, a slip of thin paper scrolled up and he tore
off the extrusion.

"Hot pumpkins! We have a red alert!"

The news team gathered close and all spoke at once.

"From who?"

"Crime?"

"Financial?"

"Our military liaison?"

"Sports?" slurped Harry. He had fifty bucks riding on Blue-
bell in the fourth at Yonkers racetrack.

"It's," the man swallowed, "from Weather?"

A pause.

"If this is some sleazy trick to keep us here to do the morning six o'clock report, you are a dead man, Box," warned
Rikka, waggling a finger. "We got places to do and people to
expose."

"It's the straight poop," said Ambocksky, offering her the
sheet. "Oh, and by the way, good job on the Martian robbery."

"Thanks." Hey! It was from Weather!

"Now about this priority one from Weather ..." started
Jhonny, scowling.

"Do we even have such a department?" asked Snyder, getting to the core of the matter.

"Yes, we do," replied Bob firmly. "And at this moment the
editor is waiting for us in Conference Room A."

"The main conference room?"

"Yep."

Always musically inclined, Michelangelo started doing the
theme song to an ancient flat TV show about bizarre events.

He had only gotten to the second set of "do-do's" when
there was a sudden flash and a translucent Maria Valdez appeared in the center of the office.

"What the prack is going on here?" she demanded hotly.
Although radiating fury, the busty woman was scantily clad in
a Fredericks of Mars French maid outfit and around her neck
was a white silk bib with the blue silhouette of a male human-
oid. Seeing their amused reactions, Valdez quickly ripped the

item from her neck and stuffed it into a pocket. Oops. Didn't have one. Damn.

"I was housecleaning," the Station Manager offered as a lame excuse. "And what is this about Weather calling an emergency session? Is there a spring comet shower? An unusually heavy crop of meteors this year? Is there a severe vacuum warning?"

Much as they hated to admit it, SNT agreed with the archbimbo. Media was situated in deep space, protected in the shadow of the moon, safe from everything but the Big Bang, Part II. What weather?

"Unknown," said Box, gathering some papers and shoving them into a desk drawer. A touch of his thumb locked the desk and activated the destruct-self. A variation of self-destruct, any attempt to broach the drawers caused the immediate annihilation of everything outside the desk.

"Let's go find out!"

Minutes later, the entourage of reporters pushed open the double doors to Conference Room A. A scanner in the jamb automatically checked them for bugs and sobriety. It was a close decision, but the machine finally allowed Jhonny and Harry entrance. There was no problem with Michelangelo, as the alien tech had long ago gimmicked the sensors to refuse to register anything he carried.

The large room was centered with a round table that would have definitely impressed the knights of King Arthur, and perhaps even Merlin. Seated above the colossal wooden ring were the heads of every news division, Media department, and a smattering of cub reporters. Fresh clean towels were placed prominently before them as an aid to drying behind their ears.

Paul Ambocksky took his position at the allocated head of the table and Maria Valdez flashed into existence one seat away. She was presently dressed in a conservative lavender jumpsuit with a froth of white lace ruffles at her throat and cuffs. As this was a business meeting, Valdez placed her attaché case on the table, snapped it open, withdrew a plastic carryall, and began filing her nails to needle-sharp points.

The ornate chair between them was blatantly empty.

Taking their usual seats, the Satellite News Team greeted friends, passed off a couple of hot tips, and accepted an invitation to a TupperWear spacesuit party next week. An astronaut might feel a bit silly burping his helmet closed, but those garments really kept a person fresh and crisp.

"Sasha! Hi, love," smiled Harry, dropping into his chair just before he went rigid with shock. What had he said! Good Lord, what had just escaped from his mouth! Ms. Parsons was half his age! Intolerable! Impossible! Shaddup you old fool! Oh, Christ.

On the video monitor filling her location, the Communications Chief grinned happily, then frowned as she saw the incredible consternation on the man's face. Okay, Snyder was weakening so it was time for her to move in for the kill.

"Hi, Harry," she purred, blowing him a kiss. "I just wanted to say how much last night meant to me."

The anchor slowly turned toward the telephone.

"Urpble?" he asked incoherently.

Parsons managed a blush. "I certainly hope after our intimacy you don't think me too presumptuous, but it was more than simply fabulous sex for me, Harold. I . . . had other dates arranged for the coming weeks, but now I've canceled them. An exclusive arrangement, that is what we discussed last night over wine, didn't we? You haven't changed your mind?"

"Urpble?" Poleaxed with the unexpected arrival of his greatest desire, the indomitable anchor suddenly found himself quite tongue-tied.

Arranging papers on the table before her, Rikka could only hide a grin and wait for the outcome. Here was the mighty Harry Snyder, the Voice and Face of the Satellite News Team. He had a wheelbarrow full of awards in his closet, could visit the King of Mars or the President of Terra unannounced, women across the planets threw themselves at his feet, and yet the big dope was stymied before the Comm Tech.

Shaking himself, Harry leaned close to the telephone and looked directly at Parsons. He knew that nothing had happened last night, and she knew that he knew that she knew.

"Exclusive," he exhaled, blue eyes twinkling. "Absolutely
. . . milady."

Sasha raised both brows. "Hmm, I like it."

"And what else do you like?"

"Forgotten already? Guess I'll just have to show you
again."

"And again and again."

"Why, you sweet talker."

"Anchors are known for the clever use of their tongues."

"Really?"

"Anyway!" interjected Ambocksky, loudly before the
whole staff died of romantic diabetes. Geez, get a grip, people. Several staff members were already gagging and retching.
"We have some business to do."

"Yeah, not to be rude, but we have another story to cover,"
said Rikka brusquely.

The editor from Weather stood to his full five feet two
inches of height and glared almost hostilely at the woman.

"Perhaps a story more important than the first natural disaster in space?" he asked, nearly being aggressive.

"A what?" asked Jhonny, amused.

"Solar flares of an unprecedented size are threatening to
destroy the solar observatory The Spot," finished the man
with a flourish.

At those words, the QSNT reporters went ramrod-straight
in their chairs.

"The Spot?" asked Harry, nearly applying his cigarette
lighter to his nose instead of the Havana Gold.

"That is its colloquial name," admitted Weather. "But the
real designation is the Solar Observatory, Limited."

Rikka and her gang looked at each other meaningfully. A
disaster at The Spot, eh? They had been planning a quick escape by setting off the fire alarm, but now dynamite couldn't
blow them out of this meeting.

Adjusting the compact control panel set in the table before
him, the Weather editor flipped a switch and a hologram appeared in the air in the middle of the room. Resembling a
plump rock edged with windows, the three-dimensional image
rotated slowly in perfect synchronization with the real station.

Dotting the hull were countless dish antennas, telescope emplacements, and hundreds of tiny orange blobs moving here and there. Spacesuits. Surrounding the station were squadrons of shuttles darting about on nameless tasks.

"Some background info," said Weather, clearing his throat.

Somebody started to snore and was rudely awoken. This was important. Could even be a good joke in it.

"Originally designed by the legendary Freeman Dyson in one of his lighter moods, The Spot is basically a huge floating mountain from the Asteroid Belt hollowed out and a small L5 colony built inside."

Sports gushed amazement at the technological achievement.

Privately, Jhonny and Mike exchanged amused glances. Of course the average person had no damn idea why the prack anybody would want to study the sun so closely. But then the average person had no damn idea how gravity worked and was endlessly amazed by the mystery and grandeur of a toaster.

Weather continued unabated. "This design was incorporated so that the delicate scientific instruments mounted on the outer rock casing did not have to be endlessly adjusted and refocused for their detailed analysis of the sun because of the spinning hull. The L5 rotates inside the asteroid."

The meteorologist adjusted his glasses and was surprised to find he wasn't wearing any. Thank God, the man had thought he was going blind. "Purely as an aside, it should be noted in passing that it was a cousin of Mr. Dyson who got the ball-bearing concession for the construction project and was presently living a life of luxury on Hedonism World theme park. The lucky bastard."

General murmurs of agreement. Nepotism strikes again!

"The hundreds of meters of space-hardened rock also served as additional protection for the scientific personnel. The Spot has ridden out storms of tremendous fury, but these coming flares will be of such unprecedented power that the executives in charge of The Spot have decided to evacuate the station as a safety precaution."

The SNT glowered at each other. So the place would soon be empty, eh?

"What?" gasped Political. "Evacuate fifty thousand inhabitants?"

A glum nod. "Yes. It is already in progress."

Assorted countenances beamed with pleasure. Wow. A mass exodus from a natural disaster of historic proportions. This was real news! Even better than the circus! Well, almost.

"You must be so proud," smiled Advertising at Weather.

Blushing, the man did admit it was their golden time.

"How should we handle this?" asked Valdez, buffing a thumb.

"I want the Satellite News Team there in the middle covering the highlights with hourly reports, up to the last great departure—and that will be live, nonstop," barked Ambocksky.

"Acceptable," said Maria, finishing a pinkie.

"We can unleash the cub reporters to interview everybody for their opinion about the disaster; from our statistical average person Joe Smith in Illinois, North America, to the Secretary-General of the United Planets. Maybe even that alleged crime lord fellow, Sheik Abduhl Benny Hassan. He's given us some good copy in the past."

The SNT pretended to write down the suggestion and said nothing.

"There's a lot of good angst in this," muttered P. J. O'Ellsion, popping the top of his namesake beer. "Even if it is only crotchety old scientists being evicted and not rosy-cheeked waifs in rags. How about we try for a few lighter moments by showing how this will increase the sale of sunglasses and establish a few deep-space nude-tanning saloons."

Ambocksky chewed the idea over and gave it a conditional acceptance. Cheesy, but good copy.

"Remington, I want your Political section to do an in-depth study of how this unforeseen development will affect the governments involved. Particularly in reference to past scientific studies that went bad, and outposts destroyed by natural phenomena."

"Such as when NASA first invented antigravity and inadvertently put a fully equipped laboratory on Luna," said the woman, chewing on the end of a stylus. "And when the Halley's Comet probe got hit and obliterated by the Kahotec Comet instead."

The room shuddered at the remembrance. Yes, that had been a particularly nasty boner. To this day, bookies won't take odds on natural disasters, or use brand-name sink cleanser.

"Where are the scientists going?" asked Crime, wondering if there was anything in this for his staff. Nyah, probably not.

"That decision has not been made as of yet," answered Weather, checking his voluminous notes. "Just away from there at present. Maybe the Hyatt, but the Sheraton has a better salad bar."

"Will this exploding sun stuff have any effect on the upcoming play-off?" asked the Sports editor in a frightened voice.

"Not a bit."

Whew. Thank God. Nothing serious then.

"However, communications will be seriously fouled by the ion particles of the solar wind," stated the picture of Sasha Parsons, removing her baseball cap to rake fingers through her ebony tresses. "We'll have to use only Z-band transmitters for the duration. X and Y will most likely lack the power to broadcast any cohesive signal over a functional distance."

"First come, first served, then," said Box. "Get your stories in on time or lose your place in line."

"How come this trillion-dollar station doesn't have any engines?" demanded Politics. "How did they move it there in the first place?"

"Miniature nuclear charges," said Real Estate. She was intimately familiar with all of the pertinent details of how damn near everything in the solar system had been originally built. Including several pneumatic actresses. "They set off a Baby Boomer to shove the asteroid out of the Belt and then detonated as Anthony Newley class 'Stop the World I Want to Get Off' to perfectly counter the inertial thrust reaction of the initial blast."

Rikka and Harry chuckled. How incredibly crude compared

to what they had just recently witnessed Prof. Ketter accomplish on Venus. Bombs had certainly come a long way since the early days of "Hey, Fritz! Hold this little metal egg to your ear. It's ticking!"

"Any chance we can get a military angle?" asked the petite Entertainment editor eagerly. Warships were a fabulous visual. All those big guns. Yum.

"The military? How?" asked Ambocksky, puzzled.

Even Maria arched a painted brow.

"Well, with this super storm front coming, this would be a prime opportunity for the United Solar Defense Alliance to field test any new force shields they recently had built for their command ship, the USDA: *Prime*."

Weather answered, "Aside from their endless studies of solar formations and research into the true origin of the universe, The Spot periodically conducts shield tests for the USDA and apparently nothing they have will stop this coming flare."

"And the scientists had no advance warning this superflare was on its way?"

"None. Very odd, indeed."

Rikka typed a question into her wrist secretary.

"Is there any danger to the inhabited worlds?" asked Classified Ads, nervously licking her SWF lips.

"No flare could be that powerful, madam," soothed Weather. "Aside from the distance, planets have natural magnetic shields."

THE ANSWER IS YES, scrolled Deitrich to Collins in response. MIKE SAYS THE SHAPED NUCLEAR BOMBS COULD HAVE BEEN USED TO MAKE FAKE FLARES.

Ah! Now they were getting someplace!

Paul Ambocksky pressed a button and his robotic gavel banged on the table. "Okay, people. Weather will stay here on coordination duty and prepare detailed up-to-date reports with full technical support from Special Effects."

"I . . . I . . ." The man had trouble with the words. "I get to be on . . . camera?" He finished in a whisper.

"This is your show," stated Box. "You're the expert. So go! Makeup and Wardrobe are waiting for you in Studio One."

Grabbing his papers, the man scampered out of the room at Fatal speed. But after a moment, his head came back in. "Ah, just where *is* the studio anyway?"

The staff tried not to laugh too loud as Box directed Security to escort the trembling meteorologist.

"Think he can do it?" asked Real Estate, chuckling.

Jotting notes on a physical sheet of paper, Ambocksky nodded. "I think he'll bust a gut doing the best job possible."

"Acceptable," said Maria, buffing industriously.

The pencil snapping in half with perfect sympathy to his temper, Paul turned on her. "Is that going to be the extent of your contribution to this meeting, Ms. Valdez, endlessly repeating the word 'acceptable'?"

Her eyes narrowed to laser slits. "I have another word," she admitted with a hiss. "And it is most assuredly not 'acceptable.' "

"Oh, yeah?"

"Yeah!"

"When was the last time you oiled the wheels on your heels?"

"When was the last time you changed the rocks in your head?"

"Bimbo!"

"Lackey!"

Just then, a pair of feet came out of the ceiling and a well-known figure drifted into his executive chair with amazing precision.

"Hi, boss!" chorused the massed reporters busy at their work.

"Hi!" cried Wilkes and he sank out of sight again.

For a split second, Ambocksky and Valdez faced each other and privately shared a moment of mutual exasperation.

"How about a sponsor?" queried Arts & Leisure. Having somebody else pay for the work was a prime requisite in her line.

"We have two already," stated Promotions proudly. "Bronco Billy's Wild West Action Junior Buffalo Flake Breakfast Cereal and an advertisement from Triad Stars Productions: *Doc Bronze, Hero With a Tan*."

" 'Part Two, in 3-D, *The Adventure Continues*!' " tagged the man reading the copy sheet.

"Wow, great tie-in," acknowledged Harry, doffing his cigar in salute.

A smiling shrug. "Hey, sometimes you get lucky."

"Anything else?" asked Box, lifting a Hush phone and starting to dial. There was no response from the reporters. "Fine, then. Meeting over! Let's get cracking, people. This is a big story!"

BIGGER THAN HE KNOWS, scrolled Deitrich, and his teammates heartily agreed. There were wheels within wheels here. Clues often led to dead ends and false trails waited for them everywhere to trick the reporters and foul their investigation. But the answers to everything seemed to be waiting for them on a doomed space station.

The Spot.

CHAPTER THIRTEEN

STEPPING TO THE edge of forever, Chief Engineer Nathan Vatore waved an orange-gloved hand at the stars. "You're in position!" he called over the helmet radio in his spacesuit. "Lower it!"

"And not on my foot again!" Vatore complained, gesturing toward his heavily bandaged boot.

A distant worker waved both gloves as an apology.

Ever so gently, the rigged derrick began to maneuver a plain metal rectangle toward the area outlined on the irregular rock hull by splotches of charred red paint. The bumps and ridges of the plate fit the contours of the asteroid perfectly, as damn well it should, and as the metal thudded into place, swarms of technicians armed with wrenches began bolting the armor down tight on the hot rock. For most of the scientific staff, this was the first time they had ever done anything and seen immediate results instead of having to wait six years, write a paper, get a grant, write another paper, rerun the original test, write a third paper, and then see that somebody else published the data two days before they did. This instant result thing was wonderful! And definitely worthy of some serious research.

Filling the galaxy behind the sweating Chief Vatore stretched the enormous igneous bulk of The Spot, its five kilometers of length seeming like a used wad of chewing gum. Or a great prune that was slowly wrapping itself in tinfoil.

Below and on both sides lay the blazing horizon of Sol. Working this close to the mighty solar orb, the naked eye could see the incredible storms of nuclear fire racing across the boiling surface. Explosions that could microwave a world into popcorn erupted toward space, only to have the crushing gravity well of the incandescent supermass pull the atomic tongues back its into burning bosom. After only a short time working here, many scientists developed a steadfast belief in God, because they soon knew for certain that hell existed and could even supply its zip code upon demand.

Nearby on the asteroid surface, a team of android workers were shuffling along a railed ramp that led from the jagged side hull to the pointed end. In his reckless youth, Nathan had boldly bypassed such conveniences, but now just looking from one endless vista to another gave him a feeling of vertigo. One wrong step out here and you could fall into the sun, receiving the kind of to-the-bone tan that no amount of soothing calamine lotion will help cure.

Thousands of orange spacesuits were everywhere on the colony. In an effort to protect the scientific station from the ravages of the coming flares, Dr. Mitchell Botwin from Physics and PsyEd had his incredibly healthy gang welding tremendously thick alloy patches over theoretically weak or supposedly vulnerable spots on The Spot. The station had been built to study the sun very closely, but the rock was quite unable to handle the results if said sun personally came knocking on their airlock door.

With the unpainted acres of gleaming steelloy dotting the pitted stone hull, it appeared as if the space station had already survived the flares or fought a major war. Many battles had been fought on board the station, but they all involved struggling with scientific truths, and trying to get the female members of the staff back to your quarters to see a collection of erotic Bunsen burners.

A vibration in the rock told Nathan that the next sheet of steelloy had been delivered. Carefully, he shuffled about in a turn and waved the go-ahead. On command, the waiting crew of technicians surged close and precisely positioned the contoured alloy plating over the external window of the Women's Shower Room and laser welding it into place. A snort. Security should have done that years ago!

Extending off to his right was an endless row of similar plates. Manufacturing and Machining had feigned a heart attack when he placed the order, but so far they had delivered quality, in the desired quantity and on schedule. Besides, it was good to roust the gang a bit occasionally. It tuned the cardiovascular system, exercised the adrenaline glands, maintained muscle tone, and even helped knock some of the dust off a few of the more sedimentary staff members.

Briefly, Nathan wondered how things were going with the Chief of Research and Reclamation? There was much to discuss. Which materials to take, what experiments to leave running, who was to get blamed for this fiasco, lots of important stuff.

A sudden rainbow flash across his visor made the engineer glance outward. Ah! Another evacuation shuttle arriving. But even from this distance he could see the bold script on the bow of the cylinder. No, it was QSNT. Damn.

Like negative ions swarming toward a exothermic flux caused by an allthropic cathode of isotope 245—the media had arrived.

Hexagonal helmets in hand, the crowd from QSNT in their distinctive white spacesuits shambled along the crowded main access corridor. Aircars hummed along in the opposite direction, stacked high with boxes, valuable equipment, and rats in cages. What the rodents had to do with solar research was anybody's guess, but scientists always have a few rats in cages. Maybe it was a union rule.

Most of the crowd were outgoing, frowning men in Vandyke beards and angry women with monocles, all of them with exceptional tans, heading for the space dock and awaiting a flotilla of USDA troop transports. Everybody had a manila envelope or pile of computer flimsies stuffed under an arm, and occasionally there was a snoring professor dressed in a lab coat strapped stiffly on a handcart being wheeled along by a sweating assistant like a deceased, but still voting board member on his way to the university luncheon.

There were signs on every wall, and while the language sort of resembled Esperanto, it made no sense. Why, the sentences only had punctuation on one end! And it was underlined with mathematical equations and weird geometric symbols. Rikka and her teammates had no idea what that could mean.

Then Michelangelo barked a laugh. "I get it! Hey, that's good."

"What?" asked Harry, looking about confused. A gang of cub reporters tagging along after them duplicated his action.

The big alien pointed at the equation. "It's a joke about quantum thermodynamics and Gottenstein's Third Law of Forcefield Reunification. Pretty funny stuff. I thought these scientists were going to be stuffy old codgers. Guess not."

"Who's a stuffy old codger, ya big aaraa?" demanded a be-spectacled oldster, his arms full of a bubbling collection of beakers, tubes, flasks, and an oddly shaped Bunsen burner.

The team smiled nicely and Jhonny took his picture.

Blinking at the flash, the grumbling elder joined the crowd going away. Reporters, bah. Obviously, community college graduates, the lot of them.

"You really don't understand the joke?" asked Mike with a half smile.

Heads shook no.

Opening his mouth, the technician paused, and closed it with a snap. Too difficult to explain. Briefly the alien wondered if you could actually do that with a petri dish? Probably not. While the Kama Sutra said yes, *Grey's Anatomy* most definitely said painful.

Taking a side corridor, the team rode an elevator to a sub-section deeper into the station and encountered another endless stream of people: janitors, accountants, lab assistants, mechanics, technicians, cooks, robots, and a gardener. Some of the transportees were grim, others laughing, crying, or fiercely silent. For some this was an adventure, for others a disaster, and a select group firmly believed this was merely some sort of bizarre experiment in sociological psychology and tried their best to give real reactions.

In passing, Harry noticed only a single hovercraft ferrying materials into the station and pointed out this abnormality to the group. Interesting.

Coming to a halt, Rikka turned about and called for the attention of their entourage of cub reporters and camera-ops. There was a moment or two of human billiards as the crowd settled into position.

"Okay, folks, this is where we part company," said Collins. "Spread out and try to cover the loading of the evac shuttles, people emptying their homes, labs deserted, a single sheet of paper blowing artistically along a deserted street. That sort of stuff."

A chorus of agreements came from the photographers.

"And you cubs," instructed Collins, crossing her arms with a clang. "I want interviews with the chief of operations, a janitor, somebody frightened, somebody happy, somebody who doesn't believe it's really happening, a young couple, preferably hetero, holding hands and gazing in awe and wonder at the mighty sun, et cetera, et cetera."

A chorus of aggressive agreements and a shy request on how to spell et cetera. The heckler was hushed with a boot to the shin.

"And don't wait for us," said Harry. "Now git!"

They happily got. Oh, boy, news!

Suddenly alone amid the streams of strangers, the SNT moved on about their real business. Stopping to study a chart on a bulkhead near an elevator bank, Collins tried comparing the directions displayed on her wrist secretary to the map on the wall. Hmm, where was the core of this can in a rock?

"Deitrich, can you locate us on your WatchDog scanners?" she asked her wrist.

. . . O . . . TERFERENCE . . . FRO . . . UNSPOTS . . . crackled the MainBrain. . . . UT . . . WAS A . . . UNNY JOKE.

"Excuse me," said a monotone voice. "Perhaps I may assist?"

Turning about, the reporters saw a hairless man with a puckered facial scar. The fellow was wearing a bright orange spacesuit. It had been the translator on his belt speaking.

"Chinese?" asked Michelangelo curiously. Oddly, some humans refused to speak Esperanto and were forced to use translators to operate in modern society. Mike had used one himself until he learned human speech. Hell, he was still learning.

"No, I am African," said the box on the orange belt.

A blush hidden by fur. "Sorry."

"No problem," came the mechanical reply.

"We're trying to find downtown," interrupted Jhonny impatiently.

The scared man gave a wry grin. "Deeper inside? Good Lord, why? Everybody else is departing with haste. Who are you people?"

That stopped the reporters in their tracks. Something nobody had ever done before sans military support.

"Who are we?" repeated Snyder, jostled by a scampering group of people in spacesuits and carrying umbrellas. "Are you serious?"

"Ah, a question for a question," said the box. "You must be reporters. This way, please."

As they started off toward a bank of turbo-lifts, Michelangelo could no longer contain himself and was forced to ask why the spacesuits on The Spot were painted that ghastly shade of orange?

The bald man glanced at his outfit as if seeing it for the first time. "Because that's the easiest color to spot against the rock hull. Why is your suit painted a drab white?"

"'It's the most efficient color for temperature control." A sly grin. "You lose a lot of folks?"

"Is your equipment so inefficient that color is an important consideration in its operation?"

Roaring with laughter, the alien thumped the large human on the shoulder, almost driving the muscular man to his knees. "A fellow technician! I knew it. Michelangelo."

Hand met paw and shook. "Toyvo."

"In a hurry," reminded Rikka, politely as possible.

Bullying and shoving a path through administrators and clerks, and turnstiles, Toyvo led the reporters to a floor tram that whisked them past a sonic curtain and down an inclined ramp toward a massive set of double doors. Here they said farewell to the friendly guide who had business to finish elsewhere. Cycling through the armored portal, the SNT stepped into suburbia.

Standing on a paved street, the four watched while a soft glow began to infuse the night, the colossal sunstrip gently pulsing into life, bathing town and country with warm light. Inside the station, the polarized windows of the downtown skyscrapers automatically darkened to the growing illumination, and the artificial waves in the lake cast playful rainbows on the evergreen trees lining the grassy shore. Rising thermals from the sunstrip created a mild breeze that rippled across the leafy corn and wheat in the agricultural fields. And precisely on cue, the tiered water fountain in the main city square began to splash merrily. And morning was officially heralded by the click of twenty thousand street lamps turning off.

Stretching into the distance, the horizon bent gently upward until the trees became farms and then houses that blurred in the distance. Only an inverted mall was visible directly above. And while the sprawling shopping center was carefully positioned to counterbalance the mass of the lake in the park, the bizarre sight still made the reporters grab their pockets to keep ahold of any loose change.

"Whew," breathed Jhonny, humming cameras pointed everywhere. "These research grant guys do themselves okay."

"Yes, they certainly do," said a chillingly familiar voice.

Turning in slow motion, the Satellite News Team found themselves face-to-face with Hardcopy and Sunshine.

"Hi. QINS, isn't it?" asked Rikka in words of acid. "Thought you two were in jail. Wasn't the charge indecent exposure? Or perhaps drug running?"

"No, it was cannibalism. We ate somebody who didn't agree with us," answered Susie Sunshine, spitting a stream of tobacco juice into a nearby flower bed. The roses immediately began to wilt. "And we got bailed out, same as you."

"Besides," smiled Jason Hardcopy, expertly flexing the perfect pects beneath his silk shirt. "Everybody is here."

"Certainly are, old chaps," drawled a cultured voice.

And Lord Hyde-White and Hanna O'Toole walked around from behind a public gas chromatography kiosk and joined the congregation.

"Hi, folks," beamed Snyder. "Find any good flying bananas lately?"

As the four aces moved closer, Jhonny and Michelangelo and several camera operators quietly stepped away. This was a meeting of the big guns and secondaries could be killed outright.

"How come you aren't still chasing those stolen bombs?" asked Hanna O'Toole suspiciously.

Rikka laughed. "Guess you haven't seen our latest broadcast. The perps accidentally blew themselves up at Titan. Case closed. This is the story of the hour."

"Mayhap you have considered that their demise could have been a ruse to forestall further pursuit?" asked Lord Hyde-White, leaning on his ebony cane.

Sunshine parked a hand on a curvaceous hip. "You know, the old 'we're dead so don't look for us any more' trick?"

"Or maybe you green cubs never heard of it?" added Hardcopy in a condescending manner.

Turning red, Harry started to speak, but Rikka cut him off fast.

"Gee, you may be right about that," she said emotionlessly. "After this assignment, we better go and check things out."

The British reporter sniffed in disdain. If they thought he was going to fall for the old "you may be right, I'm going back, but don't you come along" trick, then they were sadly mistaken.

Snyder pulled a sheaf of papers from his belt pouch. "But we can let you have a copy of our notes, if you need the assistance," the anchor said nicely, offering them his laundry list.

It was ignored. But reluctantly.

"Wouldn't want to make a major mistake like that Callistro arson goof I read about in high school," smiled Collins. "Now what was the name of the pair of idiots who did that? Hmm."

Hardcopy and Sunshine went stiff. That was their biggest failure, and directly attributable to the SNT.

"It was not that long ago," retorted the hot blonde. "And it could have been worse. Such as the Air Bank/Youth Drug corruption case on Mars. Got pulled out from underneath some old drunk and divorcee like an oiled rug."

Rikka and Harry glared at the reference to when QINS had beaten them to a scoop. And fairly too. Which made it a historical first. And doubly annoying.

"I still remember that fake blood on the butler decoy," drawled Hyde-White toward the SNT. "Dirty pool, that."

"But generally harmless," countered Harry, trying to radiate more elegance than the BBC and nearly succeeding.

"And kidnapping me to delay a report was as low as anybody could go," stormed O'Toole at the INS. "It was almost as lousy as your copy. Do you write your own, or have a trained chimpanzee on staff?"

Hardcopy threw back his head so that a laugh could slide easily from his throat. "If you're annoyed, then do something about it, toots."

"Or ain't you got the guts?" snorted Sunshine, curling a lip.

"Oh, but I already have taken my revenge," said the redhead from Venus, smiling evilly.

Nervously, QINS exchanged glances. Uh-oh. They really didn't care for the way she said that.

Several yards away, Michelangelo pulled a pack of cards from his belt pouch.

"Poker?" he suggested to the amassed support crews.

"Chess?" offered a camera-op, displaying a pocket set.

"Monopoly?" countered another, unlimbering a cardboard box, and the games began.

"That robbery on Medina!" "Those stolen engraving plates from Earth!" "But I had the notes and the dog collar!?" "But you had to pay for it!" "Your momma!"

A good hour later, the aces separated gasping for breath. Whew. They hadn't done a good donnybrook like this for years. Boy, was it fun!

When everybody was fully satisfied that every network had been properly insulted, each team regrouped with their crew and went off in different directions. The downtown area was almost entirely deserted by now, the streets vacant, the motorized sidewalks still and quiet. The attending crowd of professors and scientists had grown bored of the fight and ambled away long ago. The bloodless confrontation had been no more than a mild lover's spat compared to a Board of Regents inquiry into professional ethics. And they always had pictures.

"How did you guys do?" asked Rikka, wiping sweat from her brow. Tough crowd. Good thing she had brought along her pocket collection of heckler retorts and lethal ad-libs.

Harry drained his hip flask in silent agreement.

In answer to the question, Jhonny showed them the new watch on his wrist and Mike fanned himself with a thick wad of currency. "Not bad. CNN was a sucker for a bluff, INS al-

ways tried for a Fool's Mate, and the BBC loved to land on
Marvin Garden."

"Happily, however, there is that single special attribute that
distinguishes us from them," noted Collins proudly.

Slowly, the Satellite News Team faced each other: Harry
Snyder, the world famous reporter who had experienced a private disaster and retired from the field to become an anchor
who drank too much only to be dragged back into the real
world by—

Rikka Collins, the former secretary and ex-wife of a limp
count from Mars. A woman who lived to bust apart mysteries
and possessed more current contacts than a tokamac generator. It was she who had forced the hiring of—

Michelangelo, the alien technician from beyond the stars,
abandoned here by a slight miscalculation by his homeworld
scientists. And, Jhonny, an illegally employed android disguised as a human being so he could do the photograph work
he loved. And, of course, Captain Uther Deitrich, a pilot
whose last crash had cost him his body, but not his career.

A full minute passed as each pondered the incredible truth
of their improbable association.

"We're different because we know the truth," she stated.
"The Spot is the real goal of the crooks." God, they had been
daydreaming for a long time. Must have been thinking about
themselves again.

A stunned pause.

"Yes!"

"Of course!"

"We knew that."

Proceeding along a warm sidewalk, the team crossed at the
green, not in-between, and went into the park. There, the
leafy wilting trees offered a bit of cool respite from the thermal onslaught of the increasing storm. A sweat-damp security
guard nodded hello to them in passing. The portable radio
clipped to his belt was chatting about the evacuation and then
broke into a commercial for Solar Flares, the felt-tip pens that
could write on the surface of the sun!

Oh, geez, not that old chestnut again. Please.

Watching the exodus around them, the reporters walked

across a stone pavilion whose terrazzo stonework was laid in geometric patterns that made Michelangelo start giggling again. Momentarily, a winged zeppelin being chased by a steam-powered baroque autogyro blocked the sunstrip. On a nearby bike path, a fat man in chaps, cowboy hat, and spurs was using a small Van Der Graf generator on a stick to move along a herd of giant fifty-pound lobsters and miniature five-pound cows.

"Stock from a pet store?" asked Michelangelo quizzically.

"Menu of a restaurant," answered Snyder.

"Now what does genetically altered food animals and antique vehicles have to do with solar research?" demanded Jhonny, amused.

"Nothing," replied Rikka. "But the permanent staffs of government institutions have always been allowed to siphon off a bit of the federal funds for some private research. As the amounts involved are pretty meager, and nobody really abuses the system, the governments never care about the minor pilfering."

Just then a buxom blonde in a mink stole and tin jewelry sashayed by in the company of an ancient doddering old man with tenure.

"Mostly," she corrected hastily. "But it is not the norm."

"Definitely not normal," gagged Snyder, as the voluptuous sex kitten nuzzled the toothless centenarian and his Nobel prize. Yuck!

"This whole gig is abnormal," chuckled Jhonny, cradling his camera as he reloaded. "No stock answers in this story."

"No stock answers," muttered Rikka, her eyes closed to slits. "Stock." Grinning widely, the reporters threw her arms apart. "But that's the answer!"

"What? The stock market!" cried Harry, seeing whole new vistas of crime spread wide before him. "When these places were robbed, their public stocks went through the floor!"

"But most of them, no all, were government-owned installations," corrected Jhonny.

"Government facilities with civilian support companies," amended Collins, chewing her lips. Yeah, this made sense. "If somebody knew about the coming thefts and was prepared to buy fast, they could seize control of entire industries!"

"And/or eliminate their competition!" added Michelangelo, getting into the spirit of the discussion. Industrial espionage was an honored profession on his world. Nobody got physically hurt and there were lots of neat spy toys to play with; transparent beards, stealth sneakers, nose cameras, and disappearing white-out. His race were pacifists, not passivists!

"Now what would be the result of these robberies?" asked Rikka, staring off into the trees.

"A lot of guards would be fired, even more hired, and still more sent off for additional training," listed Snyder on his fingers. "Security will be increased. New equipment purchased. Lots of money involved, but nothing on the scale necessary to facilitate this level of scam!"

"Ah, guys," drawled Jhonny, studying his wrist. "At the scale we're chatting about, the persons who ran this bunko operation would need millions to set it up and dozens, no, hundreds of millions more to make it pay off."

"Correct," said Collins, typing notes into her secretary, and booting the uncomfortable watchband modem that connected it to the hard-drive earrings. "As soon as we reconnect with Deitrich, we can access the big files at Media and find out who has that level of available cash."

"And who has done any buying."

"Check."

Harry added, "They would also need access to a robot factory manufacturing plant to do the secret reprogramming."

"Hassan has these kinds of funds," said Mike hesitantly. "And he refused to speak to us."

Collins shrugged. "Okay, then he's on the list."

"Along with Gardner Wilkes?" asked Jhonny, feeling a bit queasy.

Four faces and a Toshiba frowned. Now there was an unpleasant notion. Wilkes might be an old fuddy-duddy, a bit absentminded, and get lost in his own station. But the man worshiped money and even made a profit when he slept by field testing experimental mattresses for a bedding company.

"If our goofy boss is actually the big boss behind this, then we nail his ass to the wall and send off résumés for new jobs."

"Deitrich will not be pleased," said Michelangelo with a chuckle. "I can see his ad now. 'Hardworking brain looking to get a head. Please call Cerebellum I-QZERO.' "

WHA . . . ? . . . LOW ME, FUZZBAL . . .

Glancing about to make sure the other networks were not in visible range, Collins started into the heart of the subterranean town at a brisk pace. "Come on, guys. We need to find a safe location to hide until everybody else is gone. And I see the perfect place!"

Staying alongside the bold brunette, Snyder hesitantly pointed a metal finger at an imposing structure ahead of them. "There?"

"Where else?" chuckled Rikka in a conspiratorial tone.

Oh. Well, at least it would be cool.

A few hours later, the warning sirens had finally stopped their incessant screaming throughout the station, and two guards were doing a last patrol down the empty street. There wasn't even a piece of paper blowing along to keep them company.

"Apparently the evacuation is total," said the younger officer, scanning the inverted horizon with a pair of trinoculars. His blue shirt was sweat-damp and stuck blackly to his skin.

"Well, there is still us," noted the older guard, observing that a thermometer on a library wall had long since expired and gone to quicksilver heaven. Even with the shields operating at emergency levels, enough heat was still leaking in to warm the giant laboratory to uncomfortable temperatures. Eggs on the sidewalk were still safe, but no sane broker would sell them any insurance.

"Hey!" The second guard tapped the WatchDog scanner in his hand to double-check the reading. "I could have sworn I got a reading of life from that building on the corner of Forth and Main!"

The younger guard turned, read the sign above the front door, and shuddered. "I really don't think so."

The WatchDog was stuffed into a sticky pocket. "Yeah, you're correct. Only a lunatic would go in there."

"Probably just a rat."

As the two began walking toward the exit, the sunstrip dimmed to evening mode adding a bit of cooling darkness to the encased city. The tactic helped, but not much. The heat endlessly rose from the very ground itself.

"And how come we have so many of those rodents on board?" asked the youngster, irritably switching on his flashlight shoes.

His own toes illuminating the sidewalk, the professional smiled at the amateur. "Because gerbils are noisy and hamsters are too fat."

Ah! Makes sense once somebody bothered to explain.

"Let's do a last sweep of the loading docks and get the prack out of this billion-dollar sauna."

"Agreed. If the shields failed with us still inside it would be a really nasty feline situation."

"A cat-tastrophe?" smiled the older man.

"Yep."

Ha! God, he loved working with this guy. Funnier than rubber bullets.

As the WatchDog scanner in his toolvest stopped beeping, Michelangelo threw off the sheet covering his body and sat upright on the marble slab.

"Clear," the technician announced, and among the score of still tables, three other sheets billowed to the floor.

"This is always the best place to hide," grinned Collins, stretching and doing some exercises. "Nobody really wants to search in a morgue, so they only do a perfunctory job at best."

"And the walls help hide us from sensors," noted Jhonny, painfully removed the stiff wires of a toe tag from his foot. Now how had that gotten there? Damn automation.

Grumbling assent, Harry stiffly walked to the closet where they had stashed their spacesuits and retrieved his pocket humidor of cigars. Gratefully lighting one, he spied something very interesting among the lines of the laboratory cadavers.

"Ah, excuse the interruption, folks, but there does not appear to be a handle on this side of the door," said the anchor with strained casualness. Snyder had started his apprenticeship on the crime beat and spent far too many nights in the lunar morgue waiting for stories to arrive to ever again appreciate its establishment's noteworthy attributes of silence, solitude, and steel.

As best they could, the rest stumbled over. The burnished portal just stood there and silently defied them to do something about it.

"Oh, hell, now what?" demanded Jhonny, standing on a leg while pulling on his boots.

"What would a staff member do if this happened legitimately?" asked Harry, puffing in concentration. "There's no keypad on the wall."

Buttoning her collar, Rikka pointed. "They would use the telephone, or just wave until the guards on the security camera saw them."

The android glanced at the machine hanging impotently in the corner of the dark ceiling. He had personally eliminated that option. And his work was too good for a fast repair.

"Are the hinges exposed?"

Collins gave a quick look. "No."

"Enough space around the jam for a lever to be shoved in?" asked Jhonny, placing his camcorder on his shoulder. Wincing from the contact, he took the Toshiba down and started blowing on its tiny metal feet. Brrr. Cold.

"Even if we had one with us," said Snyder, "no again."

"Yo, Deitrich!" shouted Collins at her wrist.

Silence.

"Okay, then stand aside," said Michelangelo, and everybody scrambled for safety. What was he going to use? A hidden laser? Explosives? Acid?

Assuming an odd stance, the huge alien swirled about lightning fast, his tree-trunk leg kicking at the door.

"HI-YAH!" the technician bellowed.

In a strident boom, his colossal boot bounced off the thick portal with no visible result. Then, the vibrating lock shattered like a dream dropped on reality, and screeching in protest, the door creaked to the floor with a loud boom. The reporters stared at the gaping doorway with matching mouths.

"Where did you learn to do that?" whispered Harry as the cool air from the morgue and hot breeze from the corridor mixed to form a misty fog that flowed about the floor.

"The kung fu? A mail-order course from the Wilkes Corporation. I used my employee discount."

Craning her neck, Rikka could only stare wordless at the two-meter-tall, 450-pound mountain of alien muscle.

"Why?" asked Jhonny succinctly.

A smile. "I just love it when a door says my name," Michelangelo admitted shyly.

Puzzlement, then understanding. Ah, yes, his last name.

"Let's go find out what was being delivered to a doomed space station hours before the hammer falls," mused Rikka, stepping over the door and into the office beyond. "Deitrich, you copy?"

... URE ... O PROBLE ... U ... EAD ME?

"No way, comrade. Static up the wazoo."

WHA ... ZOO?

Christ! Maybe they could send him a telegram. "Is everybody else gone? How much time till the big flare?"

... ESS THAN ... IVE MINUTES.

"How many minutes? Fifty-five? Twenty-five? Deitrich?"

. . .

"So much for tactical support," sighed Jhonny, rewiring a booster from his camcorder to his wrist secretary, but the result was the same. Even his mechanical arms and leg were feeling a bit stiff from the ionic bombardment. "Okay, we're inside and alone. What we need is hard data that our perps are still alive and robbing. Where first? The bridge?"

"Command center," corrected Harry, glancing up and down the corridor outside. "If you and Mike can tap into the security surveillance system, then we'll have a box seat on everything that transpires in this station."

"Until it vaporizes," said Collins, shuffling her feet.

"Oh, cheer up," scolded Michelangelo with a smile, hoisting an equipment pack on his shoulder. "We're a long way from dead, and the shuttle can remove us whenever we want!"

TWENTY-FIVE MINU ... scrolled Deitrich in a burst of power and then the signal faded to silence.

CHAPTER FOURTEEN

LEAVING THE COOL chemical mist of the morgue behind them, the SNT donned their spacesuits for protection and moved stealthily down the main corridor of the warm building. The hallway was lined with doors, all of them ajar to prevent the glass panels from exploding due to hot air expanding. As The Spot was a research community, designed, built, and staffed by PhDs, the news reporters had expected anything but common sense. Most impressive. However, those damn scientific jokes were everywhere and Michelangelo never quite stopped his guttural giggling.

Climbing up to the lobby again, Rikka and her team eased past the reception desk, silent as thieves in the night. Only it was forever high noon here and they were after the thieves.

"Hey, what did one subcritical mass of U235 say when it met the other subcritical mass of U235?" whispered Mike, hunched over to help lower his imposing profile.

Exercising iron willpower, the creeping reporters said nothing. Oh, no, not another one.

" 'China, hell, I'm headed for the Bahamas!' " chuckled the technician, tears running down his furry checks. Gods, that was a goody!

"Yeah. Great. Swell. Save it for the next party," muttered Collins, lifting a window blind with a metal fingertip to peer outside. Damn, a brown evergreen was directly in front.

As Harry and Jhonny joined her, Michelangelo assumed a dignified pose. Hurmph. He guessed intellectual jokes required a sophisticated sense of humor. Well then, he wasn't even going to tell them why chemists make such good lovers. Let 'em suffer.

On a silent request, Jhonny oiled the latch on the front door, and lubricated the exposed hinges. With gentle pressure, Collins opened the door and pulled it back a hair-thin crack.

With a strangled cry, Rikka shoved the door closed and flipped the lock. "There are orange spacesuits everywhere," she hissed. "Hundreds of them!"

Jhonny placed an ear against the door. Mike went to the window and Harry glanced at his wrist.

"But according to the posted schedule, this place should be totally deserted!" said the anchor.

"Then nobody staying here is doing so legally."

"Just us and the crooks."

Ah, perfect. Alone with an army of villains. Just another day on the job.

"What should we do?" asked the technician, his hairy face layered with slices of light from the blinds.

"Retreat," said Jhonny, only the lens of the camcorder peeking out the door.

"Back to the morgue?"

"The reception desk."

Fast, Rikka took two steps. "Okay, we're here. Now what?"

Sinking his paw-tip talons into the plastic cover on the console, Michelangelo lifted free the cover exposing a multicolored collection of wires, cables, and squat square things.

Harry blinked. Yep, definitely things. He'd seen them before.

"This is where they relay the video signals of the autopsies to the lab and switch phone calls," said Jhonny, his hand busy splicing wires, while Mike snipped others and twisted the ends together. Sparks crackled and the things began to hum.

"Can we do a link here into the station security cameras?" asked Harry, sliding a chair under the latch of the front door and using his shoe to nudge it into position as tightly as possible. Not much, but it might fool a casual search into believing the morgue was locked and vacant.

"Gosh, I don't know," came the uncertain reply. "What do you think, Mike?"

"Difficult," growled the alien. "Maybe impossible."

A split second later, in a crackling burst of light, the four monitors on the desk console flickered into life. #1 showed a view of starry space; #2, the blazing sun; #3, the morgue with a broken door; and #4 was angled to display the sky above them. A Mack truck was skimming along, conserving power by flying along the central axis of the rotating station where the gravitational pull was virtually nonexistent.

Jhonny lowered the access panel into place. "Wow, success!"

"It's a miracle!" agreed Michelangelo, tightening screws.

"Okay, you guys are fantastic," remarked Rikka, pulling a chair close to the first monitor. "Happy now?"

Taking the second, Jhonny beamed a smile. "Nothing the average genius android couldn't do."

A loud alien cough.

"Correction, the average genius android and his brilliant assistant."

Overlapping the third seat, Michelangelo raised a furry eye ridge. "I thought you were the assistant?"

"In your dreams, Yogi."

"Try recharging your brain, R2."

"Who?"

"You're both geniuses and both assistants," said Snyder, taking the last chair. "Okay, how do we . . . ah, never mind, standard Wilkes Corporation controls." Sometimes it was really useful to be a top employee of the second biggest business in existence. Harry was intimately familiar with almost every piece of equipment in use today.

"Switching to internal view," said Jhonny, hands typing effortlessly. On his shoulder, the Toshiba extended its lenses to get a better view of the monitors and switched from twenty-four lines a second to thirty so it could get a clear picture off the TV screens.

Monitor #1 showed squads of spacesuits going from house to house, smashing down the doors and coming out with electrical equipment: VCRs, monitors, toasters? On #2 was a big group working on the front door of the Sunview Bank Limited. The third zoomed in on a team loading boxes onto the railroad train that ran down the middle of the small park. #4 was filled with a small UP flag fluttering on top of the tall pole. The curious sight gave her a shock, until she spotted the tiny electric fan mounted behind the flag, blowing the material stiff. It was a humorous reminder about the blandness of the indoor climate. Air circulation pumps and thermals caused some minor breezes and that was about it for weather.

Inside, that is. Outside, hell was brewing.

"Lord, they're taking everything not nailed down," breathed Rikka, furiously typing notes into her wrist secretary.

"And now they're stealing hammers!" added Harry, frowning.

Softly, the telephone trilled.

Flipping a switch, Jhonny killed the connection to the reception console. But immediately, the telephone on the wall near the bubbling water cooler rang again. Unable to contain her curiosity, Collins lifted the receiver and placed the device into a recess in her helmet.

"Hello there, sir or madam," said a mechanical voice. "This is an official notice that you, or a living member of your family, may have just won ten million dollars in our big publisher's sweepstakes giveaway! You can be the proud owner of your own body weight in breath mints if you can just answer this simple question—who's buried in Grant's Tomb?"

"Deitrich?" asked Rikka, stunned.

"Bzzt! That's incorrect. Sorry. Now would you like to try another question for a year's supply of Pope-Sicles! those tasty frozen treats in the shape of his holiness with a stick up his robes, or go for what Jay has in the box and try for a lifetime supply of Gas-O-Lean, low-cal fuel for chubby autos?"

Hearing her cry through his helmet, Snyder jacked the telephone into the communications console for all to hear. From the woman's pained expression it was either the IRS, her mother, or their pilot doing another prank phone call.

"Deitrich, how did you track us down?" demanded Collins,

still watching the monitors. "And how did you know which phone we're near?"

"Trade secret," countered the chuckling four-pound cyborg. Besides, he liked to cultivate a certain air of mystery. And as a brain in a jar, he needed every bit of help he could get.

"He's linked into the surveillance system," said Jhonny, waving at a ceiling camera. The Toshiba did a little dip of hello.

"Spoilsport," said the telephone. "Yes, I attached my umbilical to the station, overrode a few security systems, not difficult for a MainBrain, and shazam, I see everything. In charge, on top, and that's the way I like it."

"Thank you, Big Brother," interrupted Snyder, pointing at screen two. "I'm sure old George Orwell would be proud of you. However, check out this!"

At the railroad crossing, a warning toot sounded from down the track and seconds later a northbound trolley rolled past, as it headed toward a tunnel in the great dividing wall between the housing section and life support. Moments later, a fully loaded southward train pulled away from the station and rolled off for the opposite tunnel that led to Industrial.

A dozen questions filled the reporters' minds but there was nobody to answer them. Obviously, something big was going on. Something that involved the whole station.

"They're not just here for something particular, their guys are looting the place from aft to stern," said Rikka, making a fist. "In raw materials alone, this could be their biggest heist. And if they get the plans for these military shields, the Free Police would pay gazillions for the technical schematics and blueprints."

"If these aren't the Freeps, themselves," said Jhonny woodenly.

Eh! What a horrid thought. Trapped inside a rock, with a thousand insane pirates. On the other hand, what a swell story it would make for their obituaries.

"Deitrich, can you get a message off to the USDA? UP? InterPlanetPol? Anybody?" A long pause, and Harry had to force the words out of his mouth. "Even another network?"

Everybody made retching noises.

"Absolutely not. The shields are at eighty percent excitement, and between them and the solar interference I couldn't pump a fifty-gigawatt Z-band transmission ten meters away."

"Maybe a silent alarm from the bank, or a workshop," offered Michelangelo hopefully.

"Sorry. Four have already gone off. Nobody but me can hear them." Pause. "A bit atonal, but actually rather nice for alarms."

Prack! "So what should we do?" asked Jhonny, frowning.

"Our job," said Collins, dialing for a tighter angle on a group of spacesuits cutting down a bronze statue of Prometheus. Geez, they were taking public monuments? What sleazeballs! "I want pictures of everything they take. Solid, irrefutable evidence of every crime, trespassing, breaking and entering, every misdemeanor and felony they commit."

Reaching up, Jhonny removed the camcorder from his shoulder and placed it on the console. "And when the crooks leave, we go to the police, and hand over enough evidence for them to send these bastards to jail in a term that could only be measured in geological years," said the android as the camera waddled over to sit down in front of screen #3.

"That's good copy," said Harry, giving his highest praise. "Criminal masterminds arrested on evidence supplied by the Satellite News Team. Film at eleven." Yeah, QINS, eat your heart out! "Our ratings will go through the roof!"

"Unfortunately, this appears to be more complicated than we originally imagined," said Michelangelo, working an area of the consoles at fever pitch. The meters gave the same results. So he did it again. And again.

"Explain," demanded Rikka, turning her chair around. "What? They plan to blow the place after they finish stealing the gravel from the bike path? No problem. We can leave in their wake. Correct?"

ABSOLUTELY, scrolled words at the bottom of the #2 screen. If he couldn't be there in person, Deitrich would rather do a scroll than chat. It helped ease the recent loss of his holobody. And there was less chance of somebody else receiving his transmissions.

"This is much worse than destroying the station," said the alien with deceptive calm. "I found the tin stolen from Titan."

"But that's great!" cried Jhonny.

Leaning backward in his chair, Harry frowned. "No, it is not. Why would they haul their loot to the next job? Ten tons of anything, even marshmallows, will only slow you down more than bringing along a relative."

"Options? Opinions?" asked Rikka, chewing a cheek. Carting around their loot was a stupid thing to do, but since these folks weren't fools, there must be an alternative reason.

"I have been running a theoretical on what they're stealing here in the station," said the technician slowly, choosing his words with care. "Mostly miscellaneous items: wooden doors, bronze statues, hovercar engines, a lot of it inexpensive junk, while they are ignoring the bar platinum and other valuables in the bank and the labs."

"And?" prompted Jhonny.

"I've found the reason why," said the alien, twisting a dial. "Or at least, a reason. Please give me your opinions of this."

Screen #3 dissolved from a view of the park, to the train tunnel, then inside the brick-lined passageway, and on into a view of a loading dock at the end of the railroad tracks. There dozens of spacesuits were hurriedly unloading the passenger carriage and relaying the materials to another team that was laser welding the equipment into an unholy mishmash of jutting beams, gauges, wires, light bulbs, garden hoses, superconductor cables, acres of exposed circuitry, air conditioners, electric fans, a rigid house-of-cards formed from circuit boards, a steering wheel, a gearshift, and a battered kitchen sink.

It was the dimensions that threw off recognition. The object was patently familiar to the reporters, but none of them had ever before seen one this size. Or so rudely constructed.

"An engine," breathed Collins, unable to tear her gaze from the screen. "They are building an FTL engine the size of a house!"

"These guys aren't going to rob this station," said Harry in a flash of understanding. "They're here to steal the whole goddamn station!"

"That's why they took the tin," added Jhonny, clicking away. "Not for cash, but as fuel!"

"Steal an L5?" espoused Rikka, her left hand never stopping its endless typing on her secretary. "Even a small one like this inside an asteroid? Is it possible?"

WORKING, scrolled the screen.

A tense minute passed.

PROBABILITY OF SUCCESS 15% . . .

"Ah-ha!" cried the reporters.

AGAINST.

Oh.

Suddenly, Harry placed a hand to his ear and cursed bitterly. "More bad news. They just ordered the main computer to drop the shields and forcefields in five minutes!"

"Five minutes!" cried Rikka. "What in hell for . . . power? The station tokamacs lack sufficient energy to power the FTL engine. They weren't designed for a load of that magnitude."

"The flares," whispered Jhonny. "They're going to use the sun itself to power the engine."

"Wow."

"Then we better split," said Collins firmly. "Deitrich, warm up the mains."

GOTCHA. I'M HOT TO TROT.

"Wait a minute," she corrected herself. "Are the crooks leaving?"

"Apparently not," stated Michelangelo, adjusting dials and slides. "Maybe they have some protected place, someplace safe from the radiation?"

"The morgue?" asked Snyder, looking at their poorly barricaded door. The internal temperature of his suit was a cool even seventy-four degrees Fahrenheit, but he felt as if it was subzero. Lord Almighty, this was the first time their very lives had been endangered by a story. Well, okay, the second, but they were all drunk that first time on Rhea moon. Besides, you could easily outrun lava even when handcuffed to a pogo stick.

"Could we stay if we went to the far end of the station, got as much material between us and the flare?" asked Rikka, dumping her text into their shuttle's computer. A beep tone told her the files had been archived and were safe. Whew.

Stuffing disks into the belt pouches of his spacesuit, Jhonny said no. "This isn't a little pinpoint flare, but a huge surge of plasma. The sides of the wave will slop over everything."

"Not necessarily," said Michelangelo, a bearish grin beginning to grow on his features inside the octagon helmet. "No, the wave will not spread wide, but stay tight and cohesive."

"Nonsense," snapped the android. "Why do you say that?"

The alien swept an arm across the reception desk toward the dancing monitors. "Because the shields will be used to funnel most of the solar bombardment into the engine as fuel. So we should be perfectly safe anywhere."

"You sure about this?" asked Harry, squinting out one eye, which was his way of forcing the truth from unwilling people. The gag rarely worked, but practice made perfect.

The tech returned the look. "It's my hide too."

AND HE'S GOT MORE THAN ALL OF US COMBINED, added Deitrich.

Rikka nodded. Good enough. "Okay, then, we stay."

"Deitrich, are you still hot?" asked Jhonny with a note of concern in his voice, leaning forward.

AS ALWAYS, KID.

"Then get off this station now. Pronto and fast."

GOOD LORD, WHY?

"Because when these guys go Fatal with the gigantic engine, any other denatured tin on board this station will almost definitely become activated by the infusion drive field and—"

YIKES! I'M GONE.

"But stay in touch," requested Collins as a mechanical arm in her neck ring mopped her face with a cool towelette. "This tub can't have much speed, despite the size of the engine. It should be easy for you to follow us."

Glancing at the wrist secretary on his gauntlet, Harry watched a vector graphic cartoon of an ancient slide rule quickly calculating the simplistic six-dimensional equation on lift plus force equals drag plus weight over inertia divided by time. "I give this beached whale a calculated top velocity of Fatal 3.2."

HA! A MERE STROLL. I CAN DO THAT BACKWARD!

"Oh, please don't," pleaded the camera-op.

OKAY . . . I'LL JUST TAG ALONG AND SNEAK BACK ON BOARD WHEN I CAN.

"Now get!" barked Collins.

POOF, and the line disconnected with a busy signal.

Thoughtfully, Harry rubbed a glove on the outside of his helmet exactly where his chin would be. "How soon till the shields drop?"

"Two minutes," said Michelangelo, glancing at his gauges and meters.

"What are the thieves doing?" Collins asked, retaking her chair.

"GRAA!" cried Michelangelo, clawing at his spacesuit. Nearly tearing off the chest seals, the alien opened his suit and threw a pawful of his burning toolvest onto the floor.

"That . . . was . . . a . . . fob of tin I . . . kept . . . as . . . a . . . good luck . . . piece," he gasped in response to their unasked questions.

"Idiot," scolded Collins, helping the technician close the spacesuit. "You heard what Jhonny said."

"Not denatured fuel tin . . . but raw mineral . . . tin," continued the alien, feeling very embarrassed. "I didn't think the drive field would excite it also." Then he coughed a few times. Whew. Burning fur. Nothing short of home cooking smelled worse.

"Live and learn," joshed the android, sliding a wrench-shaped air freshener through an access slot in his friend's suit.

"But just barely," adminished Snyder, offering the alien a drink from his hip flask. It was politely refused.

Without warning, the reporters heard a muffled explosion in the distance, and each fervently prayed that Deitrich had managed to get off The Spot fast enough.

Plunging in from their meticulously plotted elliptic orbit, the last two hundred of the Ketter superbombs hurtled themselves toward the endless flaming vista of the blazing sun. Grains of black sand lost in a yellow forest of nuclear fire, the bombs detonated a thousand kilometers above the surface, much closer than anybody had ever believed they could possibly get.

Which completely ruined all of the careful calculations.

Triggering into their programmed pattern of an Italian stiletto, the combined megablasts stabbed at the heart of the solar orb with a force blade equal to over 95 billion tons of dynamite; a blast that would have split Luna like ripe cheese drop-kicked by a major league quarterback, or two soccer players and a hockey center to be named later.

Barely able to sense the miniscule pinprick, the semisolid inferno of the sun dimpled under the tiny push, and gave a tiny little squirt of raw plasma into space before sealing off the irregularity in its surface.

On the other side of the solar system, a carnival psychic named Madame Olga momentarily thought she heard somebody telepathically say "ouch," but dismissed the notion as pure nonsense. Must be those damn downstairs neighbors again, and she started thumping her walking stick on the floor.

"Shut up, down there," she yelled at the empty apartment.

A fiery column of nuclear destruction formed a geyser into cold black space, the plasma flare thicker than the Earth and hotter than jalapeño snuff. Extending outward, the rushing volcano of destruction surged toward the distant stars, ever accelerating as the quadrillion tons of fusing hydrogen soared free from the death grip of home.

And directly in the path of the nuclear tsunami was a tiny speck. A barely discernible mote of rock patched with metal and surrounded by an invisible barrier of monomagnetic force lines.

Which abruptly cut off.

On board The Spot, far aft in Engineering subsection 4, quadrant 2, a pair of technicians were sitting on a catwalk and having lunch when they both heard a loud click, followed by a revving noise, and smelled the bitter stink of ozone.

"Hey, Guido, look!" munched the woman, standing and

pointing astern to the deck below the walk they were on. Nestled inside a collection of power cables and steam pipes, huge turbines were revolving in their casing, faster and faster, building to operational speed.

Stepping close to a wall display, the man wiped his greasy fingers on a napkin and punched in a request on the control monitor. "Fatima, check out those settings! Those idiot scientists must be going for half . . . two thirds, no, full power from the tokamacs!"

"Full power?" gaped the woman, dropping her peanut butter and lobster sandwich. "What in prack for? We've never been that high except for when we had to hold off an attack from the Free Police. Then some fool plugged in a hair dryer, blew every fuse on the station, and we almost got killed!"

"Don't I know it." A pause. "Maybe there's a big flare coming, or something."

"Nyah, somebody would have remembered to tell us."

"Oh, yeah?"

The tech swallowed. "I'm out of here."

Leaving her *When Dirty Harry Met Sally* lunchbox behind, the woman scampered for the nearest exit hatchway. Her associate was close behind.

In the deserted level, the muted rumble of the Chernobyl-class tokamacs steadily built to a barely contained roar of unrestrained mechanical power.

Slowly the first laps of the flare touched the magnetic forcefields of the space station. In the manner of a Bussard ramjet, the burning wisps of ethereal plasma were funneled together along the immaterial boundaries, condensing into a visible cone of flame that, for all intents and purposes, closely resembled a standard rocket exhaust. Gradually, pressure began to build along the hull of the asteroid. At the first jolt, the whole station trembled; spacesuits and reporters fell to the floor, bicycles tumbled over, the lake slopped onto its shore, retorts bounced off walls, and store windows cracked sending off an unheard cacophony of silent alarms. Then another vibration rattled the modified rock; jigsaw puzzles shook together, oil and water voluntarily mixed, and 412 little black bags discreetly tucked underneath the beds of married couples began to shamefully vibrate inside and out.

Thrust increased until it equaled, and then surpassed, the trillion tons of inertia. Sluggishly, the colony began to move, with a glowing aura of blinding flame extending far behind, which was clearly visible to half the watching population of the system, all of whom wondered what was happening. Was this a disaster or a fireworks display? Actually, either was okay. As long as there weren't too many commercials.

And then the hand-built FTL mains were activated.

"Holy . . . prack . . .!" screamed Rikka as she watched the monitors and saw the morgue go hurtling toward the distant jiggling internal wall of the station with frightening speed.

The building surged again, and the wall retracted.

"Damn . . . engine isn't . . . in sync!" cried Michelangelo, trying to hold down breakfast, lunch, and dinner.

Vibrating, Harry responded in the only way possible. "No . . . shit . . . Dick . . . Tracy . . .!"

Calmly, Jhonny took another bite from a candy bar and wondered what they were complaining about?

In a sudden locking pulse, the engine and the station dovetailed in perfect unison and The Spot disappeared from before the onrushing column of nuclear flame from the sun. On into starry space it streaked away at Fatal One . . . Two . . . Three . . . Four . . . Five . . .!

And racing along sluggishly in the wake of the rocky titan, a tiny shuttle strained its engines to the utmost heroically trying to keep pace with the colossal reverse meteor.

CHAPTER FIFTEEN

THE ARMORED DOORS to the USDA Command Center slammed open and Port Admiral Roger Sullivan stormed into the room. The elderly, gray-haired man was dressed in golfing clothes and flanked by half a dozen guards, assistants, and assistant guards.

Protected by umpteen billion tons of molecularly reenforced Florentine Plastic, a battalion of troops, missiles, Bedlow lasers, spaceships, parking meters, and numerous warning posters, the Command Center was the heart of the Geneva L5, the headquarters of the United Solar Defense Alliance, and the nerve center for SitComTac. There were two hundred doors to pass and guards who had orders to shoot on sight anybody they even considered suspicious. Which accounted for their rigid discipline, extreme politeness, and why only decaf was served in the wardroom. It required a triple Alpha class security clearance to get into the vaunted center and, occasionally, a signed note from God to get back out.

The huge, bustling room was filled with rows upon rows of control boards fronted by hundreds of busy technicians. Spanning the walls were giant, full-color holographic maps of the fourteen worlds, and glowing green vector graphics of the Earth-Mars-Titan triplanetary formation. The three worlds were not only the political leaders of humanity, but also possessed the biggest collection of weapons and trained people who loved to use them.

"Okay, what the hell happened to The Spot," demanded Admiral Sullivan in a brass voice, advancing to the metal railing of the overlook post. Frowning, the Port Admiral radiated his severe displeasure at this untoward interruption. Damn emergencies always occurred whenever he took a day off.

In the front row, a young lieutenant wearing headphones rose uncertainly to her feet and saluted. The Admiral returned the salute impatiently.

"Report, mister," snapped Sullivan, nearly hitting himself in the head with a nine iron. Demurely, an aide took the club, folded the metallic stick into a compact wafer, and tucked it into a bulging jumpsuit pocket, along with the rest of the sports equipment, an inflatable golf cart, and a midget wet bar.

"Ah . . . sir, we're not exactly sure what has happened beyond the fact that the scientific space station Solar Observatory Limited seems to no longer be in place."

Another aide brought Admiral Sullivan a chair. "So there's trouble with the equipment," he demanded gruffly, sitting down.

"No, sir. Redundancy probes show our transmitters functioning perfectly. Secondary and tertiary circuits are in the green."

"Jesus, did the flare atomize it?"

"No, and that is the problem," said a pleasant voice behind him.

Turning, the Admiral's frown softened. A tall, thin woman in the black and green uniform of the Jupiter Navy submarine corps, was coming out of the glass-enclosed Communications Booth, her left leg squeaking nosily. Major General Mindy Schwartz was an old friend. They had both served as line officers aboard the Martian superdreadnought *Thunderfish* during the Sons-of-Uncle-Bob Insurgence of '96. Scarcely forty years old, the amazing woman was already the Chief of Operations for SitComTac, and a Warrant Officer for its dreaded sister organization TacSitOn.

"Good to see you, Mindy," he said as she noisily climbed the short flight of metal stairs to the overlook. Her left knee was stiff and unbending from a hit the *Thunderfish* had taken amidships in the Great Mud Sea by an enemy missile complete with derogatory phrase painted on the side. The Sons of Uncle Bob were rude as well as ruthless. The resulting explosion had vaporized her left leg, but its robotic replacement was a modern marvel. However, she constantly forgot to oil the damn thing. Lubricates were for guns and motels, not your knee.

They shook hands. "Glad you could make it on such short notice, Rog. Looks like we have got ourselves a situation."

Glancing at the War Board on the far wall, Sullivan saw the stepladder-style sign showing the present status of the USDA at DefCon Two. Two? Oy vay! "Sneak attack by the Freeps?"

Schwartz shook her head. "Unknown."

In the Command Center, a screen flashed red, warning lights glared, and a console began a steady series of beeps, each increasing in tempo and volume. Coffee was brought in for the officers and ignored. Below them on the Operations Floor, cool technicians continued to maintain the defense of the fourteen planets, wishing they were somewhere else and awaiting for further orders.

"Sir, we have just received a signal from the head of the Satellite News Team, a Captain Deitrich," reported a sergeant, a clipboard tucked under his arm so tight it might have been nailed there. "They claim to be on board The Spot and that it has been stolen."

"Stolen? They mean somebody has boarded the station under the cover of the flares and is fortifying a strategic position?"

"Maybe using some sort of cloaking device to hide it from our sensors?" asked Schwartz.

"No, sirs. They claim criminals in spacesuits, who stole Prof. Ketter's superbombs, made a fake solar flare to evacuate the station, then built a giant FTL engine and stole the whole damn thing!" A pause. "Sirs," he added hastily.

"Ketter? The loony who made those instant statues?"

"Aye, aye, sir."

Reluctantly, Admiral Sullivan accepted that. His longest tour of duty ever had been a weekend in Ground Zero, the capital of Venus. He had almost become deaf only going to the local library! Their card files brought a whole new meaning to the Dewey Decibel system.

"Preposterous!" snorted General Schwartz. "The inverse square ratio law says that the bigger the engine and bigger the ship the more fuel it takes. Even if such a thing were possible, what kind of range would they have?"

"Computer and MainBrains estimate a maximum range of sixteen hours at Fatal Five," crisply reported a tech.

The two officers choked. Five? That was faster than a Z-band radio transmission!

"But that would enable them to reach Pluto or a bit beyond!" noted a lieutenant.

Sullivan stared at Schwartz. "Good God, you don't suppose—"

"The Linstorm Maneuver?"

"Major, where did this signal emanate from?" demanded General Schwartz formally.

"Within the orbit of Mercury but moving galactic north 180 degrees."

Straight out into space, in plain Esperanto. Oh, crap. This was bad. Very bad.

"Our jurisdiction ends at the Oort Cloud. If they can escape into interstellar space, we can't touch them!"

"Legally," growled the General, and the two officers swapped meaningful glances.

Schwartz bolted to attention. "Duty Officer, alert the United Planets General Assembly, and scramble everything we can get into the black. If The Spot is compromised, I want troops there immediately! Put those birds airborne in five, or you're a private."

"And assign fleet command to Admiral Terrance Davis!" stated Admiral Sullivan.

The Captain blanched and saluted. "Aye . . . aye, sir!"

" 'Mad Dog' Davis?" whispered Schwartz, leaning close to her friend. "Is that a wise move?"

Sullivan shrugged, making his chest full of golfing medals tinkle. "Unknown, but it should almost certainly help us to ascertain the seriousness of the situation."

"You're a cold bastard, Roger."

"Comes with the job, Mindy."

In full three-dimensional, holographic Technicolor, the tactical display on the main wall of the Command Control in Geneva L5 showed the unleashing of countless warships to chase the runaway L5.

Cresting the lot was the ultra-superdreadnought of the United Planets service, the legendary USDA: *Prime*. The massive spherical mobile command ship, controlled by the rockhard fanatic Admiral Terry Davis. A legend in its own time, the *Prime* was horribly beweaponed with guns and lawyers, ready to go in either direction should an opportunity present itself. Davis and the *Prime*. Like black lace and perfume, it was deemed a formidable combination.

Standing side by side at the railing, Admiral Sullivan and General Schwartz shared a private glance, each expressing the exact same unspoken prayer.

Fleet, don't fail me now.

Lacking attitude jets, vanes, wings, wheels, a mast, propellers, or anything even vaguely useful for steering, The Spot rammed straight on through the attending crowd of spaceships and floating laboratories whose crews had been patiently waiting to see if the rock would be destroyed when the flares hit. Caught in the virulent backwash, ships flipped over backward, people fell out of chairs, and spilled beer went everywhere. But since the observation ports and telescopes were entirely staffed by professional scientists and trained observers, no two of them could quite agree on exactly what had just happened. Except, of course, that it wasn't their fault, and could they please have a grant to study the event?

Ever increasing in velocity, the modified L5 started to plow into the planetary system of humanity like a bullet across a billiard table full of multicolored balls.

At Fatal Five, the scientific rock sliced through the orbit of Mercury unimpeded, the fiery world of metal and money safe on the far side of the mighty sun purely by chance. But sensors detected the racing giant, and quickly the Strategic Headquarters For Making a Fast Buck starting laying bets on whether the UFO would explode: 2–10; hit another world: 10–2; or simply tear itself apart: even money.

* * *

Ever onward, the space station zipped past Venus missing the gray world by only a few thousand kilometers, but close enough for each to get a passing glimpse of the other. Alarms screamed, WatchDogs howled, and QCNN shuttles frantically exploded into space, but were quickly left far behind the gargantuan speedster.

Sullenly, the reporters returned to their desk unable to report the incident to anybody, because news stories were like fish; nobody ever believes you about the size of the one that got away.

Increasing slightly in speed as the last vestiges of pull from the sun was negated by sheer distance, The Spot cannonballed past Earth and Luna, one of the rocky spires of the asteroid neatly sheering a dish antenna off the outer hull of Media, temporarily rendering the news station blind and deaf. More alarms screamed, Wilkes was disconnected from his visophone, and MacKenzie got a mop to clean up the drinks on the floor.

In the bustling control booth of Studio One, Ambocksky stared in terror as the main monitors went blank as the news network blinked off the air.

On the carefully lit stage before the silent battery of cameras, Lois Kent crumbled a sheet of paper into a ball and threw at it the wall poster of her fellow anchor. Snyder, it had to be Snyder. God, what that ham wouldn't do to unsurp one of her broadcasts. How incredibly unprofessional!

Just then the monitors crackled with static.

HI! IT'S US! scrolled the hundred screens for a split second and then the message disappeared.

"Hot damn," grinned Box, rubbing the back of his neck. "Rikka and the gang must really be embroiled in a hot story to pull a stunt like this!" Or rather, they better be, else the SNT would be doing in-depth reports on "Bathroom Mildew: Myth or Menace?" for the rest of their careers.

Just then a hologram window formed in the air next to the Producer.

"What the heck was that?" demanded the angry head of

Maria Valdez. "Did the SNT crash again? Or has the tokamac exploded?"

"Hmm? What was what?" asked Ambocksky innocently, and the technicians behind him valiantly tried to keep a bland face.

"Eh? Oh, never mind!" And with a snap, Maria turned off the hologram unit of her bedstand and turned to the naked android in bed next to her.

"Must have been you," she purred in contentment, snuggling closer to the blue male. "God, you're fabulous."

Danny allowed himself a smile and reached for the feather-covered torque wrench. "Again?" he murmured sweetly.

"Oh, yes, please, my MixMaster of love."

Gosh, he just loved it when she talked dirty!

Streaking underneath Koop Medical Hospital, the ionic turbulence of The Spot rattled bedpans from the ER to the doctors' lounge, causing a great deal of disturbance, but no significant damage. And the nursing staff really appreciated the fact that they wouldn't have to shake down another thermometer for the next ten years.

Happily Imperial Mars, and sadly QINS on Phobos moon, were both missed entirely. The Royal Navy unleashed a squadron of Tarantula pursuit jets and INS sent off a dozen of their most disposable cubs reporters, but neither succeeded in either endeavor of interception or interview.

However, on Deimos moon the bolting bulky behemoth was accidently videotaped by a wandering travel agent who instantly incorporated the dynamic visual into his latest commercial for "Mafia Vacations! Specializing in surprise car rides and one-way trips to the bottom of the sea. With a solid foundation to build on, let us be the cornerstone of your getaway plans when you want to disappear forever. Special discounts available to government agents, stoolies, and news reporters. Mafia vacations! Your friend to the end."

Yeah, good stuff.

* * *

A short while later, inside the reception area of the morgue, a thunderous pounding echoed throughout the entire volume of the straining, shuddering space station.

BOOM ... BOOM ... BOOMBOOMBOOM!

A fearful wait.

BOOMBOOM.

"What the hell was that?" demanded Rikka, vibrating inside her spacesuit helmet. "A musical interlude?"

Quivering, Jhonny checked his monitors. "The asteroid belt," he replied succinctly. "And most of our armor plating is gone!"

"Great," chortled Harry, twisting his helmet about so that he could see out the front once more. "That will make it easier for the cops to get inside."

Using a mechanical arm in his helmet to retrieve his fallen glasses, Michelangelo privately noted that the lack also would make it easier for the crooks to get out.

But maybe he could do something about the problem.

Trailing bits of metal and gravel, The Spot plowed on past the mighty Jupiter, lancing neatly between dozens of moons. Suddenly a single large mass loomed directly in front of the rocky runaway, but before the matter could even be registered in living brains, The Spot was gone past them into space.

On Ganymede moon, inside the underground control room of Experimental Lab #9, a breathless technician burst through the doors of his superior's private office.

"Okay, what the hell was that?" demanded Charles Conway, papers from the report he had been writing still fluttering about in the air around him.

A gulp. "Apparently, chief, an L5 colony ripped through the valley we're in at slightly over Fatal Five! It missed us by less than a kilometer! A single kilometer! And what's more, the damn thing was being chased by a space shuttle!"

"Ah, then," smiled the burly executive, relaxing and returning to the work scattered on his desk. "Back to work, comrade. It was probably only Rikka Collins."

Reporters? Darn, he had hoped it was one of their experi-

ments in FTL engine designs that had gone horribly correct.
Oh, well.

Saturn and its lovely lacy ice rings were spared a visit from
the rock-eteer by the simple fact of cleverly being located a
million kilometers up orbit.

However, on the snowy surface of Uranus a skier stepped
out of a mountaintop cabin and was consumed by a wild buf-
feting wind. As the hurricane quickly diminished, and the
snowstorm settled to the icy slopes, the man glanced about in
puzzlement.

Hey, the ski lodge was gone. And it was a rental!

Dark and frigid, Neptune was so far removed from the vicinity of The Spot that the only way to tell the impromptu
craft had passed the orbit of the eighth planet was when it
pulverized a small floating buoy with an arrow pointing "This
Way to the Prison."

The communications link between Pluto and its only moon,
Charon, were momentarily interrupted as something the size
of an L5 passed between the two worlds, cutting off the
punch line to the joke "Know how to stop a werewolf? Just
use an aluminum chicken! A what? Oh, you know a—"

A riot immediately erupted on the mother planet.

Minutes later, in a prismatic blurring of colors and a gut
twisting effect similar to being the main spring for a windup
clock, the SNT suffered through the space station grounding
to a halt as the last few atoms of tin in the FTL engine elements disintegrated into nothingness.

The asteroid continued onward in its original course, but at
a greatly reduced speed of only a few thousand kilometers per
hour. Barely a crawl.

And right on cue Deitrich plowed straight into it from behind.

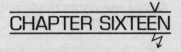
THE INSTANT THE Spot came into direct visual range, Deitrich killed his mains, but the microsecond of difference was more than enough and the QSNT shuttle plowed into the relatively motionless space station.

In a shower of glass, the craft exploded through the exposed window of the women's shower. Down a corridor the MainBrain hurtled, the wings of the craft scrapping furrows in the tiled walls. Lockers exploded into shrapnel and clothing, plastic dividers stretched to pop like bubbles, furniture disintegrated into splinters, and curtains shattered into individual threads.

Sixteen wooden doors, a stepladder, and two sonic curtains later, the bedraggled shuttle blasted through the stained-glass windows of a rotating restaurant and erupted into the very heart of the station.

Yikes! Spiraling out of control, there was ground above, below, and on both sides of the spacecraft, trees and buildings spinning about in as insane kaleidoscope of colors.

Frantically, the pilot mentally activated the emergency controls. All over the craft steering jets flared in response and the starship straightened out its course. Flying level, Deitrich could see he was diving toward an endless white floor. What the hell? Hey, there was a city beneath! Sensors fed the navigational computer precise data and the attitude jets fired in a calculated pattern, flipping the vehicle over. Now with its stern pointing toward the wall, the main engine roared into life, vomiting huge gouts of green flame from the rear of the tiny starship. Conflicting forces crushed the MainBrain in its protected jar as the crazed plummet violently reversed course and he raced from the deadly wall—only to see another impossible wall in front just a scant kilometer away!

The pilot's caustic remark was lost in the hissing of the steering jets as the spaceship flipped over and again began the braking maneuver.

A burning column of green fire stretched out in back of the craft as it hurtled toward the metal barrier, details of the landscape became momentarily discernible as he rocketed through a thin cloud. The white floor—wall?—swelled to fill the aft video monitor as the brutal G forces painfully crushed the human blob into his jar. Ouch! Then a rude kick jolted Deitrich as the chemical jets added their potent thrust to the vector battle and once more he leaped away from sudden death.

Like a flaming arrow, the news craft flashed across the sky, the MainBrain and its computer desperately trying to master the insane mixture of velocities and tangent forces of the rotating cylinder. Arbitrarily, the autopilot of the ship chose a landing place and angled downward. The cyborg only caught a fleeting glimpse of two skyscrapers before a sonic boom annihilated every window as he flashed between the buildings. De-accelerating by the second, the vessel lanced over fountains, bridge, and houses. Finally the fighting four-pounder heard the landing gear cycle into action, as empty seat belts tightened, and crash balloons expanded from the cockpit walls.

Glass shards were still falling from the skyscrapers when the darting shuttle zoomed inward, skimmed low over the town square, and smashed directly into the trees of the park. At first, the leafy boughs sheared off easily, but as their amassed drag pulled the ship lower, the thick branches fought back, snapping and cracking with every jarring crash.

Bursting free from the confines of the forest, the battered hulk arched over the empty picnic area to skip across the turbulent surface of the lake, once, twice, thrice. And finally crashed into the deserted row of cabanas on the south shore, beach balls, swimsuits, and surfboards shotgunning into the air.

"M-m-made it alive," gasped the Brain to himself, inside the upside-down smoking shuttle. "God, I'm good."

Pale and shaky, Rikka released the death grip on the reception desk and asked her pocket-doc to wack her with a few cc's of anything it damn well felt was appropriate. Soon cool sobriety flooded her body and mind. Ah, better.

HI, HONEY, I'M HOME, scrolled the four monitors.

"Deitrich, you aren't dead!" greeted Jhonny in delight.

NOT QUITE. AND BY THE WAY, WHAT THE HECK IS A SILVER PULLET?

"Beats me," answered Michelangelo, scratching his head. Something used to kill a werewolf? Nyah, stupid joke.

A mental shrug. OH, WELL. HEY! CARE TO GUESS WHERE WE ARE?

"Hell," said Harry, chomping on a handful of antacids and washing them down with a double from his hip flask. Ah, better.

CLOSE, BUT NO CIGAR. TRY JUST SHORT OF THE OORT CLOUD.

"Impossible," growled Michelangelo, sucking on a chocolate lozenge and feeling the caffeine tighten his whole body. Ah, better. Thank the gods, he had long ago gotten over his adverse reactions to traveling FTL, or else this would have given him a lethal case of light-headedness. "We would have needed to exceed Fatal Five."

YES, INDEEDY. LESSON NUMBER ONE FOR TODAY, KIDDIES: NEVER TRUST HARRY'S MATH.

Rallying to the attack, Snyder attempted a clever retort or two, but the only quips that came to mind were too flimsy for public use so he remained quiet.

"So, they almost performed the Linstrom maneuver," remarked Jhonny, sounding impressed. Many had tried but few ever managed to pull off that little miracle.

YEP, OH, BY THE WAY, HELP IS EN ROUTE.

"Who?" demanded Collins weakly. She hadn't felt this bad since her first meeting with Maria Valdez.

DAMN NEAR EVERYBODY FAR AS I CAN TELL.

Forcing herself into action, Rikka started to scan the monitors throughout the station. "Where is the military going to

break in? And how? This rock is armored for war." Damn,
had that been part of the overall plan?

"Not anymore," reminded Jhonny, rapping shave-and-a-
haircut-two-bits on the top of the reception console.

"Oh, yeah." Shudder.

"How did you get in then?" asked Michelangelo curiously,
as he lowered the temperature of his suit. Already the station
was cooling. If life support couldn't compensate fast enough
there might actually be an autumn frost.

SNUCK IN THROUGH A WINDOW.

"Ha!" What?

"And when can you connect us to Media?" asked Collins
before Snyder could.

"Tones and bars, chief," replied the android, his cameras
clicking and humming. "Mike has established a hot link with
the shuttle and we're broadcasting live straight to Media."

Twirling knobs, Harry did a visual sweep around the
morgue. Clear of any criminals. "Any response from Box?"

"Not yet. Maybe there's interference from the big flare. Give
him a while."

"The thieves are doing something," announced Mike,
switching the four monitors to a side-by-side panoramic view.

Eagerly, the news team bent closer to their video ring-side
seats to the confrontation of the century. Perhaps, now, finally, at long last, they would discover the true identities of
the criminals who had done five of the ten biggest thefts in
history. The other greatest being: the Great Train Robbery of
England, the Brinks Job of North America, Venus de Milo's
arms, and the other two were related to the Academy of Motion Pictures Oscar Award and shrouded in deepest secrecy.

Spanning the four glass screens was an aerial view of a
hundred orange spacesuits clustered around the junkyard collection forming the very dead Fatal engine.

"Did . . . did we make it past the Oort Cloud?" asked a
slim youngster, using a crowbar on the machine to pull down
the off switch fashioned from two refrigerators and a wooden
breadboard.

"No, we did not," glumly replied a mature woman in a

welder's mask, assisting with the breadboard. "But our escape has gone unnoticed, and soon everything will be ours."

With great ceremony, a huge muscular figure opened a elaborately carved wooden box, and inside was a roll of cloth on a stick. Removing the contents, the cloth unfurled into a rectangle of a rainbow marred by a slim black line. As the big spacesuit started walking toward the train tracks, the others saluted and some removed their helmets in respect.

Exposing the blue-skinned heads inside.

"Androids?" gasped Rikka, slamming backward in her chair. "No, it can't be!"

"That skin tone doesn't come from cosmetics," said Harry, scrutinizing the people on screen professionally. Androids, oh, no, please God, no.

"And that cloth thing is a flag," whispered Michelangelo, feeling ill to his stomach.

"An android nation flag," said Jhonny slowly, his camera clicking away but not pointed toward anything in particular.

"The rainbow and bar," gestured Snyder weakly. "Is that a mass spectrograph reading for the element silicon?"

Glumly, he was informed on the correctness of the assumption.

Bloody hell. What had they done!

On the screens, tiny figures marched after the flag, talking and laughing.

"Soon we will be able to rebuild this research station into a independent worldlet, smuggling thousands of our brethren on board until we can claim political status with the United Planets and get total equality for all of our people!" proudly stated an elder droid with a nasty purple scar.

"Chatty machine, ain't ya?" asked a slim female with no hair.

"On a wonderful day like this, who cares?" added a fat male with spindly arms and legs. In reply, dozens laughed in delight. Others began to sing a very old song about groups of people overcoming. The happy chorus was punctuated with the occasional spurts of cowboy wahoos and headstands tossed in for flavor.

In the morgue, Rikka groaned. Harry groaned. Then the two reporters looked at each other and groaned in unison. Michelangelo began beating his head on the wall, and Jhonny appeared to be poleaxed. Bloody hell on toast! These folks weren't thieves doing the ultimate robbery, but freedom fighters! And the SNT had just blown their cover and called the cops. The word "disaster" didn't even begin to cover the situation. Total cosmic boner was closer to the dictionary definition of the incident.

Suddenly, whole banks of glowing green meters flickered wildly above the steel-edged monitors full of dancing blue people in orange spacesuits.

MILITARY IS HERE, scrolled three of the screens. The fourth was solid static. THE USDA HAS ASSUMED AN ATTACK POSTURE AROUND THE SPOT AND A RECON TEAM IS CYCLING THROUGH THE MAIN AIRLOCKS EVEN AS WE SPEAK.

On the second monitor, amid the boisterous singers, a tiny male touched his left ear, paused, went pale, and ran over to a public kiosk. Slamming coins into the pay phone, he dialed for an external view and, to his great regret, got it.

"Alert," said a male, backing away from the horrible sight. "The USDA fleet is here!"

"And demanding our surrender," added a leglass android sitting on a hovercart jammed full of equipment.

The singing stopped abruptly and spacesuits quickly walked from one screen to gather on another. "Are you sure?"

"No question. Over a thousand warships with enough firepower to roast Uranus!"

A fast conference was held on the street.

"Is the FTL engine . . .?"

"Totally dead."

"Can we escape?"

"In what? We have no shuttles?"

"Hide in the sewers?"

"From military scanners? Impossible."

"Enough!" called the elderly woman, raising a hand. "We know what we have to do. This situation was covered in our contingency plans. We cannot fight them or else even more repressive legislation may be passed against our brothers and sisters back home."

"Surrender?" asked another.

A nod. "There is no other choice."

Sadly, the androids removed the rainbow flag from the stick and neatly folded the cloth and reverently tucked it into a pocket.

"Our dream of political freedom is dead," announced an older male. "With our own world, we could have reshuffled the balance of power in the United Planets and eventually abolished the Organic Law of 2018. But now ..."

A hundred blue heads hung low.

"But how did they find us?" asked an android child plaintively.

"How?"

All of the members of the SNT sported the appearance of people who had just drunk raw gasoline.

"We didn't know," said the anchor in heartfelt shame, a sob marring his husky voice. But to whom he was addressing the remark was unclear. "Jesus, God, Mary, and Joseph, we have done countless editorials on repealing that very same asinine law! I thought they were just crooks stealing stuff. Honestly."

Jhonny cut off his friend's denials with a curt hand chop. "It's okay. Really. None of us had any notion of their true identities."

Collins felt like barfing. Christ! Her team busted wide open the biggest story of their career, and what was the reward? The good guys go to jail. Even their idiot bosses, the money-mad Gardner Wilkes and snotty Maria Valdez, had agreed to hire Jhonny as John Smith so that the android could work as a camera-op, in spite of the laws forbidding androids to do anything but menial labor. It had been their private rebellion against an unjust law created by frightened uneducated people who had read *Frankenstein* just one too many times.

Shame burning her face, Rikka hung her head. But the

droids had taken a more direct approach, and it was her own team that had blown the plan to pieces. If only the SNT had known the truth, exposing the androids would have been the very last item on their agenda. But instead, the reporters blindly performed their job and fulfilled their requirements as law-abiding citizens of society.

"So why do I feel like such a cosmic shitheel?" she asked nobody in particular.

"Because we're so damn good at uncovering mysteries that we've just utterly destroyed any hope for androids receiving social equality for the next hundred years," snapped Harry, biting off each word as if their flavor was more bitter than he could bare.

Painfully blunt. Like being stabbed with a butter knife.

"Harry, Rikka," spoke Michelangelo, tears in his eyes. "You two are the acknowledged masters of sneakiness. Isn't there anything we can do? Anything?"

"What?" demanded Jhonny, reaching out to touch the cool glass of a monitor full of his weeping cousins. "Burn our records? Deny the events occurred? Stage a diversion so the androids can leap into space? Pointless. The military is on the way in, and the droids are on the way out. What can we do? What could anybody do?"

"Then it's finished," said Harry, slumping over. Without thinking, the anchor found the hip flask in his hand and he tossed it across the room to crash in a corner. Damn! Damn! Damn! Damn! Damn! And damn again!

Dead silence for a while, the only sound was strained breathing from the SNT and tearful good-byes from the androids. Then a sudden snap was heard and the reporters turned to see Collins holding the two halves of a computer stylus.

"It is finished?" asked Rikka, that famous glint shining silicon bright in both eyes. "Is it really over?"

Hearts beat faster in the reception room and the news team gathered close.

"Talk to us, kid," urged Snyder urgently.

YOU HAVE A PLAN?

"Maybe," admitted the woman, a hand stroking her chin

but missing by a good inch. "Deitrich, Jhonny, Mike, the main computer of this station has been seriously, and I mean seriously, damaged by the flares and an FTL trip that it was never designed to handle. Hasn't it?"

Faces furrowed in confusion, then brightened in understanding.

"Stall for time," said the alien as a question.

VIA MAJOR COMPUTER MALFUNCTIONS? CHECK.

"How much time do you need?" asked Jhonny, locking his mechanical fingers together and cracking knuckles as a prelude to action.

"Whatever you can get me," she said, accessing files on board the shuttle. "Ten minutes, five. Anything!"

Swiveling about in his chair, Harry established a link with the library computer. "Don't bother to explain details," said the grinning anchor, watching over her shoulder. "Just get going, and I'll start helping once I figure out what the hell you're doing."

Already lost in the private world of her work, Rikka just nodded, both hands typing at Fatal speeds. Her idea was crazy, insane, a long shot! But long shots do sometimes pay off, and crazy, insane, and Gertrude were her middle names.

God, she hoped this worked!

CHAPTER SEVENTEEN

"OKAY, HOW DO we handle this?" asked Jhonny, taking a seat and booting the controls. Thank God they had already interfaced with The Spot mainframe.

"First, we have got to slow down the military by closing off the hole that Deitrich made getting inside," said Michelangelo, seizing control of numerous subsystems.

ALL SHIELDS UP AND RIGID AS A TEENAGE CODPIECE AT A WET G-STRING PARTY.

"Then we should let everybody know what is going on."

"Check!"

Everywhere throughout the cubic kilometers of The Spot, doors began to open and close by themselves in irregular patterns. Streetlights dimmed and brightened with no rhythm or reason, and the sunstrips rippled in a strobe effect. Fountains geysered under far too much pressure and the streets began to flood. Radios clicked on and microwaves burned a thousand dinners. Fire alarms went off where there was no smoke and remained strangely quiet where there was flames. Janitor robots leaped from their maintenance closets with no sane goal in mind: painting windows, oiling doorknobs, waxing ladders, removing manhole covers from the streets, and generally running amuck.

As the androids were walking toward the train tunnel, emergency decompression bulkheads slammed into place, narrowly missing the lead male of the sad-faced crowd.

"How could that have happened?" called an android tech, touching his bruised nose. "It's impossible!"

"Unless the main computer has shorted out and gone crazy!" noted another critically.

"Oh, great," moaned an elder female. "And the military will think it's us!"

In the morgue, Jhonny frowned, "Damn, and they probably will."

FAIR ENOUGH. SO LET'S TELL THE USDA OTHERWISE, scrolled Deitrich to his friends.

As the MainBrain gave conflicting orders via his umbilical cable attached to the cabban payphone to life support, Mike sent off a phony distress call from the androids for help and Jhonny typed in commands with absolutely no care for misspellings.

With a strident bang, the explosive bolts on the airlock doors ignited and blew the squad of Marines in Samson powerarmor rudely through the decontamination arch and into a Spot souvenir stand.

"What the . . . is this some sort of pitiful attack?" asked a slab of UP metal, getting to his feet and brushing anatomically correct Einstein dolls off his assault rifle.

The fluorescent lights overhead exploded and a soda machine began ejecting cans of pop like a hiccuping mortar.

"No, the thieves are asking for immediate assistance," decided another, with a line of hash marks on its louvered sleeve and a "Caution: I Do Research for the Hell of It!" T-shirt draped over her head. "The main computer blew and the whole ship is out of control."

Before them, a set of double doors slammed open and closed like a human-size vegetable slicer. Nobody noticed that the pounding was also an incredibly rude phrase in Morse code.

"Orders, sir?" asked a corporal, attempting to release the safety of his Gibraltar Assault Rifle, and then remembering this weapon didn't possess one.

A grunt. "We take the stairs."

But even that innocent structure had been affected and the escalator started going forward/backward, forward/backward until even the hardiest of the space veterans was feeling sea-sick. Then the mechanical stairs did their very best to go side-ways. And actually succeeded, to everybody's astonishment.

On the bridge of the USDA: *Prime*, Admiral Davis swiv-eled about in his command chair and scowled at the circle of officers before him.

"What do you mean the computer raised their shields?" de-manded the Naval officer, puffing hostilely on his pipe. "Well, blast it down!"

"Sir, those adamantine shields were designed and augmented to withstand the raw unbridled fury of a primordial solar flare," stated a brash lieutenant at the weapons console. He had a col-lege degree in poetry and tried to use his talent whenever pos-sible. "Our vaunted guns could only punch a hole through the immaterial forcefield barrier by using enough concentrated power to also annihilate The Spot beyond."

The steel pipe drooped. "So we can only get the crooks, by killing them. Is that it?"

"Aye, sir. And our own recon team."

Hmm. Tough choice. Davis would have to think about this for a minute.

Watching the androids leave the sealed train tracks and head for the cargo corridors, Jhonny overrode another security code and mere microseconds before the partisans turned a corner the signs changed; arrows pointing in the wrong direc-tion toward incorrect goals.

"That will slow them down," sighed the camera-op.

TRUE. HOWEVER, THE UP IS IN SAMSON POWERARMOR AND THERE IS NO NEED FOR US TO PULL OUR PUNCHES WITH THEM, scrolled Deitrich.

"Go for it," urged Michelangelo.

And the MainBrain unleashed his talents at seriously re-tarding the advance of the invasion force of law-and-order.

Crawling off the wreck of the escalator, the troops stag-gered dizzily across a hallway and stumbled into a turbo-lift whose doors were conveniently parted and waiting.

As the doors of the elevator closed, the turbo-lift safeties disengaged, the emergency cables snapped, the secondary brakes locked into an open position, and the capsule full of Marines plummeted downward at an ever-increasing speed.

Ten stories below, the turbo-lift punched through the bottom of the shaft and a platoon of metal figures shotgunned out of the ceiling, slamming into a chemical laboratory that immediately detonated in a strident blast.

"Ouch," said a bruised private, standing amid the crackling hellish flames. "I broke a nail!"

"So far, so good," said Rikka, throwing switches on the reception desk console, duplicating files madly. "There are only two points more to cover and we may have this sussed."

"He's on the line and waiting for you," announced Harry, thumbing a sensor pad. "I had to use a bribe, some threatened muscle, and several whoppers, but here he is."

The center section of the control panel clouded over and then cleared into a picture of a tall, handsome man, his dark skin perfectly accented by his electric-blue robes and titanium-white turban. He was breathing very heavily, seated in a gilded throne behind an elaborate business desk of gold coins welded together into a homogeneous mass.

Rikka placed her palms together and gave what of a salaam she could while sitting in a chair. "Sheik Hassan, thank you for taking our call."

"Argh!" cried the criminal boss, and he pointed a pistol at the TV screen. The phone went blank.

Rikka hit redial.

"AIYEE . . .!" screeched the Arab. And a chair went flying toward the phone this time.

Redial. With a finger on the pause button.

"Argh!" shouted the man, shaking both fists toward the ceiling, or perhaps heaven. From this angle it was hard to tell.

"Auction went badly?"

With a jerk, the crime lord went still, turned toward the telephone, and looked at the reporter with newfound respect. "So, you know," he said as a statement.

"Yep. Everything," lied Harry with a poker face.

The sheik rolled his eyes about and gnashed his teeth. "I was gypped! Rooked! Robbed and swindled!"

"How? They paid you off in counterfeit bucks? Fool's gold? Artificial tin?"

"Worse," said the man, slumping so far down that his turban threatened to drop off. "Fake bombs."

Instantly the morgue went dead quiet and everybody turned about to stare at the furious man.

"No kidding?" asked Snyder, a surge of adrenaline making his spine tingle with excitement.

On the view screen alongside her, Rikka could see the androids struggling to pry open doors, while the military was blasting holes in the walls, which at least offered them a stationary target. So far. But how long could her teammates keep this up?

"Let me get this straight," she spoke hastily. "An auction was arranged, the price was some blueprints, and you were paid off in fake bombs?"

"Yes, exactly," raged the man. "I was robbed!"

Then suddenly the Arab went still and gave a sickly smile at the video phone. "Although, of course, I was only acting as a civilian sting operation to remove these potentially lethal weapons from the open market. Afterward I would have immediately turned the nukes over to the proper authorities."

Rikka leaned closer to the phone. "Sheik Hassan, this transmission is triple scrambled and encoded on both ends. Nobody else can hear us."

"Dead!" screamed the sheik, tearing at his hair. "I want them dead, dead, dead! And then brought back to life so I can kill 'em again!"

Now that was more like the Hassan they knew and feared.

"And torture! Did I mention torture?"

"We would love to help you get revenge," offered Harry sweetly.

Hassan stopped his tirade and smiled benignly at the reporters. He had always liked the team. He didn't watch the news, but if he ever did, it would surely be their show.

"But we gotta go," amended Collins, stabbing a button. "Bye!"

The line went dead.

"If the androids didn't use the bombs to pay for the blue-prints, then that eliminates the crime of selling stolen goods and trafficking in illegal weapons," said Rikka, crossing an-other item off her list.

"And that was the biggy," said Snyder, withdrawing sup-plies from his belt pouch and laying the contents about on the reception desk before him. "Who's next?"

"Media," snapped Rikka, punching numbers as if she had palsy. Thank goodness at least they would be easy to get ahold of!

Air vents spewed forth raw sewage while robotic pizza de-livery trucks arrived everywhere and wouldn't take no for an answer. Both of the north- and southbound trains took off at full speed and, upon entering a specifically chosen access tun-nel, immediately hit the brakes. Buckling in half, the trains then flipped over, filling the tunnels solid with smashed wood, red-hot metal, spinning wheels, and tiny complimen-tary packets of hickory smoked peanuts.

Their Samson armor barely scratched, the soldiers re-grouped and proceeded deeper into the scientific base. Good thing these weren't serious attacks. They suffered worse just visiting a library on Venus.

Suddenly Michelangelo appeared with torn sheets and started binding the reporters to their chairs.

READY! announced Deitrich.

Jhonny pressed a single button.

In the aft section of the space station, relays actually blew, power transformers crackled into lightning storms and melted into puddles. Gears broke into metallic confetti, ball bearings disengaged, and the cylinder began to slow.

Having reached the inside of The Spot, the departing an-droids found themselves moving along the sidewalks with surprising grace, but then every step was too large and they began slowly, oh, so casually, falling over. Attempted tries to stand correctly again only made them flounder and bounce a bit into the air.

"We've lost gravity!" cried a pretty female in disgust.

"Centrifugal force, actually," corrected a dapper male, suspended above the crowd.

"Nuts and bolts!" cursed another. "This dump is falling apart!"

Behind them, the waves of the lake did not stop at the shore but rolled up onto the banks and gently drifted about as weird undulating globules of clear fluid. With the occasional very surprised-looking fish trapped inside.

"No matter," shouted the ebony-haired spokeswoman. "We cannot let the military capture us. We must willingly surrender to them for the sake of future generations. Onward!"

And the androids bobbled on, a few simply diving forward and swimming above the motionless turbowalk.

At the extreme other end of the station, the Samson powerarmor was unfortunately equipped with gravity boots and the lack of attraction only sped the troops along as they could now easily walk along the walls and ceiling, bypassing many of the hasty impediments shoved before them by the struggling SNT technicians.

A hundred million kilometers away, a lovely young human with volumes of luxurious copper-red hair pressed a button on her desk activating the answer function of her communications monitor.

"Media news network!" she called gaily. "Home of the Satellite News Team. Sorry we've been off the air, but unforeseen—"

"Stuff it, Gwen," snapped the brunette on the monitor. "I'm calling in the favor you owe me. Give me Wilkes five seconds ago."

"Or else," added Snyder dramatically off-camera.

The line crackled and snapped with static. Or maybe it was only the secretary.

Inside the presidential office of Media, Gardner Wilkes was sitting cross-legged and mediating on his living carpet of thick green grass, when the phone rang in a perfect B flat, the emergency tone. In one smooth motion, Wilkes rose and stabbed a finger at his smooth blank desktop.

"Wilkes," said the boss. "Okay, what is the problem?" That was the only reason anybody ever called him. Even on birthdays.

Above the desk formed a picture of a slim brunette tied to a chair with what resembled a bed sheet. On the wall behind her was a chart of the disassembled human body on display.

Good Lord, what had the SNT gotten into this time? Cannibals?

"Chief? Rikka Collins, here, your top ace," said the woman in the hologram window, just in case the old man had forgotten. "We're on top of the biggest, THE biggest news story for the past and future decade, but it's Sunday supplement filler unless you instantly donate The Spot to the United Planets for a tax loss."

A short pause. "How did you ever discover I owned the company that owned the company that owns the university that owns The Spot?" Gardner asked, impressed.

"Sir . . ." she implored through gritted teeth. Geez, her team was the top reporters in the solar system! What didn't they know?

Taking a seat in his hoverchair, Wilkes toyed with a cuff link. It came loose, dropped to the grass, and rolled away. The billionaire ignored it. He had lots of replacements, and they were everywhere. "Are you quite serious? The story of the decade?"

"Deadly. Utterly. Totally. I'd stake my pension."

The owner of QSNT and the multiplanet Wilkes Corporation took three slow breaths. Wow. For reporters that was the tops.

"Accepted," he stated. "However, what's in it for me?"

The SNT reporters gagged and choked on the replay.

"Ah, the scoop of the year?" suggested Collins.

"That is your job and QSNT's glory."

Unseen, Harry chimed in, "Increased revenues from advertising!"

"I do most of the advertising here. All in-house."

"What do you want?" demanded Rikka rudely.

Ah, so it was a real superstory and not some sort of fanciful practical joke. Fine. His options were many, but the choices few. "Be nice to Valdez."

Rikka pulled her face away from the telephone and screamed. Mike and Jhonny halted in their work and stared.

WHAT DOES HE WANT? BLOOD?

"That I'd give him," she retorted hotly. "Now listen to me, sir . . ."

"Gosh, it's not too late already, is it?" the bald man on the monitor asked in concern.

"Whew, he's good," admitted Snyder in a whisper.

In surrender, Rikka threw up her hands. There was no time left for negotiations. "Okay, we'll be nice for a week."

"Six months."

"One month."

"Three."

"Two, and we'll cancel the first fourteen annual 'Name your favorite picture to paint of Maria's butt' contest," contributed Snyder loudly.

Wilkes blinked. My God, then that wasn't just a rumor!

"Done," said their boss, and he disconnected the transmission. Even before the hologram faded, he hit the intercom. "Ms. Pickerington?"

"Sir?" asked another featureless area of the desk.

"This is priority one business call. Immediately contact the United Planets Purchases and Acquisitions department on Geneva L5 and inform them that this is a courtesy backup call on the physical hard-copy letter I sent them a month ago donating The Spot to the UP."

After the appropriate gasp, the human secretary got busy.

Releasing the hidden button, Gardner Wilkes reclined in his flying chair. Well, well, there went fifty or sixty million Earth dollars. The SNT had better bring this story home and it better be a nova-hot, front-page doozy on wheels!

Or else.

On two of the other monitors on the reception desk was a view of the Samson powerarmor-clad soldiers trying to undog the locking wheel of a closed bulkhead door.

The third monitor showed the same portal, but from the other side. There, a team of sweaty androids had shoved a

steelloy bar through the spokes of the locking wheel and were
straining to free the mechanism by shoving in unison.

Meanwhile, Jhonny, Mike, and Deitrich were shutting
down whole areas of the research station to gather more electrical power to shunt through the mammoth stereo speakers
on the RecRoom level below the door, and the industrial can
opener in the kitchen on the level above; the combination
forming a crude but powerful electromagnetic seal holding the
portal rigidly in place. For the moment.

"It that it?" demanded Harry, busy at his own work. "Did
we cover everything?"

Panting with her mental exertions, Rikka couldn't speak as
her mind was frantically reviewing everything. If they missed
a single item, one tiny loophole, then the whole situation
would go down the drain. Taking their careers with it. And
there would be no second chance. She either got this perfect
the first time, or her news team would be personally responsible for destroying the most amazingly heroic attempt for
freedom in the history of the worlds since that Cassandra
Peterson clone unhooked her bra live on camera.

"Well?" shouted Snyder, combing his hair.

On the staggered monitors facing each other, the androids
and soldiers valiantly struggled to get through the stubborn
portal. Without warning, the wheel snapped off and the droids
went tumbling. The SNT technicians cheered. But then a soldier with a WatchDog scanner pointed toward the ceiling and
the floor. The troops emptied their weapons in the indicated
directions, the ceiling and floor were volatilized and the machinery beyond was annihilated. Instantly, the magnetic seals
vanished and the door started to creak open.

"Prepare to drop the external shields and fields," ordered
Rikka to her cursing technicians. "Harry, you ready?"

Swiveling away from his cosmetics kits, the anchor faced
his teammates. The elderly man's hair was solid black and
combed flat to his skull. His nose had been enlarged, his lips
thinned, ears glued flat, eyebrows arched, and his skin was a
smooth silicon blue.

"Yes, mistress, I am quite ready," he spoke in a calm artificial voice.

CHAPTER EIGHTEEN

THE BULKHEAD DOOR swung open wide enough for the powersuits to see the androids, and vice versa.

The shields dropped and Admiral Davis called off the final bombardment of proton lasers and disrupter beams.

On command, Michelangelo, Jhonny, and Deitrich stopped the fake malfunctions and allowed the secondary subsystems to reclaim control of the station: streets started to drain of sewage and water, the air cleared of smoke and smells, fire alarms turned off, ceiling extinguishers killed countless small blazes, the sunstrips ceased their photonic pulsations, and the cylinder began to turn again, soon restoring gravity.

"Centrifugal force," corrected one of the androids to another.

Watching the monitors, the reporters saw the hundred orange spacesuits cluster near the open doorway as the score of troopers in Samson powerarmor assumed a double-layered firing line.

Then a hologram window formed above the soldiers and the foggy square cleared into the picture of Fleet Admiral Davis. His infamous stainless-steel pipe stuck out of the corner of his mouth and there was a glint in his eyes of mixed fury and suspicion. But for him, that was normal.

"Okay, all of you pracking yahoos are under arrest!" his amplified voice boomed. "Drop your weapons, raise your hands, and hit the deck ... androids?" gasped Admiral Davis. "What in the three hells of divorce court is going on here? A bunch of droids stole this space station?"

An elderly blue woman stepped forward to speak.

But before she could utter a word a masculine voice boomed a strident denial from every speaker, computer, monitor, radio, TV, and wrist secretary within and without The Spot.

As everybody glanced around in surprise, another hologram window formed above the droids. It was an android male with a large nose, thin lips, and really bad haircut. The floating colossi stared belligerently at each other in a classic faceoff.

"What was that again?" rumbled the mammoth hologram Navy Officer.

"Sir, no crime has been committed," spoke the mysterious translucent android.

"What? You people stole The Spot!"

"No, we did not."

Slowly understanding came to Davis. "Ah, then some human did and you're covering for him. Okay, tell us where the bastard is hiding and we will hit 'em so hard his grandmother will fall over stunned."

"A truly formidable visual," replied the disguised Harry. "But I reiterate. Nobody made us do anything. We took this station of our own free will."

The androids on the ground started buzzing among themselves.

"Ah-ha!" gloated Davis. "You admit it!"

"We admit nothing, because no crime has been committed."

The Admiral scowled. A terrible thing to see.

"Gimme that again, Yankee," drawled the officer, his Southern Earth accent boiling to the surface of his rage.

The troops stood motionless and ready, fingers on triggers.

Snyder cleared his throat. "Sir, under the Organic Law of 2018, androids are not allowed to own property. Indeed, under the strict interpretation of the law, we are, in practice, if not de facto, ourselves to be considered property under the law.

"And as even a child knows," continued the floating speaker. "Property cannot steal property."

Among the delighted androids by the door, a large woman

spoke, "Indeed, Admiral, can your desk lamp steal your stapler? Your coffee maker rob you of the pencil sharpener?"

There was a long pause. Then the Admiral's head turned off screen to address somebody privately.

"What?" Mad Dog demanded hotly. A pause. "You sure about that? God's teeth, it's true?"

The ebony-haired woman advanced, spreading her arms in welcome. "We are pleased to have you representatives of the human military forces here as visitors, but we must formally ask you to lower your weapons."

A few of the gun barrels sagged and then stiffened with resolve.

Silently, Harry applauded the assistance. What a woman! No wonder she had been in charge before he arrived. They made a great team.

"Okay, you got us," admitted the officer in oily smooth terms. "As androids, you cannot be arrested for the . . . relocation of this space station. However, the personal property of the scientists—"

"Will be returned to them forthwith," interrupted a burly blue male, taking the cue. "As soon as we can be furnished with a list of the materials and the correct addresses of their rightful owners."

Accepting a pencil from a bodiless hand, off camera, Davis made a checked mark on a list. "So, who claims this station as salvage?"

There was a moment of confusion.

"Beg pardon?" asked Harry, tilting his aerial head. "Salvage? There is no salvage. We are here and legally lay claim to the abandoned property."

"Oh, I am so sorry," said Admiral Davis in a contradictory voice. "But you cannot do that. If you operate on the premise that property cannot steal property, then my legal staff advises me that you cannot lay claim to the station, because . . ."

"Property cannot own property," whispered Collins, holding a hand over her microphone. Talk about circular logic!

"I lay claim to this station," announced Jhonny, flipping switches and looking directly into the monitor.

On the screens, everybody turned to stare at the new hologram head.

"And who are you?" said the Admiral, frowning.

Oops. The camera-op removed his spacesuit helmet. "I am a human, nonfelon, and believe me one hell of a property owner," stated the manchine, mostly telling the truth. "My name is John Smith, a camera operator for QSNT, and I do hereby and formally claim this station as abandoned UP property!"

"This station is a private civilian concern!"

"No. It was donated to the United Planets a while ago." Sort of, anyway.

The androids on the monitors pooled their heads, while the Admiral had another off-camera discussion.

"What in hell are you doing?" demanded Rikka, killing her collar mike.

"Trying to help the good guys win and save our story," replied Jhonny out of the corner of his mouth.

"But you can't claim salvage," whispered Michelangelo.

The photographer turned upward to gaze at his giant friend. "Eh? And why not?"

"United Solar Defense Alliance, general law #98876257!" intoned the translucent Admiral from all four screens. "Official noncombatants, such as news reporters, doctors, and prostitutes, are forbidden to use, and thus exempt from the usage, of the salvage law blah-blah-blah, you get the idea."

"That's why I didn't try and use that trick," muttered Snyder sotto voce.

"Oh, poop," sighed the camera-op, slumping. Then he straightened upright. "What if I was to quit SNT?" he asked hopefully.

"Too late," rumbled Mike, monitoring the status of the soldiers' weapons. "The military was here before you were a civilian, and thus they have first option."

On the reception desk monitor and above the soldiers and androids, Mad Dog grinned a grin of total triumph. "So, you folks gonna depart quietly, or must my troops escort you from the premises?" he asked sweetly. His preference in the matter was painfully clear.

Nervously watching the powerarmor, the androids conferred among themselves.

Yanking a cable from her belt, Rikka jacked herself into the communications console and started typing.

"Well?" asked Admiral Davis impatiently. "I'll give you to the count of three. One!"

Suddenly the black-haired spokeswoman jerked her attention down at the neck ring of her spacesuit and her eyes went round as flying saucers.

"Two!"

"Hold!" boomed the female, trying not to openly read from the words scrolling across her neck monitor. "I apologize for the misunderstanding of my earlier statement, and for referring to an obviously improper flaw in the law, you big lunkhead."

The woman gasped, and Davis fumed.

Rikka spoke to her wrist. "Kept it clean."

SORRY, scrolled the MainBrain. I GOT CARRIED AWAY.

"I misspoke when declaring that my fellow patriots and I claimed this station as salvage."

"Damn straight you did," growled Davis, looming over them.

"What I meant to say," went on the woman smoothly. "Is that"—her vision flicked across the crude teleprompter—"we declare this space station as a new and independent political entity."

Dead silence.

Opening and closing his mouth like a beached whale, Davis jerked his face off camera and started silently yelling at somebody.

"Geez, that's brilliant," said Harry softly. "They can't be innocent of the crime and claim this place a salvage, but even androids can start a country."

"Hopefully," said Rikka, typing madly on her wrist secretary. "I'm doing this from a half-credit law course I took in college back in the Pliocene age. Whether or not it's going to work is another matter entirely."

"What do you mean they can?" came from the hologram window in the dock air. "But they're pracking androids!" A pause. "Even them? God damn it to hell, then why did HQ send me off after them?"

The droids buzzed with excitement.

"Ah, better," smiled the Admiral, and he returned to the waiting crowd of nouveau diplomats. "Okay, fine, swell. Under these unusual circumstances, I am forced to allow you to do that. But there are a few formalities to observe, before my troops will be withdrawn."

The female spokesperson wet her azure lips. "Such as?" she asked politely as possible, a trickle of sweat running down her cheek.

Mike turned from the video screens. "Oh, crap, he's going for the recognition trick," muttered the alien. "They tried this on us when we first arrived. You can't just declare yourself an independent country. There are basic criteria that must be followed."

"Shaddup and get me a dictionary," growled Rikka, typing. "Fast!"

Jhonny calmly reached into a back pocket of his spacesuit belt and handed her a slim booklet. Collins snatched it away from him and started flipping. Every dictionary had what she needed tucked away in the back pages. No, every dictionary from Earth had it. Where was this one made? Chicago? Which Chicago? The town, the L5, or the asteroid with the gay disco bikers tavern?

Killing his microphone, Harry started dialing fast.

"May I see a copy of your official declaration of independence?" asked Admiral Davis in forced politeness.

The spokeswoman started to marshal a terrific lie, when her belt fax began to hum and out scrolled a single sheet of paper.

"But this is the American Declaration of Independence!"

stormed the Navy officer, staring at a duplicate sheet from his own belt. "Only with the word 'England' crossed out and the word 'Humanity' written in!"

"And why shouldn't we use as basic text the most stirring document on freedom in the history of the worlds?" asked the woman, sounding innocently puzzled.

"Whew. Is that one of yours?" asked Michelangelo.

A head shake. "That's her words, and good stuff." Briefly, the reporter wondered if the lady had originally been a secretary, as those unsung stalwarts mostly ran civilization anyway.

Despite automatic color control, the Admiral's face was getting longer and redder by the moment. Failure was not a word normally found in his personal lexicon. "You are indeed a tricky bastard," stated the soldier. "And I like that in a leader. Although there is another little matter. Has any charter member of the United Planets recognized your fleding country?"

And The Spot chilled. This was the catch. Not just anybody could claim they were a free country. Centuries ago, legislation had been passed to protect society from some drunk meteor miner standing on an asteroid, planting a dirty handkerchief flag, and announcing that he was the independent county of Zip-A-Dee-Doo-Da-Land and thus didn't have to pay any taxes. Ha-ha, so there. A dastardly tactic that was soon absolutely forbidden by every bureaucrat in existence.

"Well?" demanded the Admiral impatiently.

Strained expressions among the crowd of droids as they plotted, planned, and schemed like sonsabitches.

"Oh, I am terribly sorry, but in accordance with the rules and regulations of the United Planets charter, unless your country has the authorized backing of at least one member nation or world, then we do not legally HAVE to recognize your status and thus, sadly, we will reclaim this station."

The troops hardened into an attack posture.

"Any way necessary," growled the grizzled Navy officer.

And there flickered into existence a hologram window off to the side of the groups. The picture was badly out of focus,

and danced with static, but the facial features enclosed within
the square were still readily discernible.

"I am Lord Burgess d'Coultier the Ex-Eye-Eye-Eye, king
errant of New-Olde-South Mars, and may I be the first to officially recognize the independent status of this sovereign nation of androids."

The crowd held their breath in anticipation.

On Snyder's wrist secretary words began to scroll.

DOES THIS MAKE US EVEN? asked the monitor in a royal font.

"More than even," he replied with a smile. "We owe you
a favor."

OH, GOD, NO, PLEASE. EVEN IS FINE.

"And thank you for answering so fast, Your Majesty,"
added Rikka.

NO PROBLEM, I WAS GLAD TO. AS A FORMER COLONY WORLD OF
EARTH, I DON'T LIKE TO SEE ANY PEOPLE GET BULLIED AROUND,
AND BESIDES, MY NATION DOESN'T MAKE OR USE ANDROIDS.

"Thanks anyway," winked the anchor.

NOW CAN I HAVE THE NEGATIVES? pleaded the screen.

A billion kilometers away, King d'Coultier wiped a brow
with a mink-trimmed sleeve and sighed. Whew. Free again!
He must resolutely remember to never have an affair during
a full lunar eclipse. Especially on a dairy farm.

"Troops, stand down!" called the Admiral reluctantly.

The Samson powerarmor pulled in their weapons and assumed a more friendly posture.

"Who is your leader, president, premier, king, whatever?"

Safe from view behind a large android, a group of five held
a fast game of paper rock, scissors. Paper won.

"I am, sir," proudly announced the elderly female. "President Shahra J 992745."

The Admiral bowed and saluted. Not sure which was
proper. "Greetings, madam. Oh, by the way, how many troops
would you like for us to leave as an honorary guard until you
have a chance to form your own protective militia," asked the
Naval Officer.

"I am sure whatever you think sufficient will be more than enough."

"Probably twice that," muttered a rude droid in the crowd.

"Well, I don't want to leave more than an amount greater than ten percent of your population, or else that, technically, could be considered an act of war. What is your population?

"Just under a thousand," said the President proudly.

"Under?"

"Yes."

"Oh, I am so sorry," cried the officer gleefully. "There's a minimum requirement for a country of this size of an even thousand. Sorry. Now please give the nice scientists back their lab, or we start blasting."

Several androids clutched their heads and tried to use hand pressure to keep their brains inside their skulls. More than a few dropped to their knees in prayer.

"Unless you have somebody in the woodwork to try the claim for salvage," added the Navy commander in grim formality.

"Hi!" said the Fatima, toolbox in hand as she and her partner joined the crowd. "What is going on?"

Everybody converged on the two workers and explained in mere seconds.

"Well, sure then, no problem," smiled Guido. "I then do like hereby and forthwith claim The Spot as abandoned property and give it as gift to these android guys."

"That good enough?" asked Fatima, squinting. "Or should we ask you to pay a dollar in cash?"

"No checks," warned Guido.

President Shahra extended a hand to the workers and they shook. "More than enough," she beamed. "How can we ever thank you?"

"Cash," reminded Fatima.

"No checks," added Guido.

"HOLD IT!" rumbled Davis. "If you two work here on the station, then it was not abandoned and there's no salvage."

"Sorry, but we were hired to come and check the fittings for the Wilkes Corporation," stated the man.

"Who formerly owned The Spot, but still assists in its up-

keep," added Snyder, fast to cover any inconsistencies in their
story.

"Ah-ha, you're kidnappers then!"

"We refuse to prosecute," said Fatima, crossing her arms.

Radiating indignation, Guido added. "In fact, we both
formally apply for immigration!" Bloody bureaucrats, always
getting in the way of common folk.

"Granted," responded President Shahra, in a cool executive
tone.

Precious seconds passed as the nettled Admiral digested
this unsavory information.

"I must say, sir, you have behaved as a real gentleman during this whole delicate incident," stated Jhonny in a good
mimic of Harry. "And I am sure our viewers on all the fourteen worlds, ah, the fifteen worlds, will agree after seeing our
recordings of these historic proceedings."

Admiral Terrance "Mad Dog" Davis stared at the SNT
camera-op with barbed-wire annoyance. "I can confiscate that
tape under the Top Secret Act of 2259," he warned brutally.

Everybody had heard of the law, but nobody knew any details. Which was only fitting and proper for a Top Secret Act.

"However, this will be difficult to do since we have been
broadcasting live the whole time," said Rikka, smiling
broadly as she joined the android on screen. "Hi, Terry! Remember me?"

Obviously he did as Davis did a superb imitation of a man
being hit with a brick.

"Activate the ESL!" the Navy officer bellowed to off-
camera.

At the rear of the bridge of the *Prime*, a sealed cyrogenix
closet opened and out from the clouds of minty steam there
stepped the USDA Emergency Strategic Lawyer.

In a single glance, his trained esquire vision swept across
the myriad of faces, the external view of the bow windows
and the navigational monitors pinpointing their location. The
Spot was just barely moving a thousand kilometers per hour,
but even as the man watched, it crossed the immaterial
boundary of the Oort Cloud and went from interplanetary to
interstellar space.

Outside everybody's jurisdiction.

"Admiral Davis," said the somber man. "You're screwed."

And the ESL stepped back into his refrigerated closet and closed the door.

In extreme slow motion, the supreme commander of the United Solar Defense Alliance turned about in his command chair to face the banks of monitors full of anxious, weary, frightened, hopeful faces. Oh, what the hell, can't win 'em all, or else war would be boring. Besides, personally he had always thought the Organic Law of 2018 was a pracking stupid rule.

"Pax," the giant Navy hologram sighed in defeat. "Madam President, please allow me to be the first military official to welcome the new independent state of what-ever-the-hell-you're-going-to-call-yourselves to the United Planets."

Cheering erupted, everybody hugged everybody, and a convenient clothing store was broken into so that the traditional celebration motif of hats in the air could be properly filled.

As always, it was the little details that were so important.

EPILOGUE

THE HUGE CROWD of Humans, Androids—with a capital "A"—and Gremlins in The Horny Toad all began to shout. "Ten! Nine! Eight! Seven!"

"Oh, I hate countdowns," said Prof. Ketter and he hit the button on the box in his hand.

Instantly, there was a tremendous explosion in the center of the room, and for a moment, a mushroom cloud formed over table #3. Soon a brisk breeze from life support cleared the atmosphere, and revealed sitting atop the table, where a solid marble block was only seconds ago, was now a perfect stone likeness of Bruno, surrounded by a tiny school of jade piranha.

The crowd erupted into applause.

"It's . . . ah, really lovely," said Rikka, not sure if she should laugh or cry.

Harry forced a grin and a nod. "Sure will look great in our office." In the closet of our office, he privately corrected.

"And it's functional," cried Ketter proudly.

"Come again?" asked Michelangelo, removing the earmuffs from his head.

Smiling broadly, the professor walked to the monument and slid a couple of sheets of paper between the mighty jaws. In a resounding crash they snapped together and Ketter removed the sheets neatly stapled.

"Oh, well, now that we like!" cried Jhonny in delight, the Toshiba on his shoulder zooming its telephoto lens in for a frightening close-up. "Good show! Bravo!"

AND IT WILL BE SWELL PROTECTION FROM ANY STRAY DANISH, scrolled Deitrich.

228

Over by the bathroom, the CD player formed the picture of a muscular man with no shirt and very bad tailored pants, who immediately launched into a kicking rendition of how he was far too legal to ever stop . . . but from doing what was never made exactly clear. Uncaring of the logic lapse in the lyrics, dancing commenced among the happy patrons of the bar. Along with a lot of drinking.

"Just a little gift from the grateful people of Silicon Valley," said President Shahra, walking closer. The female was dressed in a dazzling white jumpsuit, her left breast adorned with a tasteful rendition of the android flag.

"Much appreciated," smiled Collins.

She waved that aside. "A trifle really."

"I do believe that you will find this a bit more pragmatic," said Ambassador Ralph J 7979160, offering them a sealed letter covered with seals and ribbons.

"Thanks, what is it?" asked Harry, accepting the five-pound message.

"Official notice of your status as the exclusive reporters for Silicon Valley."

The SNT wobbled.

"Exclusive?" whispered Collins. "You gave us the exclusive rights for an entire world?"

The androids glanced at each other.

"A very small world," the President reminded them.

"DRINKS ARE ON THE HOUSE!" bellowed Snyder, raising the letter in a fist toward the ceiling and God. And the four reporters joined the joyous throng in twirling about and generally acting goofy. This has been a very heavy letter, indeed!

With a human on one arm, and an android on the other, Michelangelo still managed to send off a copy of the authorization to QINS. Ha! Suffer, you bozos.

As MacKenzie poured endless drinks and shots at the bar, in the fish tank behind him, Bruno gave a heartfelt sigh at the magnificent stone vision on the table and fell hopelessly in love.

Over in a corner by the comic wall photo of Heraldo Raveria, Prof. Ketter was holding court with a dozen news reporters from different departments.

"No," he corrected. "This is my second Nobel Prize. The

first was for solving the second inconsistency of the Time/ Space continuum."

"And this was for?" prompted a pretty white-haired lady from Science and Diet.

Reaching into his shoulder pouch of explosives and subway tokens, the scientist retrieved a second metallic statue. "This was awarded to me for Artistic Achievement." His Valley of Statues had become a big thing in more ways than one.

A zaftig woman from Arts and Entertainment saddled closer to the professor. "I just love to ravish men with Noble prizes," she whispered hotly into his ear.

"Me too," breathed the lady from Science.

"Of course, in sex, artistic flair is the most important attribute," snorted Entertainment.

"Nonsense, knowledge and skill are paramount," snapped Science.

"Only for a paramour!"

"Want a word to rhyme with that?"

"Ladies, please," said the professor, stepping between the combatants, brandishing his awards as crude swords. "As a trained mathematician, I can absolutely assure you that the number one can be infinitely divided by such prime numbers as your lovely selves."

The two reporters stared at each other. Hmm.

"Deal," they said, shaking hands, and each grabbing an arm they hauled the startled scientist out the door.

Laughing and breathless, the SNT reclaimed the seats at their table, loosened their tuxedo jumpsuits, and ordered a round of drinks for themselves. The tiny MacKenzie hologram took their order and vanished in a puff of smoke. Hey, nice touch that.

"Okay, I can't stand it anymore, why do chemists make such good lovers?" asked the alien as they relaxed amid the wild celebration. It wasn't every day that a new world was forged.

"Because they do it just for the reaction," answered Rikka, salting the popcorn.

"And then they do it again, to test the reaction," added Harry, taking a handful.

Mike's face fell. "How did you know?"

"I wrote it," said Collins with a smirk.

Damn.

Just then a short plump man came out of the crowd and tugged on Michelangelo's vest.

"Sir, aaraa, I am a chemist and would like to thank you very much for saying that joke in a public place."

"No problem," smiled the alien as the short human strode proudly into the boisterous mob.

With a musical ding the center of the table irised and a vast collection of drinks arrived. Much more than the reporters had ever ordered in their lives.

"Complimentary drinks from your admirers," said the tiny hologram Mack, standing amid the tumblers and glasses. "Except for this one. It's a Spotini, a brand-new drink I just created in honor of the fifteen worlds."

"We have to try that," said Harry with a grin. "Honor demands no less."

Mack stepped in front of the bubbling shot glasses. "Sorry, it's for androids only. A subtle mixing of methyl ethol ketone, horseradish, hydraulic fluid, vodka, and strawberry jam."

Even Jhonny stared at the drink in horror.

"But there's no MSG," said the miniature bartender quickly to dispel any false fears.

"Oh, well, then, okay," smiled the android. Might as well die a fool rather than a coward. Raising the tiny glass thimble, he took a deep breath and downed the sizzling brew in a single gulp.

"Hey that's good," coughed Jhonny, turning violent in the face and licking the glass. "Strong, but really good! Gimme 'round and send a batch to the ambassadors on me." Oh, heck, he was already tipsy from the stuff.

"The hell, you say, laddie boyyo. The first round is on the house!" burred the Scotsman. "However, you can pay for their seconds."

"Done!"

Just then, a tall blonde forced a path through the crowd around the drinking team of reporters, stared at them hard, and broke into a smile that threatened to tear off her lips.

"Hello. I wanted to compliment you on the fine job you did

covering The Spot," said Maria Valdez, apparently battling the stomach flu. "Superb, exemplary. Really good."

The SNT took deeps breaths and returned the smile.

"Thanks, Maria. Have a seat and join us," offered Rikka.

Suspiciously, the Station Manager stared at the empty chair and wondered what had they done to it. Sawed off the legs? Glue on the seat? Placed it over a trapdoor with a greased chute that ended in a pool of lime Jell-O?

"Ah, thank you, but no. Gotta go. Kids on the stove." And she hurried off before something really terrible happened to her.

"This forced truce may yet prove to be highly entertaining after all," chortled Michelangelo in glee.

Eyes twinkling, Harry agreed. "She is so sure we're out for a practical joke, the woman will go mad the nicer we act!"

Evilly, the reporters rubbed their hands together and started planning for surprise parties, gifts in the mail, and cash deposits into her personal account. God, the next two months were going to be great!

Amassing the notes and disks, Snyder slid them into a small box that he then locked and stuffed into his belt pouch.

"What else is in there?" asked Michelangelo curiously, adding sugar at his gallon pitcher of ice tea. Alcohol did nothing to his race, it was caffeine that got them stiff.

"Oh, not much really," said the anchor in a professional manner. "Some personal letters, a few stolen access cards for government installations, and the hindquarters of a unusually large rodent that we once found at a major Indonesian seaport on Terra."

"A giant rat from Sumatra?" sipped the alien. "But why do you have that particular item locked in the box?"

"Because," said Snyder, milking this precious moment for all it was worth. "Because this is a tail the worlds are not yet ready for."

UGH!

In agreement, Rikka sputtered into her beer, Michelangelo dropped his glasses into his tea. Even passers-by groaned and reached for something to throw at the grinning anchor.

"How long have you waited to say that joke?" asked Jhonny, massaging his temples trying to ease the pain.

"Years," sighed the anchor. "And it was worth it."

As additional neural inhibitors were quickly administered to ease the pain of that god-awful pun, the crowd of celebrities and functionaries parted and P. J. O'Ellison strolled into view talking to a microphone floating near his head.

". . . and so this lone brave soul used his own hair to stitch his clothes together into a crude parachute and dove naked from the giant statue, wafting down into the icy cold winds of Whatadump Valley . . ."

Hiccuping softly, P. J. ambled away celebrating in the best way he knew how. Alone with himself.

"I wish we could keep tabs on that guy," said Rikka wistfully. "I got a feeling he's going to cause us nothing but trouble in the future."

"No problem," answered Michelangelo, displaying a handheld WatchDog. "Or, at least we'll know where his shuttle goes."

"What did you do?" asked Jhonny, the tiny Toshiba struggling mightily to keep its boss upright and in the chair.

"Place a homing device inside the blast chamber."

Snyder scoffed. "Won't it be vaporized in only seconds?"

Michelangelo shook his head with difficulty. "No. It is made of Florentine Plastic. Will last for months back there."

ZOUNDS. HOW MUCH DID A NIFTY LITTLE DEVICE LIKE THAT COST? scrolled Deitrich. His own repairs had been astronomical, but Silicon Valley had covered the cost.

"$47,839.14." answered the technician, glancing at his wrist.

Harry stopped in the act of waving hello to Parsons as she entered The Horny Toad. That amount was vaguely familiar to him.

"You!" cried the anchor, pointing a finger at the alien.

Valiantly, Mike attempted to look innocent.

"You're the reason InterPlanetary Express canceled my account!"

"Well I certainly don't have that kind of money," explained the huge Gremlin.

Snorting through his nose, Harry exploded into laughter. "Damn, son. But you're really getting good at this news biz."

A furry bow. "Thank you, Obiwon."

"You're welcome, Grasshopper."

Jhonny lowered his shot glass and hiccuped. "Hey, I'm Grasshopper, he's the fuzzy mountain."

"I'm Grasshopper," said Rikka, blowing the foam off her mug of beer. "You're Tobor. He's Methuselah."

WELL NOW THAT MOUSEKETEER ROLL CALL IS FINISHED I ALSO HAVE SOME NEWS.

"Speak and be heard, Donovan!" encouraged Snyder grandly.

Sheesh. I CAME UP WITH A NAME FOR OUR SHUTTLE.

"What is it?" asked Collins, dropping a shot glass of whiskey into her next beer. But first making damn sure it was whiskey and not that . . . that rocket fuel for androids.

THE SPIRIT OF 66.

Stiffly, Michelangelo finished off his pitcher of ice tea and brushed off his whiskers with the back of a paw. "Which '66 is that? 1966? 2266?"

"And you left off the little apostrophe before the sixes," noted Jhonny, his words already slurring. Whew, they could use this stuff for rocket fuel. Then he mentally reviewed the components of the drink. Hey, it was rocket fuel! Mostly.

WRONG ON ALL COUNTS.

Collins snapped her fingers. "It's antiquarian reporter slang. He means 66 as in, 'more to come.' "

YEP. BECAUSE OUR WORK NEVER REALLY ENDS.

"Ladies and gentlemen!" shouted Snyder, standing and raising his glass of Scotch as high as he was. "Here's to *The Spirit of 66!*"

"No! Here's to the Satellite News Team!" cried President Shahra from the crowd and a toast was raised to them.

In embarrassment, the reporters sat down. Then they stood back up and toasted Gardner Wilkes, Prof. Ketter, Sheik Hassan, Admiral Davis, and everybody else they could think of or remember through their alcoholic fog. What the hell, why hold a grudge? Life was a 66!

And that was the straight poop.